Gawain

and the

Green Knight

Gawain
and the
Green
Knight

Introduction by Alan Lupack

General Editor: Jake Jackson

**FLAME TREE
PUBLISHING**

This is a FLAME TREE Book

FLAME TREE PUBLISHING
6 Melbray Mews
Fulham, London SW6 3NS
United Kingdom
www.flametreepublishing.com

First published 2023
Copyright © 2023 Flame Tree Publishing Ltd

23 25 27 26 24
3 5 7 9 8 6 4 2

ISBN: 978-1-80417-583-5

The cover image is created by Flame Tree Studio, adapted from a photo © Tim Green, licensed under the Creative Commons Attribution 2.0 Generic license.

Decorations courtesy of Shutterstock.com and the following:
Cattallina, KindMan, Nikolaenko, Panos Karas and Robert Voight.

The classic texts in this book are adapted from:
Sir Gawain and the Green Knight: A Middle-English Arthurian Romance Retold in Modern Prose, with Introduction & Notes, by Jessie L. Weston, 1898;
Sir Gawain at the Grail Castle, translated by Jessie L. Weston, 1903;
Sir Gawain and the Lady of Lys, translated by Jessie L. Weston from Wauchier de Denain's section of the *Conte del Graal*, 1907.
The Turke and Gowin was originally published in Volume 1 of the Percy Folio Manuscript, *The Grene Knight* is from Volume 2, and *The Carle of Carlisle* is from Volume 3, 1867–68, reproduced here without the additional notes.
The concluding chapter extracts are taken from *The Legend of Sir Gawain: Studies upon Its Original Scope and Significance* by Jessie L. Weston, 1897.

A copy of the CIP data for this book is available from the British Library.

Printed and bound in China

Contents

Series Foreword

STRETCHING BACK to the oral traditions of thousands of years ago, tales of heroes and disaster, creation and conquest have been told by many different civilizations in many different ways. Their impact sits deep within our culture even though the detail in the tales themselves are a loose mix of historical record, transformed narrative and the distortions of hundreds of storytellers.

Today the language of mythology lives with us: our mood is jovial, our countenance is saturnine, we are narcissistic and our modern life is hermetically sealed from others. The nuances of myths and legends form part of our daily routines and help us navigate the world around us, with its half truths and biased reported facts.

The nature of a myth is that its story is already known by most of those who hear it, or read it. Every generation brings a new emphasis, but the fundamentals remain the same: a desire to understand and describe the events and relationships of the world. Many of the great stories are archetypes that help us find our own place, equipping us with tools for self-understanding, both individually and as part of a broader culture.

For Western societies it is Greek mythology that speaks to us most clearly. It greatly influenced the mythological heritage of the ancient Roman civilization and is the lens through which we still see the Celts, the Norse and many of the other great peoples and religions. The Greeks themselves learned much from their neighbours, the Egyptians, an older culture that became weak with age and incestuous leadership.

It is important to understand that what we perceive now as mythology had its own origins in perceptions of the divine and the rituals of the sacred. The earliest civilizations, in the crucible of the Middle East, in the Sumer of the third millennium BC, are the source to which many of the mythic archetypes can be traced. As humankind collected together in cities for the first time, developed writing and industrial scale agriculture, started to irrigate the rivers and attempted to control rather than be at the mercy of its environment, humanity began to write down its tentative explanations of natural events, of floods and plagues, of disease.

Early stories tell of Gods (or god-like animals in the case of tribal societies such as African, Native American or Aboriginal cultures) who are crafty and use their wits to survive, and it is reasonable to suggest that these were the first rulers of the gathering peoples of the earth, later elevated to god-like status with the distance of time. Such tales became more political as cities vied with each other for supremacy, creating new Gods, new hierarchies for their pantheons. The older Gods took on primordial roles and became the preserve of creation and destruction, leaving the new gods to deal with more current, everyday affairs. Empires rose and fell, with Babylon assuming the mantle from Sumeria in the 1800s BC, then in turn to be swept away by the Assyrians of the 1200s BC; then the Assyrians and the Egyptians were subjugated by the Greeks, the Greeks by the Romans and so on, leading to the spread and assimilation of common themes, ideas and stories throughout the world.

The survival of history is dependent on the telling of good tales, but each one must have the 'feeling' of truth, otherwise it will be ignored. Around the firesides, or embedded in a book or a computer, the myths and legends of the past are still the living materials of retold myth, not restricted to an exploration of origins. Now we have devices and global communications that give us unparalleled access to a diversity of traditions. We can find out about Indigenous American, Indian, Chinese and tribal African mythology in a way that was denied to our ancestors, we can find connections, match the archaeology, religion and the mythologies of the world to build a comprehensive image of the human adventure.

The great leaders of history and heroes of literature have also adopted the mantle of mythic experience, because the stories of historical figures – Cyrus the Great, Alexander, Genghis Khan – and mytho-poetic warriors such as Beowulf achieve a cultural significance that transcends their moment in the chronicles of humankind. Myth, history and literature have become powerful, intwined instruments of perception, with echoes of reported fact and symbolic truths that convey the sweep of human experience. In this series of books we are glad to share with you the wonderful traditions of the past.

Jake Jackson
General Editor

Introduction

The Alliterative Revival

THE ALLITERATIVE REVIVAL was a literary movement of the late fourteenth and fifteenth centuries, predominantly in the north and west of England, in which poets used alliteration as the controlling metrical device. Some would argue that the movement is not actually a 'revival' but a reflection of a continuing tradition dating back to Old English verse and found in *Layamon's Brut*, an early Middle English poem, and other works that make heavy use of alliteration. The Alliterative Revival produced poems in a variety of genres. These include 'historical' poems like *Siege of Jerusalem* and *The Wars of Alexander*; debate poems like *Winner and Wastoure*, *The Parlement of the Thre Ages*, and *Death and Liffe*; religious poems like *St. Erkenwald* and *Susannah*; dream visions like *Piers Plowman* and *Pearl*; and Arthurian romances like the *Alliterative Morte Arthure*, *Golagros and Gawain*, *The Awntyrs off Arthure* and, of course, *Sir Gawain and the Green Knight*.

Early criticism on the poems of the Alliterative Revival assumed that, with a few notable exceptions, they were provincial and generally poorly crafted and constructed – certainly not in the same league as the works of Chaucer and Gower. Study of the broad scope of this body of literature, however, reveals that this is not the case. Although the alliterative line these poets used is less strict than that of Old English verse, the best poets of the movement used it to great effect. And the structure of many of the works is less haphazard than some early scholars recognized. A number of the poems combine two different narrative episodes, but they are usually linked thematically in a manner comparable to the diptychs so common in medieval art.

In short, the movement produced many fine poems, some of which are masterpieces not only of alliterative verse but of medieval literature in general – and chief among these is *Sir Gawain and the Green Knight* (*SGGK*).

The *Gawain* Poet

Most of the authors of alliterative poems are unknown. (One notable exception is William Langland, the author of *Piers Plowman*, who names himself in the text.) Since four poems – *SGGK*, *Pearl*, *Cleanness* and *Patience*, written in the same northwest Midland dialect late in the fourteenth century and surviving in a single manuscript, Cotton Nero A X – are surely by the same anonymous author, he is referred to as the *Gawain* Poet (and sometimes as the *Pearl* Poet). A fifth work, *St. Erkenwald*, not appearing in the Cotton Nero manuscript, has sometimes been attributed to the *Gawain* Poet, but most scholars consider this unlikely and certainly unproven.

Each of the four is clearly the work of a master craftsman; and *Pearl* and *SGGK* are among the best literary works of the Middle Ages. The genres and subject matter of these poems vary. *Pearl* is a dream vision, rich in symbolism and imagery, in which a father sees his 'pearl', his dead daughter, across a river that separates him from her and from the heavenly realm; and, in a reversal of roles, he is instructed by her. *Patience* and *Cleanness* are homiletic poems that use lively accounts of Biblical stories – such as 'Jonah and the Whale' and 'Belshazzar's Feast' – as exempla to teach about their eponymous virtues. The moral concerns of these three works help to explain the interest of the author of *SGGK* in the ethical dilemma with which Gawain is faced.

Gawain's Reputation

Gawain is King Arthur's nephew, and in much Arthurian literature he is considered the best of Arthur's knights. In his *Perceval*, Chrétien de Troyes asserts that Gawain is the most courteous knight in the world.

In this work, as in numerous others, Gawain is contrasted to Kay, whose boorishness is a foil to Gawain's courtliness. In several Dutch romances, Gawain is called the Father of Adventure, and he has great skill in healing as well as in fighting and diplomacy. In many of the French romances of the twelfth through to the fourteenth century, Gawain is the most important hero, although Lancelot eventually replaces him in this role. In the thirteenth-century Vulgate Cycle, for example, Gawain is said to be the second-best worldly knight after Lancelot.

In Malory's *Morte d'Arthur*, Gawain is at times brave and noble and at times vengeful and treacherous. He keeps alive the feud between the house of Lot and the house of Pellinore by unchivalrously killing Pellinore and then Lamorak. He is also unforgiving when Lancelot accidentally kills Gareth, and Gawain refuses to allow Arthur to make peace with him. Before this, however, he tried to dissuade Mordred and Agravain from accusing Lancelot; and he ultimately realizes that Lancelot is noble and Mordred wicked. In the English verse romances featuring Gawain, however, he is typically nearly flawless in his courage and courtesy.

Gawain's Reputation in Alliterative Romances

In the alliterative romances besides *SGGK* in which Gawain appears, he is presented as the epitome of knightly courtesy and chivalry. In the late-fourteenth-century northern romance *The Awntyrs off Arthure at the Terne Wathelyne* (*The Adventures of Arthur at Tarn Wadling*), a knight named Galeron accuses Arthur of wrongfully winning his lands in war and giving them to Gawain. Galeron offers to fight for the disputed territory, and Gawain accepts the challenge, thus placing his right to the lands in dramatic opposition to Galeron's. Neither knight wins the battle, but Galeron is so moved by Gawain's courage that he renounces his claim. Arthur, in turn, impressed with Galeron's respect for knightly valour, offers Gawain lands and castles in return for yielding the disputed land to Galeron, a gesture that Gawain willingly makes. Galeron is made a member of the Round Table, and tranquillity is restored. Similarly, in the fifteenth-century alliterative poem *Golagros and Gawain*, Gawain is able to win the allegiance of Golagros for Arthur by defeating him in battle but then claiming that he had been overcome so that the proud knight can maintain his honour. Inspired by Gawain's exceptional courtesy, Golagros admits that he lost and pledges loyalty to Arthur, who shows his magnanimity by releasing Golagros from his pledge of fealty, thus leaving him as free as he was before.

In *SGGK*, Gawain's 'honour' is said to be 'praised above that of all men on earth'. This reputation is scrutinized by the poem and by Gawain himself. Therefore, it becomes a question that readers must consider, and that is one of the keys to understanding and enjoying the poem.

Sir Gawain and the Green Knight

Sir Gawain and the Green Knight is the greatest and most intricately crafted of the English verse romances. Written in alliterative stanzas of irregular length with a rhyming bob and wheel (a short one-stress line followed by four three-stress lines, rhyming ABABA) at the end, *SGGK* employs intricate patterns of parallelism through which its meaning is revealed. Narrative elements reflect one another and interweave to bind the poem together much as the alliterating syllables bind lines together.

SGGK begins with a reference to the fall of Troy and to Brutus, a descendant of Aeneas. Geoffrey of Monmouth and many other medieval chroniclers considered Brutus to be the founder of Britain and the first in the line of British kings that leads to Arthur. This legendary origin story aggrandizes Arthur by giving him a heroic and historic heritage and by declaring that he is the 'most valiant' of all the British kings since Brutus.

Camelot at Christmas-time is the setting for the opening action. As often happens in Arthurian romance, something strange from outside the court intrudes and challenges its people and values. A knight, green not just in his livery but also in his person, enters astride a green horse and carrying contrasting symbols: a holly bob (a symbol of peace) and a great axe. Interpreted by critics as everything from a force of nature to a demon, the Green Knight proposes to the court a beheading contest: he will endure a stroke of the axe and then give one in return. (Morgan le Fay, the old woman Gawain meets later in the poem, is said to have instigated the challenge in order to test the Round Table and to frighten Guinevere.)

The beheading contest is a motif that is found in several other medieval works, from its earliest appearance in the French *La Mule sans frein* (*The Mule Without a Bridle*) to the late English poems *The Carle of Carlisle* and *The Grene Knight*. It is typically Gawain who undertakes the adventure. In the French prose romance *Perlesvaus*, however, Lancelot accepts the challenge. But nowhere is that motif interwoven into the structure or integrated with the theme of the work as skilfully as in *SGGK*.

The initial reluctance of any of Arthur's knights to accept the Green Knight's challenge prompts him to question the reputation of the court. He asks, "Is this Arthur's hall, and these the knights whose renown hath run through many realms?" This question introduces a controlling theme, that of renown or reputation. Gawain underplays his own reputation: when he accepts the challenge, he says that he is the weakest and the least of Arthur's knights. It is not clear that he or anyone else believes this; after all, the device on his shield is a pentangle, which is a symbol of perfection. As we learn in the extended explanation of its significance, the pentangle implies that Gawain is the 'truest of heroes and gentlest of knights'.

In order to keep his vow, Gawain endures the hardships of winter and the dangers of travel through lands outside the protection of Arthur. When he prays that he might find lodging where he can hear Mass on Christmas Day, almost immediately he sees a castle belonging to a lord named Bernlak (as Weston, whose version is used in this book, gives the name – though the standard edition of *SGGK* reads 'Bertilak' and some editions and translations call the lord 'Bercilak').

There, he is well received and honoured because he possesses 'all fame, and valour, and courtesy'. At the castle, he enters into a second bargain, which parallels the beheading contest begun at Camelot. He agrees to an exchange of winnings with the lord of the castle, who goes out hunting each of the three mornings that Gawain is his guest. In return for the game the lord brings home, Gawain must give him whatever he wins during the day.

On each of the three days, while his host hunts a deer, a boar and a fox respectively, Gawain is tempted by Bernlak's wife. As critics generally agree, there is a correspondence between the animals being hunted and the actions of Gawain as he responds to his host's wife. On the first day, he is shy and elusive like the hart; on the second day, he faces his pursuer and resists like the boar; and on the third day, he is deceitful like the fox.

In her temptations of Gawain, Bernlak's wife uses his reputation to undermine his resistance to her. She first praises his fame. As he was in Arthur's court, Gawain is self-deprecating. But when she says that she can hardly believe he is Gawain because a man such as he is reputed to be would not have spent time with a lady without asking for a kiss, he does kiss her – once on the first day, twice on the second, and three times on the third. On the third day, she also tries to give him a ring, which he refuses; then she offers her ominously green 'lace' (a girdle or belt) and tells him that it will protect him from harm. Seeing a chance to save his life, he accepts the gift. To fulfil his part of the bargain, each evening when the lord returns from the hunt, Gawain gives him the kisses he has received (without saying from whom he received them) in exchange for the game the lord has brought home. But when he exchanges the winnings with the lord on the third evening, he gives him only the three kisses and not the green girdle.

Before Gawain sets out from the castle to fulfil his obligation to meet the Green Knight, he is armed again; in this instance, however, the arming culminates not in his taking of the shield with the device symbolic of virtue, but in his putting on the green girdle, perhaps an indication of a lack of faith or at least a shift in faith from virtue to magic. As he rides to fulfil his pledge to the Green Knight, he undergoes another temptation, this time of his courage. The guide Bernlak has provided to take Gawain to the Green Chapel advises that he ride away without meeting the Green Knight and swears not to tell anyone what Gawain did. Gawain responds that even if the guide were true to his word, he, Gawain, would be a coward if he took this advice, and so he rides on to meet his fate. This brief scene is significant because it shows Gawain beginning to understand that he must define – and act according to – his own moral code.

As he prepares to receive the blow from the Green Knight's axe, Gawain swerves aside, prompting the Green Knight to say that he cannot be Gawain, who never feared any opponent, because he flinches before he feels the blow. The attack on Gawain's reputation steels him, and he does not move as the axe descends a second time; but it stops before striking him. The third time, the stroke nicks Gawain's neck and draws blood but does no real harm. As the Green Knight explains, the three strokes reflect the three days of temptation and exchanges. On the first two, Gawain kept the bargain. On the third, he was not completely faithful to his pledge, and so he receives a slight wound. Though Gawain is greatly ashamed at his failing, the Green Knight says he lacked only 'a little' (was only slightly at fault). For the Green Knight, the fact that Gawain acted as he did because he loved his life is a mitigating factor. Nevertheless, Gawain says he will now wear the green girdle 'in sign of my frailty' – that is, as a symbol of his failing.

When Gawain returns to Camelot, the court views the adventure much as the Green Knight did. Arthur orders that the green girdle be worn by each member of the court in recognition of the fame that Gawain has brought to the Round Table. Like the displaying of the axe with which he beheaded the Green Knight so that all men might see it and know of Gawain's deed, this act is another visible sign of the honour in which he is held. But the girdle that the court considers a sign of his renown, Gawain perceives as a reminder of his shame. Thus, he has come to the realization that virtue and honour are not matters of public approval and that his knowledge of his own deeds is more important than the regard of others. Yet the poem seems to appreciate that people of honour sometimes hold themselves to a higher standard than others might. It also displays a joy in life that is reflected in the lively scenes of feasts, hunts and temptations; in its elaborate structure; in the vitality of the alliterative verse supplemented by rhyme; and in its recognition that imperfections are a part of life that need not overshadow heroic action.

With Gawain's return to Camelot, the court's display of this second symbol of Gawain's courage (the girdle paralleling the axe), and the reference, as at the beginning, to the legendary founding of Britain by Brutus, the poem has come full circle and has completed the pattern of parallels around which it is so artfully structured.

Modern Renderings of *Sir Gawain* and the Green Knight

Though *The Grene Knight* (which is printed later in this volume) is the only medieval work to show direct influence of *SGGK*, quite a few modern authors and artists have responded to the earlier romance or reworked it in verse, drama, opera, fiction and film. Such adaptation, however, did not begin until early in the twentieth century. *SGGK* was virtually unknown in the modern period until it was edited for the first time in 1839 by Frederic Madden, who gave it the name by which it has been known ever since. Of course, it was some time after Madden's edition before the poem was widely read and recognized as the masterpiece that it is. The monumental 1925 edition of *SGGK* by J.R.R. Tolkien and E.V. Gordon was instrumental in introducing it into classrooms and to a wider audience.

In the twentieth and twenty-first centuries, illustrated editions, translations and adaptations of *SGGK* abound. Poets such as Yvor Winters and Loren Eiseley, novelists such as Thomas Berger, Iris Murdoch and Vera Chapman, and several dramatists (including David Harsent, whose verse play *Gawain* was written as a libretto for music by Harrison Birtwistle) have been inspired by *SGGK*.

There have also been three films based on *SGGK*. Two of them were directed by Stephen Weeks. The first of these, *Gawain and the Green Knight* (1973), starring rock singer Murray Head as Sir Gawain, inserts into the middle of the events of the medieval poem an episode borrowed from Chrétien's *Yvain*. A decade later, Stephen Weeks remade his version of *SGGK* as *Sword of the Valiant: The Legend of Sir Gawain and the Green Knight* (1983), starring Sean Connery as the Green Knight and Miles O'Keeffe as Sir Gawain. This version adds to the plot an elaborate riddle that the Green Knight poses to Gawain, the solving of which would free him from the return stroke. Like these two films, *The Green Knight* (2021), directed by David Lowery and starring Dev Patel as Gawain, adds material not in the poem – the story of St. Winifred, for example – and it radically alters Gawain's story, in the process removing much of the poem's exuberant joy.

None of these adaptations comes close to the quality of *SGGK*, yet the numerous illustrated versions and the reworkings of its story in a variety of genres are a testament to its brilliance.

Alan Lupack (Introduction) is the author of *The Oxford Guide to Arthurian Literature and Legend*. Former President of the North American Branch of the International Arthurian Society, he is co-author (with Barbara Tepa Lupack) of *King Arthur in America* and editor of medieval and post-medieval Arthurian texts. He is the Associate editor of the TEAMS Middle English Texts series and the creator of the electronic database *The Camelot Project*.

Sir Gawain and the Green Knight

THE TRANSLATION of *Sir Gawain and the Green Knight* (*SGGK*) that appears in this volume was written by Jesse Weston, who is best known today for her once influential study *From Ritual to Romance* (1920). Although her approach – seeing the Grail stories as Christianized versions of a pagan fertility rite – and most of the conclusions of her book have since been rejected by scholars, it did influence the most influential modern Grail poem, T.S. Eliot's *The Waste Land* (1922).

Weston, who herself wrote a Grail poem, 'Knights of King Arthur's Court', that celebrated Perceval's spirituality, had a wide-ranging knowledge of texts and was more conversant with medieval romance than almost any other scholar of her day. Her translations of 'romances unrepresented in Malory' included *SGGK* and some of the other Gawain episodes in this volume. In addition to her study of the grail legend, she also wrote monographs on Lancelot and Perceval and one on Gawain (titled *The Legend of Sir Gawain: Studies upon Its Original Scope and Significance* – some chapters of which are included in this book), whom she considered 'one of the most puzzling, and at the same time most fascinating, characters of the Arthurian cycle'.

Even if we do not accept all of her conclusions, she made valuable contributions to the study of Arthurian literature by considering, in her scholarly writings, texts in many languages – thus emphasizing the undeniable intertextuality of those stories – and by making accessible to the English-speaking world, through her translations, French, German, and Dutch Arthurian romances.

Preface

THE POEM of which the following pages offer a prose rendering is contained in a MS., believed to be unique, of the Cottonian Collection, Nero A. X., preserved in the British Museum. The MS. is of the end of the fourteenth century, but it is possible that the composition of the poem is somewhat earlier; the subject matter is certainly of very old date. There has been a considerable divergence of opinion among scholars on the question of authorship, but the view now generally accepted is that it is the work of the same hand as *Pearl*, another poem of considerable merit contained in the same MS.

Our poem, or, to speak more correctly, metrical romance, contains over 2500 lines, and is composed in staves of varying length, ending in five short rhyming lines, technically known as a bob and a wheel, – the lines forming the body of the stave being not rhyming, but alliterative. The dialect in which it is written has been decided to be West Midland, probably Lancashire, and is by no means easy to understand. Indeed, it is the real difficulty and obscurity of the language, which in spite of careful and scholarly editing will always place the poem in its original form outside the range of any but professed students of mediaeval literature, which has encouraged me to make an attempt to render it more accessible to the general public, by giving it a form that shall be easily intelligible, and at the same time preserve as closely as possible the style of the author.

For that style, in spite of a certain roughness, unavoidable at a period in which the language was still in a partially developed and amorphous stage, is really charming. The author has a keen eye for effect; a talent for description, detailed without becoming wearisome; a genuine love of Nature and sympathy with her varying moods; and a real refinement and elevation of feeling which enable him to deal with a *risqué* situation with an absence of coarseness, not, unfortunately, to be always met with in a mediaeval writer. Standards of taste vary with the age, but even judged by that of our own day the author of *Sir Gawain and the Green Knight* comes not all too badly out of the ordeal!

The story with which the poem deals, too, has claims upon our interest. I have shown elsewhere [in *The Legend of Sir Gawain*, Grimm Library, Vol. VII. (Chapter IX. Sir Gawain and the Green Knight)] that the beheading challenge is an incident of very early occurrence in heroic legend, and that the particular form given to it in the English poem is especially interesting, corresponding as it does to the variations of the story as preserved in the oldest known version, that of the old Irish *Fled Bricrend*.

But in no other version is the incident coupled with that of a temptation and testing of the hero's honour and chastity, such as meets us here. At first sight one is inclined to assign the episode of the lady of the castle to the class of stories of which the oldest version is preserved in Biblical record – the story of Joseph and Potiphar's wife; a *motif* not unseldom employed by mediaeval writers, and which notably occurs in what we may call the *Launfal* group of stories. But there are certain points which may make us hesitate as to whether in its first conception the tale was really one of this class.

It must be noted that here the lady is acting throughout with the knowledge and consent of the husband, an important point of difference. In the second place, it is very doubtful whether her entire attitude was not a *ruse*. From the Green Knight's words to Gawain when he finally reveals himself, "I wot we shall soon make peace with my wife, who was thy bitter enemy," her conduct hardly seems to have been prompted by real passion.

In my *Studies on the Legend of Sir Gawain*, already referred to, I have suggested that the character of the lady here is, perhaps, a reminiscence of that of the Queen of the Magic Castle or Isle, daughter or niece of an enchanter, who at an early stage of Gawain's story was undoubtedly his love. I think it not impossible that she was an integral part of the tale as first told, and her rôle here was determined by that which she originally played. In most versions of the story she has dropped out altogether. It is, of course, possible that, there being but a confused reminiscence of the original tale, her share *may* have been modified by the influence of the *Launfal* group; but I should prefer to explain the episode on the whole as a somewhat distorted survival of an original feature.

But in any case we may be thankful for this, that the author of the most important English metrical romance dealing with Arthurian legend faithfully adheres to the original conception of Gawain's character, as drawn before the monkish lovers of edification laid their ruthless hands on his legend, and turned the model of knightly virtues and courtesy into a mere vulgar libertine.

Brave, chivalrous, loyally faithful to his plighted word, scrupulously heedful of his own and others' honour, Gawain stands before us in this poem. We take up Malory or Tennyson, and in spite of their charm of style, in spite of the halo of religious mysticism in which they have striven to enwrap their characters, we lay them down with a feeling of dissatisfaction. How did the Gawain of their imagination, this empty-headed, empty-hearted worldling, cruel murderer, and treacherous friend, ever come to be the typical English hero? For such Gawain certainly was, even more than Arthur himself. Then we turn back to these faded pages, and read the quaintly earnest words in which the old writer reveals the hidden meaning of that mystic symbol, the pentangle, and vindicates Gawain's title to claim it as his badge – and we smile, perhaps; but we cease to wonder at the widespread popularity of King Arthur's famous nephew, or at the immense body of romance that claims him as its hero.

Scholars know all this, of course; they can read the poem for themselves in its original rough and intricate phraseology; perhaps they will be shocked at an attempt to handle it in simpler form. But this little book is not for them, and if to those to whom the tale would otherwise be a sealed treasure these pages bring some new knowledge of the way in which our forefathers looked on the characters of the Arthurian legend, the tales they told of them (unconsciously betraying the while how they themselves lived and thought and spoke) – if by that means they gain a keener appreciation of our national heroes, a wider knowledge of our national literature, – then the spirit of the long-dead poet will doubtless not be the slowest to pardon my handling of what was his masterpiece, as it is, in M. Gaston Paris' words, "The jewel of English medieval literature."

Jessie L. Weston
Bournemouth, June 1898

Part I

Of the Making of Britain

AFTER the siege and the assault of Troy, when that burg was destroyed and burnt to ashes, and the traitor slain for his treason, the noble Aeneas and his kin sailed forth to become princes and patrons of well-nigh all the Western Isles. Thus Romulus built Rome (and gave to the city his own name, which it bears even to this day); and Ticius turned him to Tuscany; and Langobard raised him up dwellings in Lombardy; and Felix Brutus sailed far over the French flood, and founded the kingdom of Britain, wherein have been war and waste and wonder, and bliss and bale, oft-times since.

And in that kingdom of Britain have been wrought more gallant deeds than in any other; but of all British kings Arthur was the most valiant, as I have heard tell, therefore will I set forth a wondrous adventure that fell out in his time. And if ye will listen to me, but for a little while, I will tell it even as it stands in story stiff and strong, fixed in the letter, as it hath long been known in the land.

How Arthur Held High Feast at Camelot

King Arthur lay at Camelot upon a Christmas-tide, with many a gallant lord and lovely lady, and all the noble brotherhood of the Round Table. There they held rich revels with gay talk and jest; one while they would ride forth to joust and tourney, and again back to the court to make carols;[1] for there was the feast holden fifteen days with all the mirth that men could devise, song and glee, glorious to hear, in the daytime, and dancing at night. Halls and chambers were crowded with noble guests, the bravest of knights and the loveliest of ladies, and Arthur himself was the comeliest king that ever held a court. For all this fair folk were in their youth, the fairest and most fortunate under heaven, and the king himself of such fame that it were hard now to name so valiant a hero.

New Year's Day

Now the New Year had but newly come in, and on that day a double portion was served on the high table to all the noble guests, and thither came the king with all his knights, when the service in the chapel had been sung to an end. And they greeted each other for the New Year, and gave rich gifts, the one to the other (and they that received them were not wroth, that may ye well believe!), and the maidens laughed and made mirth till it was time to get them to meat. Then they washed and sat them down to the feast in fitting rank and order, and Guinevere the queen, gaily clad, sat on the high daïs. Silken was her seat, with a fair canopy over her head, of rich tapestries of Tars, embroidered, and studded with costly gems; fair she was to look upon, with her shining grey eyes, a fairer woman might no man boast himself of having seen.

But Arthur would not eat till all were served, so full of joy and gladness was he, even as a child; he liked not either to lie long, or to sit long at meat, so worked upon him his young blood and his wild brain. And another custom he had also, that came of his nobility, that he would never eat upon an high day till he had been advised of some knightly deed, or some strange and marvellous tale, of his ancestors, or of arms, or of other ventures. Or till some knight should seek of him leave to joust with another, that they might set their lives in jeopardy, one against another, as fortune might favour them. Such was the king's custom when he sat in hall at each high feast with his noble knights, therefore on that New Year tide, he abode, fair of face, on the throne, and made much mirth withal.

Of the Noble Knights There Present

Thus the king sat before the high table, and spake of many things; and there good Sir Gawain was seated by Guinevere the queen, and on her other side sat Agravain,[2] *à la dure main*; both were the king's sister's sons and full gallant knights. And at the end of the table was Bishop Bawdewyn, and Ywain, King Urien's son, sat at the other side alone. These were worthily served on the daïs, and at the lower tables sat many valiant knights. Then they bare the first course with the blast of trumpets and waving of banners, with the sound of drums and pipes, of song and lute, that many a heart was uplifted at the melody. Many were the dainties, and rare the meats, so great was the plenty they might scarce find room on the board to set on the dishes. Each helped himself as he liked best, and to each two were twelve dishes, with great plenty of beer and wine.

The Coming of the Green Knight

Now I will say no more of the service, but that ye may know there was no lack, for there drew near a venture that the folk might well have left their labour to gaze upon. As the sound of the music ceased, and the first course had been fitly served, there came in at the hall door one terrible to behold, of stature greater than any on earth; from neck to loin so strong and thickly made, and with limbs so long and so great that he seemed even as a giant. And yet he was but a man, only the mightiest that might mount a steed; broad of chest and shoulders and slender of waist, and all his features of like fashion; but men marvelled much at his colour, for he rode even as a knight, yet was green all over.

The Fashion of the Knight

For he was clad all in green, with a straight coat, and a mantle above; all decked and lined with fur was the cloth and the hood that was thrown back from his locks and lay on his shoulders. Hose had he of the same green, and spurs of bright gold with silken fastenings richly worked; and all his vesture was verily green. Around his waist and his saddle were bands with fair stones set upon silken work, 'twere too long to tell of all the trifles that were embroidered thereon – birds and insects in gay gauds of green and gold.

Of the Knight's Steed

All the trappings of his steed were of metal of like enamel, even the stirrups that he stood in stained of the same, and stirrups and saddle-bow alike gleamed and shone with green stones. Even the steed on which he rode was of the same hue, a green horse, great and strong, and hard to hold, with broidered bridle, meet for the rider.

The knight was thus gaily dressed in green, his hair falling around his shoulders, on his breast hung a beard, as thick and green as a bush, and the beard and the hair of his head were clipped all round above his elbows. The lower part of his sleeves were fastened with clasps in the same wise as a king's mantle. The horse's mane was crisped and plaited with many a knot folded in with gold thread about the fair green, here a twist of the hair, here another of gold. The tail was twined in like manner, and both were bound about with a band of bright green set with many a precious stone; then they were tied aloft in a cunning knot, whereon rang many bells of burnished gold. Such a steed might no other ride, nor had such ever been looked upon in that hall ere that time; and all who saw that knight spake and said that a man might scarce abide his stroke.

The Arming of the Knight

The knight bore no helm nor hauberk, neither gorget nor breast-plate, neither shaft nor buckler to smite nor to shield, but in one hand he had a holly-bough, that is greenest when the groves are bare, and in his other an axe, huge and uncomely, a cruel weapon in fashion, if one would picture it. The head was an ell-yard long, the metal all of green steel and gold, the blade burnished bright, with a broad edge, as well shapen to shear as a sharp razor. The steel was set into a strong staff, all bound round with iron, even to the end, and engraved with green in cunning work. A lace was twined about it, that looped at the head, and all adown the handle it was clasped with tassels on buttons of bright green richly broidered.

The knight halted in the entrance of the hall, looking to the high daïs, and greeted no man, but looked ever upwards; and the first words he spake were, "Where is the ruler of this folk? I would gladly look upon that hero, and have speech with him." He cast his eyes on the knights, and mustered them up and down, striving ever to see who of them was of most renown.

Then was there great gazing to behold that chief, for each man marvelled what it might mean that a knight and his steed should have even such a hue as the green grass; and that seemed even greener than green enamel on bright gold. All looked on him as he stood, and drew near unto him wondering greatly what he might be; for many marvels had they seen, but none such as this, and phantasm and faërie did the folk deem it. Therefore were the gallant knights slow to answer, and gazed astounded, and sat stone still in a deep silence through that goodly hall, as if a slumber were fallen upon them. I deem it was not all for doubt, but some for courtesy that they might give ear unto his errand.

Then Arthur beheld this adventure before his high daïs, and knightly he greeted him, for discourteous was he never. "Sir," he said, "thou art welcome to this place – lord of this hall am I, and men call me Arthur. Light thee down, and tarry awhile, and what thy will is, that shall we learn after."

Of the Knight's Challenge

"Nay," quoth the stranger, "so help me He that sitteth on high, 'twas not mine errand to tarry any while in this dwelling; but the praise of this thy folk and thy city is lifted up on high, and thy warriors are holden for the best and the most valiant of those who ride mail-clad to the fight. The wisest and the worthiest of this world are they, and well proven in all knightly sports. And here, as I have heard tell, is fairest courtesy, therefore have I come hither as at this time. Ye may be sure by the branch that I bear here that I come in peace, seeking no strife. For had I willed to journey in warlike guise I have at home both hauberk and helm, shield and shining spear, and other weapons to mine hand, but since I seek no war my raiment is that of peace. But if thou be as bold as all men tell thou wilt freely grant me the boon I ask."

And Arthur answered, "Sir Knight, if thou cravest battle here thou shalt not fail for lack of a foe."

And the knight answered, "Nay, I ask no fight, in faith here on the benches are but beardless children, were I clad in armour on my steed there is no man here might match me. Therefore I ask in this court but a Christmas jest, for that it is Yule-tide, and New Year, and there are many here. If any one in this hall holds himself so hardy,[3] so bold both of blood and brain, as to dare strike me one stroke for another, I will give him as a gift this axe, which is heavy enough, in sooth, to handle as he may list, and I will abide the first blow, unarmed as I sit. If any knight be so bold as to prove my words let him come swiftly to me here, and take this weapon, I quit claim to it, he may keep it as his own, and I will abide his stroke, firm on the floor. Then shalt thou give me the right to deal him another, the respite of a year from to-day shall he have. Now pledge me thy word, and let see whether any here dare say aught."

The Silence of the Knights

Now if the knights had been astounded at the first, yet stiller were they all, high and low, when they had heard his words. The knight on his steed straightened himself in the saddle, and rolled his eyes fiercely round the hall, red they gleamed under his green and bushy brows. He frowned and twisted his beard, waiting to see who should rise, and when none answered he cried aloud in mockery, "What, is this Arthur's hall, and these the knights whose renown hath run through many realms? Where are now your pride and your conquests, your wrath, and anger, and mighty words? Now are the praise and the renown of the Round Table overthrown by one man's speech, since all keep silence for dread ere ever they have seen a blow!"

With that he laughed so loudly that the blood rushed to the king's fair face for very shame; he waxed wroth, as did all his knights, and sprang to his feet, and drew near to the stranger and said, "Now by heaven foolish is thine asking, and thy folly shall find its fitting answer. I know no man aghast at thy great words. Give me here thine axe and I shall grant thee the boon thou hast asked." Lightly he sprang to him and caught at his hand, and the knight, fierce of aspect, lighted down from his charger.

Then Arthur took the axe and gripped the haft, and swung it round, ready to strike. And the knight stood before him, taller by the head than any in the hall; he stood, and stroked his beard, and drew down his coat, no more dismayed for the king's threats than if one had brought him a drink of wine.

How Sir Gawain Dared the Venture

Then Gawain, who sat by the queen, leaned forward to the king and spake, "I beseech ye, my lord, let this venture be mine. Would ye but bid me rise from this seat, and stand by your side, so that my liege lady thought it not ill, then would I come to your counsel before this goodly court. For I think it not seemly that such challenge should be made in your hall that ye yourself should undertake it, while there are many bold knights who sit beside ye, none are there, methinks, of readier will under heaven, or more valiant in open field. I am the weakest, I wot, and the feeblest of wit, and it will be the less loss of my life if ye seek sooth. For save that ye are mine uncle naught is there in me to praise, no virtue is there in my body save your blood, and since this challenge is such folly that it beseems ye not to take it, and I have asked it from ye first, let it fall to me, and if I bear myself ungallantly then let all this court blame me."

Then they all spake with one voice that the king should leave this venture and grant it to Gawain.

Then Arthur commanded the knight to rise, and he rose up quickly and knelt down before the king, and caught hold of the weapon; and the king loosed his hold of it, and lifted up his hand, and gave him his blessing, and bade him be strong both of heart and hand. "Keep thee well, nephew," quoth Arthur, "that thou give him but the one blow, and if thou redest him rightly I trow thou shalt well abide the stroke he may give thee after."

The Making of the Covenant

Gawain stepped to the stranger, axe in hand, and he, never fearing, awaited his coming. Then the Green Knight spake to Sir Gawain, "Make we our covenant ere we go further. First, I ask thee, knight, what is thy name? Tell me truly, that I may know thee."

"In faith," quoth the good knight, "Gawain am I, who give thee this buffet, let what may come of it; and at this time twelvemonth will I take another at thine hand with whatsoever weapon thou wilt, and none other."

Then the other answered again, "Sir Gawain, so may I thrive as I am fain to take this buffet at thine hand," and he quoth further, "Sir Gawain, it liketh me well that I shall take at thy fist that which I have asked here, and thou hast readily and truly rehearsed all the covenant that I asked of the king, save that thou shalt swear me, by thy troth, to seek me thyself wherever thou hopest that I may be found, and win thee such reward as thou dealest me to-day, before this folk."

"Where shall I seek thee?" quoth Gawain. "Where is thy place? By Him that made me, I wot never where thou dwellest, nor know I thee, knight, thy court, nor thy name. But teach me truly all that pertaineth thereto, and tell me thy name, and I shall use all my wit to win my way thither, and that I swear thee for sooth, and by my sure troth."

"That is enough in the New Year, it needs no more," quoth the Green Knight to the gallant Gawain, "if I tell thee truly when I have taken the blow, and thou hast smitten me; then will I teach thee of my house and home, and mine own name, then mayest thou ask thy road and keep covenant. And if I waste no words then farest thou the better, for thou canst dwell in thy land, and seek no further. But take now thy toll, and let see how thy strikest."

"Gladly will I," quoth Gawain, handling his axe.

The Giving of the Blow

Then the Green Knight swiftly made him ready, he bowed down his head, and laid his long locks on the crown that his bare neck might be seen. Gawain gripped his axe and raised it on high, the left foot he set forward on the floor, and let the blow fall lightly on the bare neck. The sharp edge of the blade sundered the bones, smote through the neck, and clave it in two, so that the edge of the steel bit on the ground, and the head rolled even to the horse's feet.

The Marvel of the Green Knight

The blood spurted forth, and glistened on the green raiment, but the knight neither faltered nor fell; he started forward with out-stretched hand, and caught the head, and lifted it up; then he turned to his steed, and took hold of the bridle, set his foot in the stirrup, and mounted. His head he held by the hair, in his hand. Then he seated himself in his saddle as if naught ailed him, and he were not headless. He turned his steed about, the grim corpse bleeding freely the while, and they who looked upon him doubted them much for the covenant.

For he held up the head in his hand, and turned the face towards them that sat on the high daïs, and it lifted up the eye-lids and looked upon them, and spake as ye shall hear. "Look, Gawain, that thou art ready to go as thou hast promised, and seek leally till thou find me, even as thou hast sworn in this hall in the hearing of these knights. Come thou, I charge thee, to the Green Chapel, such a stroke as thou hast dealt thou hast deserved, and it shall be promptly paid thee on New Year's morn. Many men know me as the knight of the Green Chapel, and if thou askest thou shalt not fail to find me. Therefore it behoves thee to come, or to yield thee as recreant."

With that he turned his bridle, and galloped out at the hall door, his head in his hands, so that the sparks flew from beneath his horse's hoofs. Whither he went none knew, no more than they wist whence he had come; and the king and Gawain they gazed and laughed, for in sooth this had proved a greater marvel than any they had known aforetime.

Though Arthur the king was astonished at his heart, yet he let no sign of it be seen, but spake in courteous wise to the fair queen: "Dear lady, be not dismayed, such craft is well suited to Christmas-tide when we seek jesting, laughter and song, and fair carols of knights and ladies. But now I may well get me to meat, for I have seen a marvel I may not forget." Then he looked on Sir Gawain, and said gaily, "Now, fair nephew, hang up thine axe, since it has hewn enough," and they hung it on the dossal above the daïs, where all men might look on it for a marvel, and by its true token tell of the wonder. Then the twain sat them down together, the king and the good knight, and men served them with a double portion, as was the share of the noblest, with all manner of meat and of minstrelsy. And they spent that day in gladness, but Sir Gawain must well bethink him of the heavy venture to which he had set his hand.

Part II

THIS BEGINNING of adventures had Arthur at the New Year, for he yearned to hear gallant tales, though his words were few when he sat at the feast. But now had they stern work on hand. Gawain was glad to begin the jest in the hall, but ye need have no marvel if the end be heavy. For though a man be merry in mind when he has well drunk, yet a year runs full swiftly, and the beginning but rarely matches the end.

The Waning of the Year

For Yule was now over-past,[4] and the year after, each season in its turn following the other. For after Christmas comes crabbed Lent, that will have fish for flesh and simpler cheer. But then the weather of the world chides with winter; the cold withdraws itself, the clouds uplift, and the rain falls in warm showers on the fair plains. Then the flowers come forth, meadows and groves are clad in green, the birds make ready to build, and sing sweetly for solace of the soft summer that follows thereafter. The blossoms bud and blow in the hedgerows rich and rank, and noble notes enough are heard in the fair woods.

After the season of summer, with the soft winds, when zephyr breathes lightly on seeds and herbs, joyous indeed is the growth that waxes thereout when the dew drips from the leaves beneath the blissful glance of the bright sun. But then comes harvest and hardens the grain, warning it to wax ripe ere the winter. The drought drives the dust on high, flying over the face of the land; the angry wind of the welkin wrestles with the sun; the leaves fall from the trees and light upon the ground, and all brown are the groves that but now were green, and ripe is the fruit that once was flower. So the year passes into many yesterdays, and winter comes again, as it needs no sage to tell us.

Sir Gawain Bethinks Him of His Covenant

When the Michaelmas moon was come in with warnings of winter, Sir Gawain bethought him full oft of his perilous journey. Yet till All Hallows Day he lingered with Arthur, and on that day they made a great feast for the hero's sake, with much revel and richness of the Round Table. Courteous knights and comely ladies, all were in sorrow for the love of that knight, and though they spake no word of it many were joyless for his sake.

And after meat, sadly Sir Gawain turned to his uncle, and spake of his journey, and said, "Liege lord of my life, leave from you I crave. Ye know well how the matter stands without more words, to-morrow am I bound to set forth in search of the Green Knight."

Then came together all the noblest knights, Ywain and Erec, and many another. Sir Dodinel le Sauvage, Launcelot and Lionel, and Lucan the Good, Sir Bors and Sir Bedivere, valiant knights both, and many another hero, with Sir Mador de la Porte, and they all drew near, heavy at heart, to take counsel with Sir Gawain. Much sorrow and weeping was there in the hall to think that so worthy a knight as Gawain should wend his way to seek a deadly blow, and should no more wield his sword in fight. But the knight made ever good cheer, and said, "Nay, wherefore should I shrink? What may a man do but prove his fate?"

The Arming of Sir Gawain

He dwelt there all that day, and on the morn he arose and asked betimes for his armour; and they brought it unto him on this wise: first, a rich carpet was stretched on the floor[5] (and brightly did the gold gear glitter upon it), then the knight stepped on to it, and handled the steel; clad he was in a doublet of silk, with a close hood, lined fairly throughout. Then they set the steel shoes upon his feet, and wrapped his legs with greaves, with polished knee-caps fastened with knots of gold. Then they cased his thighs in cuisses closed with thongs, and brought him the byrny of bright steel rings sewn upon a fair stuff. Well burnished braces they set on each arm with good elbow-pieces, and gloves of mail, and all the goodly gear that should shield him in his need. And they cast over all a rich surcoat, and set the golden spurs on his heels, and girt him with a trusty sword fastened with a silken bawdrick. When he was thus clad his harness was costly, for the least loop or latchet gleamed with gold. So armed as he was he hearkened Mass and made his offering at the high altar. Then he came to the king, and the knights of his court, and courteously took leave of lords and ladies, and they kissed him, and commended him to Christ.

With that was Gringalet ready, girt with a saddle that gleamed gaily with many golden fringes, enriched and decked anew for the venture. The bridle was all barred about with bright gold buttons, and all the covertures and trappings of the steed, the crupper and the rich skirts, accorded with the saddle; spread fair with the rich red gold that glittered and gleamed in the rays of the sun.

Then the knight called for his helmet, which was well lined throughout, and set it high on his head, and hasped it behind. He wore a light kerchief over the vintail, that was broidered and studded with fair gems on a broad silken ribbon, with birds of gay colour, and many a turtle and true-lover's knot interlaced thickly, even as many a maiden had wrought them. But the circlet which crowned his helmet was yet more precious, being adorned with a device in diamonds. Then they brought him his shield, which was of bright red, with the pentangle painted thereon in gleaming gold.[6]

Wherefore Sir Gawain Bare the Pentangle

And why that noble prince bare the pentangle I am minded to tell you, though my tale tarry thereby. It is a sign that Solomon set ere-while, as betokening truth; for it is a figure with five points and each line overlaps the other, and nowhere hath it beginning or end, so that in English it is called "the endless knot." And therefore was it well suiting to this knight and to his arms, since Gawain was faithful in five and five-fold, for pure was he as gold, void of all villainy and endowed with all virtues. Therefore he bare the pentangle on shield and surcoat as truest of heroes and gentlest of knights.

For first he was faultless in his five senses; and his five fingers never failed him; and all his trust upon earth was in the five wounds that Christ bare on the cross, as the Creed tells. And wherever this knight found himself in stress of battle he deemed well that he drew his strength from the five joys which the Queen of Heaven had of her Child. And for this cause did he bear an image of Our Lady on the one half of his shield, that whenever he looked upon it he might not lack for aid. And the fifth five that the hero used were frankness and fellowship above all, purity and courtesy that never failed him, and compassion that surpasses all; and in these five virtues was that hero wrapped and clothed. And all these, five-fold, were linked one in the other, so that they had no end, and were fixed on five points that never failed, neither at any side were they joined or sundered, nor could ye find beginning or end. And therefore on his shield was the knot shapen, red-gold upon red, which is the pure pentangle. Now was Sir Gawain ready, and he took his lance in hand, and bade them all *Farewell*, he deemed it had been for ever.

How Sir Gawain Went Forth

Then he smote the steed with his spurs, and sprang on his way, so that sparks flew from the stones after him. All that saw him were grieved at heart, and said one to the other, "By Christ, 'tis great pity that one of such noble life should be lost! I' faith, 'twere not easy to find his equal upon earth. The king had done better to have wrought more warily. Yonder knight should have been made a duke; a gallant leader of men is he, and such a fate had beseemed him better than to be hewn in pieces at the will of an elfish man, for mere pride. Who ever knew a king to take such counsel as to risk his knights on a Christmas jest?" Many were the tears that flowed from their eyes when that goodly knight rode from the hall. He made no delaying, but went his way swiftly, and rode many a wild road, as I heard say in the book.

Of Sir Gawain's Journey

So rode Sir Gawain through the realm of Logres, on an errand that he held for no jest. Often he lay companionless at night, and must lack the fare that he liked. No comrade had he save his steed, and none save God with whom to take counsel. At length he drew nigh to North Wales, and left the isles of Anglesey on his left hand, crossing over the fords by the foreland over at Holyhead, till he came into the wilderness of Wirral,[7] that is loved neither of God nor of man, and there he abode but a little time. And ever he asked, as he fared, of all whom he met, if they had heard any tidings of a Green Knight in the country thereabout, or of a Green Chapel? And all answered him, Nay, never in their lives had they seen any man of such a hue. And the knight wended his way by many a strange road and many a rugged path, and the fashion of his countenance changed full often ere he saw the Green Chapel.

Many a cliff did he climb in that unknown land, where afar from his friends he rode as a stranger. Never did he come to a stream or a ford but he found a foe before him, and that one so marvellous, so foul and fell, that it behoved him to fight. So many wonders did that knight behold that it were too long to tell the tenth part of them. Sometimes he fought with dragons and wolves; sometimes with wild men that dwelt in the rocks; another while with bulls, and bears, and wild boars, or with giants of the high moorland that drew near to him. Had he not been a doughty knight, enduring, and of well-proved valour, doubtless he had been slain, for he was oft in danger of death. Yet he cared not so much for the strife, what he deemed worse was when the cold clear water was shed from the clouds, and froze ere it fell on the fallow ground. More nights than enough he slept in his harness on the bare rocks, near slain with the sleet, while the stream leapt bubbling from the crest of the hills, and hung in hard icicles over his head.

Thus in peril and pain, and many a hardship, the knight rode alone till Christmas Eve, and in that tide he made his prayer to the Blessed Virgin that she would guide his steps and lead him to some dwelling. On that morning he rode by a hill, and came into a thick forest, wild and drear; on each side were high hills, and thick woods below them of great hoar oaks, a hundred together, of hazel and hawthorn with their trailing boughs intertwined, and rough ragged moss spreading everywhere. On the bare twigs the birds chirped piteously, for pain of the cold. The knight upon Gringalet rode lonely beneath them, through marsh and mire, much troubled at heart lest he should fail to see the service of the Lord, who on that self-same night was born of a Maiden for the cure of our grief; and therefore he said, sighing, "I beseech Thee, Lord, and Mary Thy gentle Mother, for some shelter where I may hear Mass, and Thy mattins at morn. This I ask meekly, and thereto I pray my Paternoster, Ave, and Credo." Thus he rode praying, and lamenting his misdeeds, and he crossed himself, and said, "May the Cross of Christ speed me."

How Sir Gawain Came to a Fair
Castle on Christmas Eve

Now that knight had crossed himself but thrice ere he was aware in the wood of a dwelling within a moat, above a lawn, on a mound surrounded by many mighty trees that stood round the moat. 'Twas the fairest castle that ever a knight owned;[8] built in a meadow with a park all about it, and a spiked palisade, closely driven, that enclosed the trees for more than two miles. The knight was ware of the hold from the side, as it shone through the oaks. Then he lifted off his helmet, and thanked Christ and S. Julian that they had courteously granted his prayer, and hearkened to his cry. "Now," quoth the knight, "I beseech ye, grant me fair hostel." Then he pricked Gringalet with his golden spurs, and rode gaily towards the great gate, and came swiftly to the bridge end.

The bridge was drawn up and the gates close shut; the walls were strong and thick, so that they might fear no tempest. The knight on his charger abode on the bank of the deep double ditch that surrounded the castle. The walls were set deep in the water, and rose aloft to a wondrous height; they were of hard hewn stone up to the corbels, which were adorned beneath the battlements with fair carvings, and turrets set in between with many a loophole; a better barbican Sir Gawain had never looked upon. And within he beheld the high hall, with its tower and many windows with carven cornices, and chalk-white chimneys on the turreted roofs that shone fair in the sun. And everywhere, thickly scattered on the castle battlements, were pinnacles, so many that it seemed as if it were all wrought out of paper, so white was it.

The knight on his steed deemed it fair enough, if he might come to be sheltered within it to lodge there while that the Holy-day lasted. He called aloud, and soon there came a porter of kindly countenance, who stood on the wall and greeted this knight and asked his errand.

"Good sir," quoth Gawain, "wilt thou go mine errand to the high lord of the castle, and crave for me lodging?"

"Yea, by S. Peter," quoth the porter. "In sooth I trow that ye be welcome to dwell here so long as it may like ye."

How Sir Gawain Was Welcomed

Then he went, and came again swiftly, and many folk with him to receive the knight. They let down the great drawbridge, and came forth and knelt on their knees on the cold earth to give him worthy welcome. They held wide open the great gates, and he greeted them courteously, and rode over the bridge. Then men came to him and held his stirrup while he dismounted, and took and stabled his steed. There came down knights and squires to bring the guest with joy to the hall. When he raised his helmet there were many to take it from his hand, fain to serve him, and they took from him sword and shield.

Sir Gawain gave good greeting to the nobles and the mighty men who came to do him honour. Clad in his shining armour they led him to the hall, where a great fire burnt brightly on the floor; and the lord of the household came forth from his chamber to meet the hero fitly. He spake to the knight, and said: "Ye are welcome to do here as it likes ye. All that is here is your own to have at your will and disposal."

"Gramercy!" quote Gawain, "may Christ requite ye."

As friends that were fain each embraced the other; and Gawain looked on the knight who greeted him so kindly, and thought 'twas a bold warrior that owned that burg.

Of mighty stature he was, and of high age; broad and flowing was his beard, and of a bright hue. He was stalwart of limb, and strong in his stride, his face fiery red, and his speech free: in sooth he seemed one well fitted to be a leader of valiant men.

Then the lord led Sir Gawain to a chamber, and commanded folk to wait upon him, and at his bidding there came men enough who brought the guest to a fair bower. The bedding was noble, with curtains of pure silk wrought with gold, and wondrous coverings of fair cloth all embroidered. The curtains ran on ropes with rings of red gold, and the walls were hung with carpets of Orient, and the same spread on the floor. There with mirthful speeches they took from the guest his byrny and all his shining armour, and brought him rich robes of the choicest in its stead. They were long and flowing, and became him well, and when he was clad in them all who looked on the hero thought that surely God had never made a fairer knight: he seemed as if he might be a prince without peer in the field where men strive in battle.

Then before the hearth-place, whereon the fire burned, they made ready a chair for Gawain, hung about with cloth and fair cushions; and there they cast around him a mantle of brown samite, richly embroidered and furred within with costly skins of ermine, with a hood of the same, and he seated himself in that rich seat, and warmed himself at the fire and was cheered at heart. And while he sat thus the serving men set up a table on trestles, and covered it with a fair white cloth, and set thereon salt-cellar, and napkin, and silver spoons; and the knight washed at his will, and set him down to meat.

The folk served him courteously with many dishes seasoned of the best, a double portion. All kinds of fish were there, some baked in bread, some broiled on the embers, some sodden, some stewed and savoured with spices, with all sorts of cunning devices to his taste. And often he called it a feast, when they spake gaily to him all together, and said, "Now take ye this penance, and it shall be for your amendment." Much mirth thereof did Sir Gawain make.

Sir Gawain Tells His Name

Then they questioned that prince courteously of whence he came; and he told them that he was of the court of Arthur, who is the rich royal King of the Round Table, and that it was Gawain himself who was within their walls, and would keep Christmas with them, as the chance had fallen out. And when the lord of the castle heard those tidings he laughed aloud for gladness, and all men in that keep were joyful that they should be in the company of him to whom belonged all fame, and valour, and courtesy, and whose honour was praised above that of all men on earth. Each said softly to his fellow, "Now shall we see courteous bearing, and the manner of speech befitting courts. What charm lieth in gentle speech shall we learn without asking, since here we have welcomed the fine father of courtesy. God has surely shewn us His grace since He sends us such a guest as Gawain! When men shall sit and sing, blithe for Christ's birth, this knight shall bring us to the knowledge of fair manners, and it may be that hearing him we may learn the cunning speech of love."

By the time the knight had risen from dinner it was near nightfall. Then chaplains took their way to the chapel, and rang loudly, even as they should, for the solemn evensong of the high feast. Thither went the lord, and the lady also, and entered with her maidens into a comely closet, and thither also went Gawain. Then the lord took him by the sleeve and led him to a seat, and called him by his name, and told him he was of all men in the world the most welcome. And Sir Gawain thanked him truly, and each kissed the other, and they sat gravely together throughout the service.

The Lady of the Castle

Then was the lady fain to look upon that knight; and she came forth from her closet with many fair maidens. The fairest of ladies was she in face, and figure, and colouring, fairer even than Guinevere, so the knight thought. She came through the chancel to greet the hero, another lady held her by the left hand, older than she, and seemingly of high estate, with many nobles about her. But unlike to look upon were those ladies, for if the younger were fair, the elder was yellow. Rich red were the cheeks of the one, rough and wrinkled those of the other; the kerchiefs of the one were broidered with many glistening pearls, her throat and neck bare, and whiter than the snow that lies on the hills; the neck of the other was swathed in a gorget, with a white wimple over her black chin. Her forehead was wrapped in silk with many folds, worked with knots, so that naught of her was seen save her black brows, her eyes, her nose, and her lips, and those were bleared, and ill to look upon. A worshipful lady in sooth one might call her! In figure was she short and broad, and thickly made – far fairer to behold was she whom she led by the hand.

When Gawain beheld that fair lady, who looked at him graciously, with leave of the lord he went towards them, and, bowing low, he greeted the elder, but the younger and fairer he took lightly in his arms, and kissed her courteously, and greeted her in knightly wise. Then she hailed him as friend, and he quickly prayed to be counted as her servant, if she so willed. Then they took him between them, and talking, led him to the chamber, to the hearth, and bade them bring spices, and they brought them in plenty with the good wine that was wont to be drunk at such seasons. Then the lord sprang to his feet and bade them make merry, and took off his hood, and hung it on a spear, and bade him win the worship thereof who should make most mirth that Christmas-tide. "And I shall try, by my faith, to fool it with the best, by the help of my friends, ere I lose my raiment." Thus with gay words the lord made trial to gladden Gawain with jests that night, till it was time to bid them light the tapers, and Sir Gawain took leave of them and gat him to rest.

Of the Christmas Feast

In the morn when all men call to mind how Christ our Lord was born on earth to die for us, there is joy, for His sake, in all dwellings of the world; and so was there here on that day. For high feast was held, with many dainties and cunningly cooked messes. On the daïs sat gallant men, clad in their best. The ancient dame sat on the high seat, with the lord of the castle beside her. Gawain and the fair lady sat together, even in the midst of the board, when the feast was served; and so throughout all the hall each sat in his degree, and was served in order. There was meat, there was mirth, there was much joy, so that to tell thereof would take me too long, though peradventure I might strive to declare it. But Gawain and that fair lady had much joy of each other's company through her sweet words and courteous converse. And there was music made before each prince, trumpets and drums, and merry piping; each man hearkened his minstrel, and they too hearkened theirs.

How the Feast Came to an End but Gawain Abode at the Castle

So they held high feast that day and the next, and the third day thereafter, and the joy on S. John's Day was fair to hearken, for 'twas the last of the feast, and the guests would depart in the grey of the morning. Therefore they awoke early, and drank wine, and danced fair carols, and at last, when it was late, each man took his leave to wend early on his way. Gawain would bid his host farewell, but the lord took him by the hand, and led him to his own chamber beside the hearth, and there he thanked him for the favour he had shown him in honouring his dwelling at that high season, and gladdening his castle with his fair countenance. "I wis, sir, that while I live I shall be held the worthier that Gawain has been my guest at God's own feast."

"Gramercy, sir," quoth Gawain, "in good faith, all the honour is yours, may the High King give it ye, and I am but at your will to work your behest, inasmuch as I am beholden to ye in great and small by rights."

Then the lord did his best to persuade the knight to tarry with him, but Gawain answered that he might in no wise do so. Then the host asked him courteously what stern behest had driven him at the holy season from the king's court, to fare all alone, ere yet the feast was ended?

"Forsooth," quoth the knight, "ye say but the truth: 'tis a high quest and a pressing that hath brought me afield, for I am summoned myself to a certain place, and I know not whither in the world I may wend to find it; so help me Christ, I would give all the kingdom of Logres an I might find it by New Year's morn. Therefore, sir, I make request of ye that ye tell me truly if ye ever heard word of the Green Chapel, where it may be found, and the Green Knight that keeps it. For I am pledged by solemn compact sworn between us to meet that knight at the New Year if so I were on life; and of that same New Year it wants but little – I' faith, I would look on that hero more joyfully than on any other fair sight! Therefore, by your will, it behoves me to leave ye, for I have but barely three days, and I would as fain fall dead as fail of mine errand."

Then the lord quoth, laughing, "Now must ye needs stay, for I will show ye your goal, the Green Chapel, ere your term be at an end, have ye no fear! But ye can take your ease, friend, in your bed, till the fourth day, and go forth on the first of the year, and come to that place at mid-morn to do as ye will. Dwell here till New Year's Day, and then rise and set forth, and ye shall be set in the way; 'tis not two miles hence."

Then was Gawain glad, and he laughed gaily. "Now I thank ye for this above all else. Now my quest is achieved I will dwell here at your will, and otherwise do as ye shall ask."

Then the lord took him, and set him beside him, and bade the ladies be fetched for their greater pleasure, tho' between themselves they had solace. The lord, for gladness, made merry jest, even as one who wist not what to do for joy; and he cried aloud to the knight, "Ye have promised to do the thing I bid ye: will ye hold to this behest, here, at once?"

"Yea, forsooth," said that true knight, "while I abide in your burg I am bound by your behest."

"Ye have travelled from far," said the host, "and since then ye have waked with me, ye are not well refreshed by rest and sleep, as I know. Ye shall therefore abide in your chamber, and lie at your ease to-morrow at Mass-tide, and go to meat when ye will with my wife, who shall sit with ye, and comfort ye with her company till I return; and I shall rise early and go forth to the chase." And Gawain agreed to all this courteously.

Sir Gawain Makes a Covenant with His Host

"Sir knight," quoth the host, "we will make a covenant. Whatsoever I win in the wood shall be yours, and whatever may fall to your share, that shall ye exchange for it. Let us swear, friend, to make this exchange, however our hap may be, for worse or for better."

"I grant ye your will," quoth Gawain the good; "if ye list so to do, it liketh me well."

"Bring hither the wine-cup, the bargain is made," so said the lord of that castle. They laughed each one, and drank of the wine, and made merry, these lords and ladies, as it pleased them. Then with gay talk and merry jest they arose, and stood, and spoke softly, and kissed courteously, and took leave of each other. With burning torches, and many a serving man, was each led to his couch; yet ere they gat them to bed the old lord oft repeated their covenant, for he knew well how to make sport.

Part III

The First Day's Hunting

FULL EARLY, ere daylight, the folk rose up; the guests who would depart called their grooms, and they made them ready, and saddled the steeds, tightened up the girths, and trussed up their mails. The knights, all arrayed for riding, leapt up lightly, and took their bridles, and each rode his way as pleased him best.

The lord of the land was not the last. Ready for the chase, with many of his men, he ate a sop hastily when he had heard Mass, and then with blast of the bugle fared forth to the field.[9] He and his nobles were to horse ere daylight glimmered upon the earth.

Then the huntsmen coupled their hounds, unclosed the kennel door, and called them out. They blew three blasts gaily on the bugles, the hounds bayed fiercely, and they that would go a-hunting checked and chastised them. A hundred hunters there were of the best, so I have heard tell. Then the trackers gat them to the trysting-place and uncoupled the hounds, and the forest rang again with their gay blasts.

At the first sound of the hunt the game quaked for fear, and fled, trembling, along the vale. They betook them to the heights, but the liers in wait turned them back with loud cries; the harts they let pass them, and the stags with their spreading antlers, for the lord had forbidden that they should be slain, but the hinds and the does they turned back, and drave down into the valleys. Then might ye see much shooting of arrows. As the deer fled under the boughs a broad whistling shaft smote and wounded each sorely, so that, wounded and bleeding, they fell dying on the banks. The hounds followed swiftly on their tracks, and hunters, blowing the horn, sped after them with ringing shouts that well-nigh burst the cliffs asunder. What game escaped those that shot was run down at the outer ring. Thus were they driven on the hills, and harassed at the waters, so well did the men know their work, and the greyhounds were so great and swift that they ran them down as fast as the hunters could slay them. Thus the lord passed the day in mirth and joyfulness, even to nightfall.

How the Lady of the Castle Came to Sir Gawain

So the lord roamed the woods, and Gawain, that good knight, lay ever a-bed, curtained about, under the costly coverlet, while the daylight gleamed on the walls. And as he lay half slumbering, he heard a little sound at the door, and he raised his head, and caught back a corner of the curtain, and waited to see what it might be. It was the lovely lady, the lord's wife; she shut the door softly behind her, and turned towards the bed; and Gawain laid him down softly and made as if he slept. And she came lightly to the bedside, within the curtain, and sat herself down beside him, to wait till he wakened. The knight lay there awhile, and marvelled within himself what her coming might betoken; and he said to himself, "'Twere more seemly if I asked her what hath brought her hither." Then he made feint to waken, and turned towards her, and opened his eyes as one astonished, and crossed himself; and she looked on him laughing, with her cheeks red and white, lovely to behold.

"Good morrow, Sir Gawain," said that fair lady; "ye are but a careless sleeper, since one can enter thus. Now are ye taken unawares, and lest ye escape me I shall bind you in your bed; of that be ye assured!" Laughing, she spake these words.

"Good morrow, fair lady," quoth Gawain blithely. "I will do your will, as it likes me well. For I yield me readily, and pray your grace, and that is best, by my faith, since I needs must do so." Thus he jested again, laughing. "But an ye would, fair lady, grant me this grace that ye pray your prisoner to rise. I would get me from bed, and array me better, then could I talk with ye in more comfort."

"Nay, forsooth, fair sir," quoth the lady, "ye shall not rise, I will rede ye better. I shall keep ye here, since ye can do no other, and talk with my knight whom I have captured. For I know well that ye are Sir Gawain, whom all the world worships, wheresoever ye may ride. Your honour and your courtesy are praised by lords and ladies, by all who live. Now ye are here and we are alone, my lord and his men are afield; the serving men in their beds, and my maidens also, and the door shut upon us. And since in this hour I have him that all men love, I shall use my time well with speech, while it lasts. Ye are welcome to my company, for it behoves me in sooth to be your servant."

"In good faith," quoth Gawain, "I think me that I am not he of whom ye speak, for unworthy am I of such service as ye here proffer. In sooth, I were glad if I might set myself by word or service to your pleasure; a pure joy would it be to me!"

"In good faith, Sir Gawain," quoth the gay lady, "the praise and the prowess that pleases all ladies I lack them not, nor hold them light; yet are there ladies enough who would liever now have the knight in their hold, as I have ye here, to dally with your courteous words, to bring them comfort and to ease their cares, than much of the treasure and the gold that are theirs. And now, through the grace of Him who upholds the heavens, I have wholly in my power that which they all desire!"

Thus the lady, fair to look upon, made him great cheer, and Sir Gawain, with modest words, answered her again: "Madam," he quoth, "may Mary requite ye, for in good faith I have found in ye a noble frankness. Much courtesy have other folk shown me, but the honour they have done me is naught to the worship of yourself, who knoweth but good."

"By Mary," quoth the lady, "I think otherwise; for were I worth all the women alive, and had I the wealth of the world in my hand, and might choose me a lord to my liking, then, for all that I have seen in ye, Sir Knight, of beauty and courtesy and blithe semblance, and for all that I have hearkened and hold for true, there should be no knight on earth to be chosen before ye!"

"Well I wot," quoth Sir Gawain, "that ye have chosen a better; but I am proud that ye should so prize me, and as your servant do I hold ye my sovereign, and your knight am I, and may Christ reward ye."

So they talked of many matters till mid-morn was past, and ever the lady shewed her love to him, and the knight turned her speech aside. For though she were the brightest of maidens, yet had he forborne to shew her love for the danger that awaited him, and the blow that must be given without delay.

Then the lady prayed her leave from him, and he granted it readily. And she gave him good-day, with laughing glance, but he must needs marvel at her words:

"Now He that speeds fair speech reward ye this disport; but that ye be Gawain my mind misdoubts me greatly."

"Wherefore?" quoth the knight quickly, fearing lest he had lacked in some courtesy.

And the lady spake: "So true a knight as Gawain is holden, and one so perfect in courtesy, would never have tarried so long with a lady but he would of his courtesy have craved a kiss at parting."

How the Lady Kissed Sir Gawain

Then quoth Gawain, "I wot I will do even as it may please ye, and kiss at your commandment, as a true knight should who forbears to ask for fear of displeasure."

At that she came near and bent down and kissed the knight, and each commended the other to Christ, and she went forth from the chamber softly.

Then Sir Gawain arose and called his chamberlain and chose his garments, and when he was ready he gat him forth to Mass, and then went to meat, and made merry all day till the rising of the moon, and never had a knight fairer lodging than had he with those two noble ladies, the elder and the younger.

And ever the lord of the land chased the hinds through holt and heath till eventide, and then with much blowing of bugles and baying of hounds they bore the game homeward; and by the time daylight was done all the folk had returned to that fair castle. And when the lord and Sir Gawain met together, then were they both well pleased. The lord commanded them all to assemble in the great hall, and the ladies to descend with their maidens, and there, before them all, he bade the men fetch in the spoil of the day's hunting, and he called unto Gawain, and counted the tale of the beasts, and showed them unto him, and said, "What think ye of this game, Sir Knight? Have I deserved of ye thanks for my woodcraft?"

"Yea, I wis," quoth the other, "here is the fairest spoil I have seen this seven year in the winter season."

How the Covenant Was Kept

"And all this do I give ye, Gawain," quoth the host, "for by accord of covenant ye may claim it as your own."

"That is sooth," quoth the other, "I grant you that same; and I have fairly won this within walls, and with as good will do I yield it to ye." With that he clasped his hands round the lord's neck and kissed him as courteously as he might. "Take ye here my spoils, no more have I won; ye should have it freely, though it were greater than this."

"'Tis good," said the host, "gramercy thereof. Yet were I fain to know where ye won this same favour, and if it were by your own wit?"

"Nay," answered Gawain, "that was not in the bond. Ask me no more: ye have taken what was yours by right, be content with that."

They laughed and jested together, and sat them down to supper, where they were served with many dainties; and after supper they sat by the hearth, and wine was served out to them; and oft in their jesting they promised to observe on the morrow the same covenant that they had made before, and whatever chance might betide to exchange their spoil, be it much or little, when they met at night. Thus they renewed their bargain before the whole court, and then the night-drink was served, and each courteously took leave of the other and gat him to bed.

Of the Second Day's Hunting

By the time the cock had crowed thrice the lord of the castle had left his bed; Mass was sung and meat fitly served. The folk were forth to the wood ere the day broke, with hound and horn they rode over the plain, and uncoupled their dogs among the thorns. Soon they struck on the scent, and the hunt cheered on the hounds who were first to seize it, urging them with shouts. The others hastened to the cry, forty at once, and there rose such a clamour from the pack that the rocks rang again. The huntsmen followed hard after with shouting and blasts of the horn; and the hounds drew together to a thicket betwixt the water and a high crag in the cliff beneath the hillside. As the rough rocks were ill for riding the huntsmen sprang to earth and hastened on foot, and cast about round the hill and the thicket. The knights wist well what beast was within, and would drive him forth with the bloodhounds. And as they beat the bushes, suddenly over the beaters there rushed forth a wondrous great and fierce boar, long since had he left the herd to roam by himself. Grunting, he cast many to the ground, and fled forth at his best speed, without more mischief. The men hallooed loudly and cried, "*Hay! Hay!*" and blew the horns to urge on the hounds, and rode swiftly after the boar. Many a time did he turn to bay and tare the hounds, and they yelped, and howled shrilly. Then the men made ready their arrows and shot at him, but the points were turned on his thick hide, and the barbs would not bite upon him, for the shafts shivered in pieces, and the head but leapt again wherever it hit.

But when the boar felt the stroke of the arrows he waxed mad with rage, and turned on the hunters and tare many, so that, affrighted, they fled before him. But the lord on a swift steed pursued him, blowing his bugle; as a gallant knight he rode through the woodland chasing the boar till the sun grew low.

So did the hunters this day, while Sir Gawain lay in his bed lapped in rich gear; and the lady forgat not to salute him, for early was she at his side, to cheer his mood.

Of the Lady and Sir Gawain

She came to the bedside and looked on the knight, and Gawain gave her fit greeting, and she greeted him again with ready words, and sat her by his side and laughed, and with a sweet look she spoke to him:

49

"Sir, if ye be Gawain, I think it a wonder that ye be so stern and cold, and care not for the courtesies of friendship, but if one teach ye to know them ye cast the lesson out of your mind. Ye have soon forgotten what I taught ye yesterday, by all the truest tokens that I knew!"

"What is that?" quoth the knight. "I trow I know not. If it be sooth that ye say, then is the blame mine own."

"But I taught ye of kissing," quoth the fair lady. "Wherever a fair countenance is shown him, it behoves a courteous knight quickly to claim a kiss."

"Nay, my dear," said Sir Gawain, "cease that speech; that durst I not do lest I were denied, for if I were forbidden I wot I were wrong did I further entreat."

"I' faith," quoth the lady merrily, "ye may not be forbid, ye are strong enough to constrain by strength an ye will, were any so discourteous as to give ye denial."

"Yea, by Heaven," said Gawain, "ye speak well; but threats profit little in the land where I dwell, and so with a gift that is given not of good will! I am at your commandment to kiss when ye like, to take or to leave as ye list."

Then the lady bent her down and kissed him courteously.

How the Lady Strove to Beguile Sir Gawain with Words of Love

And as they spake together she said, "I would learn somewhat from ye, an ye would not be wroth, for young ye are and fair, and so courteous and knightly as ye are known to be, the head of all chivalry, and versed in all wisdom of love and war – 'tis ever told of true knights how they adventured their lives for their true love, and endured hardships for her favours, and avenged her with valour, and eased her sorrows, and brought joy to her bower; and ye are the fairest knight of your time, and your fame and your honour are everywhere, yet I have sat by ye here twice, and never a word have heard of love! Ye who are so courteous and skilled in such lore ought surely to teach one so young and unskilled some little craft of true love! Why are ye so unlearned who art otherwise so famous? Or is it that ye deem me unworthy to hearken to your teaching? For shame, Sir Knight! I come hither alone and sit at your side to learn of ye some skill; teach me of your wit, while my lord is from home."

"In good faith," quoth Gawain, "great is my joy and my profit that so fair a lady as ye are should deign to come hither, and trouble ye with so poor a man, and make sport with your knight with kindly countenance, it pleaseth me much. But that I, in my turn, should take it upon me to tell of love and such like matters to ye who know more by half, or a hundred fold, of such craft than I do, or ever shall in all my lifetime, by my troth 'twere folly indeed! I will work your will to the best of my might as I am bounden, and evermore will I be your servant, so help me Christ!"

Then often with guile she questioned that knight that she might win him to woo her, but he defended himself so fairly that none might in any wise blame him, and naught but bliss and harmless jesting was there between them. They laughed and talked together till at last she kissed him, and craved her leave of him, and went her way.

How the Boar Was Slain

Then the knight arose and went forth to Mass, and afterward dinner was served, and he sat and spake with the ladies all day. But the lord of the castle rode ever over the land chasing the wild boar, that fled through the thickets, slaying the best of his hounds and breaking their backs in sunder; till at last he was so weary he might run no longer, but made for a hole in a mound by a rock. He got the mound at his back and faced the hounds, whetting his white tusks and foaming at the mouth. The huntsmen stood aloof, fearing to draw nigh him; so many of them had been already wounded that they were loth to be torn with his tusks, so fierce he was and mad with rage. At length the lord himself came up, and saw the beast at bay, and the men standing aloof. Then quickly he sprang to the ground and drew out a bright blade, and waded through the stream to the boar.

When the beast was ware of the knight with weapon in hand, he set up his bristles and snorted loudly, and many feared for their lord lest he should be slain. Then the boar leapt upon the knight so that beast and man were one atop of the other in the water; but the boar had the worst of it, for the man had marked, even as he sprang, and set the point of his brand to the beast's chest, and drove it up to the hilt, so that the heart was split in twain, and the boar fell snarling, and was swept down by the water to where a hundred hounds seized on him, and the men drew him to shore for the dogs to slay.

Then was there loud blowing of horns and baying of hounds, the huntsmen smote off the boar's head, and hung the carcase by the four feet to a stout pole, and so went on their way homewards. The head they bore before the lord himself, who had slain the beast at the ford by force of his strong hand.

It seemed him o'er long ere he saw Sir Gawain in the hall, and he blew a blast on his horn to let all men know that he was come again to take his part in the covenant. And when he saw Gawain the lord laughed aloud, and bade them call the ladies and the household together, and he showed them the game, and told them the tale, how they had hunted the wild boar through the woods, and of his length and breadth and height; and Sir Gawain commended his deeds and praised him for his valour, well proven, for so mighty a beast had he never seen before.

The Keeping of the Covenant

Then they handled the huge head, and the lord said aloud, "Now, Gawain, this game is your own by sure covenant, as ye right well know."

"'Tis sooth," quoth the knight, "and as truly will I give ye all I have gained." He took the host round the neck, and kissed him courteously twice. "Now are we quits," he said, "this eventide, of all the covenants that we made since I came hither."

And the lord answered, "By S. Giles, ye are the best I know; ye will be rich in a short space if ye drive such bargains!"

Then they set up the tables on trestles, and covered them with fair cloths, and lit waxen tapers on the walls. The knights sat and were served in the hall, and much game and glee was there round the hearth, with many songs, both at supper and after; songs of Christmas, and new carols, with all the mirth one may think of. And ever that lovely lady sat by the knight, and with still stolen looks made such feint of pleasing him, that Gawain marvelled much, and was wroth with himself, but he could not for his courtesy return her fair glances, but dealt with her cunningly, however she might strive to wrest the thing.

When they had tarried in the hall so long as it seemed them good, they turned to the inner chamber and the wide hearth-place, and there they drank wine, and the host proffered to renew the covenant for New Year's Eve; but the knight craved leave to depart on the morrow, for it was nigh to the term when he must fulfil his pledge. But the lord would withhold him from so doing, and prayed him to tarry, and said,

"As I am a true knight I swear my troth that ye shall come to the Green Chapel to achieve your task on New Year's morn, long before prime. Therefore abide ye in your bed, and I will hunt in this wood, and hold ye to the covenant to exchange with me against all the spoil I may bring hither. For twice have I tried ye, and found ye true, and the morrow shall be the third time and the best. Make we merry now while we may, and think on joy, for misfortune may take a man whensoever it wills."

Then Gawain granted his request, and they brought them drink, and they gat them with lights to bed.

Of the Third Day's Hunting

Sir Gawain lay and slept softly, but the lord, who was keen on woodcraft, was afoot early. After Mass he and his men ate a morsel, and he asked for his steed; all the knights who should ride with him were already mounted before the hall gates.

'Twas a fair frosty morning, for the sun rose red in ruddy vapour, and the welkin was clear of clouds. The hunters scattered them by a forest side, and the rocks rang again with the blast of their horns. Some came on the scent of a fox, and a hound gave tongue; the huntsmen shouted, and the pack followed in a crowd on the trail. The fox ran before them, and when they saw him they pursued him with noise and much shouting, and he wound and turned through many a thick grove, often cowering and hearkening in a hedge. At last by a little ditch he leapt out of a spinney, stole away slily by a copse path, and so out of the wood and away from the bounds. But he went, ere he wist, to a chosen tryst, and three started forth on him at once, so he must needs double back, and betake him to the wood again.

Then was it joyful to hearken to the hounds; when all the pack had met together and had sight of their game they made as loud a din as if all the lofty cliffs had fallen clattering together. The huntsmen shouted and threatened, and followed close upon him so that he might scarce escape, but Reynard was wily, and he turned and doubled upon them, and led the lord and his men over the hills, now on the slopes, now in the vales, while the knight at home slept through the cold morning beneath his costly curtains.

How the Lady Came for the Third Time to Sir Gawain

But the fair lady of the castle rose betimes, and clad herself in a rich mantle that reached even to the ground, and was bordered and lined with costly furs. On her head she wore no golden circlet, but a network of precious stones, that gleamed and shone through her tresses in clusters of twenty together. Thus she came into the chamber and set open a window, and called to him gaily, "Sir Knight, how may ye sleep? The morning is so fair."

Sir Gawain was deep in slumber, and in his dream he vexed him much for the destiny that should befall him on the morrow, when he should meet the knight at the Green Chapel, and abide his blow; but when the lady spake he heard her, and came to himself, and roused from his dream and answered swiftly. The lady came laughing, and kissed him courteously, and he welcomed her fittingly with a cheerful countenance. He saw her so glorious and gaily dressed, so faultless of features and complexion, that it warmed his heart to look upon her.

They spake to each other smiling, and all was bliss and good cheer between them. They exchanged fair words, and much happiness was therein, yet was there a gulf between them, and she might win no more of her knight, for that gallant prince watched well his words – he would neither take her love, nor frankly refuse it. He cared for his courtesy, lest he be deemed churlish, and yet more for his honour lest he be traitor to his host. "God forbid," quoth he to himself, "that it should so befall." Thus with courteous words did he set aside all the special speeches that came from her lips.

Then spake the lady to the knight, "Ye deserve blame if ye hold not that lady who sits beside ye above all else in the world, if ye have not already a love whom ye hold dearer, and like better, and have sworn such firm faith to that lady that ye care not to loose it – as I scarce may believe. And now I pray ye straitly that ye tell me that in truth, and hide it not."

And the knight answered, "By S. John" (and he smiled as he spake) "no such love have I, nor do I think to have yet awhile."

"That is the worst word I may hear," quoth the lady, "but in sooth I have mine answer; kiss me now courteously, and I will go hence; I can but mourn as a maiden that loves much."

Sighing, she stooped down and kissed him, and then she rose up and spake as she stood, "Now, dear, at our parting do me this grace: give me some gift, if it were but thy glove, that I may bethink me of my knight, and lessen my mourning."

The Lady Would Fain Have a Parting Gift from Gawain

"Now, I wis," quoth the knight, "I would that I had here but the least thing that I possess on earth that I might leave ye as love-token, great or small, for ye have deserved forsooth more reward than I might give ye. But it is not to your honour to have at this time a glove for reward as gift from Gawain, and I am here on a strange errand, and have no man with me, nor mails with goodly things – that mislikes me much, lady, at this time; but each man must fare as he is taken, if for sorrow and ill."

She Would Give Him Her Ring

"Nay, knight highly honoured," quoth that lovesome lady, "though I have naught of yours, yet shall ye have somewhat of mine." With that she reached him a ring of red gold with a sparkling stone therein, that shone even as the sun (wit ye well, it was worth many marks); but the knight refused it, and spake readily,

"I will take no gift, lady, at this time. I have none to give, and none will I take."

She prayed him to take it, but he refused her prayer, and sware in sooth that he would not have it.

Or Her Girdle

The lady was sorely vexed, and said, "If ye refuse my ring as too costly, that ye will not be so highly beholden to me, I will give ye my girdle[10] as a lesser gift." With that she loosened a lace that was fastened at her side, knit upon her kirtle under her mantle. It was wrought of green silk, and gold, only braided by the fingers, and that she offered to the knight, and besought him though it were of little worth that he would take it, and he said nay, he would touch neither gold nor gear ere God give him grace to achieve the adventure for which he had come hither. "And therefore, I pray ye, displease ye not, and ask me no longer, for I may not grant it. I am dearly beholden to ye for the favour ye have shown me, and ever, in heat and cold, will I be your true servant."

The Virtue of the Girdle

"Now," said the lady, "ye refuse this silk, for it is simple in itself, and so it seems, indeed; lo, it is small to look upon and less in cost, but whoso knew the virtue that is knit therein he would, peradventure, value it more highly. For whatever knight is girded with this green lace, while he bears it knotted about him there is no man under heaven can overcome him, for he may not be slain for any magic on earth."

How Sir Gawain Took the Girdle

Then Gawain bethought him, and it came into his heart that this were a jewel for the jeopardy that awaited him when he came to the Green Chapel to seek the return blow – could he so order it that he should escape unslain, 'twere a craft worth trying. Then he bare with her chiding, and let her say her say, and she pressed the girdle on him and prayed him to take it, and he granted her prayer, and she gave it him with good will, and besought him for her sake never to reveal it but to hide it loyally from her lord; and the knight agreed that never should any man know it, save they two alone. He thanked her often and heartily, and she kissed him for the third time.

Then she took her leave of him, and when she was gone Sir Gawain arose, and clad him in rich attire, and took the girdle, and knotted it round him, and hid it beneath his robes. Then he took his way to the chapel, and sought out a priest privily, and prayed him to teach him better how his soul might be saved when he should go hence; and there he shrived him, and showed his misdeeds, both great and small, and besought mercy and craved absolution; and the priest assoiled him, and set him as clean as if Doomsday had been on the morrow. And afterwards Sir Gawain made him merry with the ladies, with carols, and all kinds of joy, as never he did but that one day, even to nightfall; and all the men marvelled at him, and said that never since he came thither had he been so merry.

The Death of the Fox

Meanwhile the lord of the castle was abroad chasing the fox; awhile he lost him, and as he rode through a spinney he heard the hounds near at hand, and Reynard came creeping through a thick grove, with all the pack at his heels. Then the lord drew out his shining brand, and cast it at the beast, and the fox swerved aside for the sharp edge, and would have doubled back, but a hound was on him ere he might turn, and right before the horse's feet they all fell on him, and worried him fiercely, snarling the while.

Then the lord leapt from his saddle, and caught the fox from their jaws, and held it aloft over his head, and hallooed loudly, and the hunters hied them thither, blowing their horns; all that bare bugles blew them at once, and all the others shouted. 'Twas the merriest meeting that ever men heard, the clamour that was raised at the death of the fox. They rewarded the hounds, stroking them and rubbing their heads, and took Reynard and stripped him of his coat; then blowing their horns, they turned them homewards, for it was nigh nightfall.

How Sir Gawain Kept Not All the Covenant

The lord was gladsome at his return, and found a bright fire on the hearth, and the knight beside it, the good Sir Gawain, who was in joyous mood for the pleasure he had had with the ladies. He wore a robe of blue, that reached even to the ground, and a surcoat richly furred, that became him well. A hood like to the surcoat fell on his shoulders, and all alike were done about with fur. He met the host in the midst of the floor, and jesting, he greeted him, and said, "Now shall I be first to fulfil our covenant which we made together when there was no lack of wine." Then he embraced the knight, and kissed him thrice, as solemnly as he might.

"Of a sooth," quoth the other, "ye have good luck in the matter of this covenant, if ye made a good exchange!"

"Yea, it matters naught of the exchange," quoth Gawain, "since what I owe is swiftly paid."

"Marry," said the other, "mine is behind, for I have hunted all this day, and naught have I got but this foul fox-skin, and that is but poor payment for three such kisses as ye have here given me."

"Enough," quoth Sir Gawain, "I thank ye, by the Rood."

Then the lord told them of his hunting, and how the fox had been slain.

With mirth and minstrelsy, and dainties at their will, they made them as merry as a folk well might till 'twas time for them to sever, for at last they must needs betake them to their beds. Then the knight took his leave of the lord, and thanked him fairly.

"For the fair sojourn that I have had here at this high feast may the High King give ye honour. I give ye myself, as one of your servants, if ye so like; for I must needs, as ye know, go hence with the morn, and ye will give me, as ye promised, a guide to show me the way to the Green Chapel, an God will suffer me on New Year's Day to deal the doom of my weird."

"By my faith," quoth the host, "all that ever I promised, that shall I keep with good will." Then he gave him a servant to set him in the way, and lead him by the downs, that he should have no need to ford the stream, and should fare by the shortest road through the groves;

and Gawain thanked the lord for the honour done him. Then he would take leave of the ladies, and courteously he kissed them, and spake, praying them to receive his thanks, and they made like reply; then with many sighs they commended him to Christ, and he departed courteously from that folk. Each man that he met he thanked him for his service and his solace, and the pains he had been at to do his will; and each found it as hard to part from the knight as if he had ever dwelt with him.

How Sir Gawain Took Leave of His Host

Then they led him with torches to his chamber, and brought him to his bed to rest. That he slept soundly I may not say, for the morrow gave him much to think on. Let him rest a while, for he was near that which he sought, and if ye will but listen to me I will tell ye how it fared with him thereafter.

Part IV

NOW THE NEW YEAR drew nigh, and the night passed, and the day chased the darkness, as is God's will; but wild weather wakened therewith. The clouds cast the cold to the earth, with enough of the north to slay them that lacked clothing. The snow drave smartly, and the whistling wind blew from the heights, and made great drifts in the valleys. The knight, lying in his bed, listened, for though his eyes were shut he might sleep but little, and hearkened every cock that crew.

He arose ere the day broke, by the light of a lamp that burned in his chamber, and called to his chamberlain, bidding him bring his armour and saddle his steed. The other gat him up, and fetched his garments, and robed Sir Gawain.

The Robing of Sir Gawain

First he clad him in his clothes to keep off the cold, and then in his harness, which was well and fairly kept. Both hauberk and plates were well burnished, the rings of the rich byrny freed from rust, and all as fresh as at first, so that the knight was fain to thank them. Then he did on each piece, and bade them bring his steed, while he put the fairest raiment on himself; his coat with its fair cognizance, adorned with precious stones upon velvet, with broidered seams, and all furred within with costly skins. And he left not the lace, the lady's gift, that Gawain forgot not, for his own good. When he had girded on his sword he wrapped the gift twice about him, swathed around his waist. The girdle of green silk set gaily and well upon the royal red cloth, rich to behold, but the knight ware it not for pride of the pendants, polished though they were, with fair gold that gleamed brightly on the ends, but to save himself from sword and knife, when it behoved him to abide his hurt without question. With that the hero went forth, and thanked that kindly folk full often.

How Sir Gawain Went Forth from the Castle

Then was Gringalet ready, that was great and strong, and had been well cared for and tended in every wise; in fair condition was that proud steed, and fit for a journey. Then Gawain went to him, and looked on his coat, and said by his sooth, "There is a folk in this place that thinketh on honour; much joy may they have, and the lord who maintains them, and may all good betide that lovely lady all her life long. Since they for charity cherish a guest, and hold honour in their hands, may He who holds the heaven on high requite them, and also ye all. And if I might live anywhile on earth, I would give ye full reward, readily, if so I might." Then he set foot in the stirrup and bestrode his steed, and his squire gave him his shield, which he laid on his shoulder. Then he smote Gringalet with his golden spurs, and the steed pranced on the stones and would stand no longer.

By that his man was mounted, who bare his spear and lance, and Gawain quoth, "I commend this castle to Christ, may He give it ever good fortune." Then the drawbridge was let down, and the broad gates unbarred and opened on both sides; the knight crossed himself, and passed through the gateway, and praised the porter, who knelt before the prince, and gave him good-day, and commended him to God. Thus the knight went on his way with the one man who should guide him to that dread place where he should receive rueful payment.

The two went by hedges where the boughs were bare, and climbed the cliffs where the cold clings. Naught fell from the heavens, but 'twas ill beneath them; mist brooded over the moor and hung on the mountains; each hill had a cap, a great cloak, of mist. The streams foamed and bubbled between their banks, dashing sparkling on the shores where they shelved downwards. Rugged and dangerous was the way through the woods, till it was time for the sun-rising. Then were they on a high hill; the snow lay white beside them, and the man who rode with Gawain drew rein by his master.

The Squire's Warning

"Sir," he said, "I have brought ye hither, and now ye are not far from the place that ye have sought so specially. But I will tell ye for sooth, since I know ye well, and ye are such a knight as I well love, would ye follow my counsel ye would fare the better.

Of the Knight of the Green Chapel

"The place whither ye go is accounted full perilous, for he who liveth in that waste is the worst on earth, for he is strong and fierce, and loveth to deal mighty blows; taller is he than any man on earth, and greater of frame than any four in Arthur's court, or in any other. And this is his custom at the Green Chapel: there may no man pass by that place, however proud his arms, but he does him to death by force of his hand, for he is a discourteous knight, and shews no mercy. Be he churl or chaplain who rides by that chapel, monk or mass-priest, or any man else, he thinks it as pleasant to slay them as to pass alive himself. Therefore, I tell ye, as sooth as ye sit in saddle, if ye come there and that knight know it, ye shall be slain, though ye had twenty lives; trow me that truly! He has dwelt here full long and seen many a combat; ye may not defend ye against his blows. Therefore, good Sir Gawain, let the man be, and get ye away some other road; for God's sake seek ye another land, and there may Christ speed ye! And I will hie me home again, and I promise ye further that I will swear by God and the saints, or any other oath ye please, that I will keep counsel faithfully, and never let any wit the tale that ye fled for fear of any man."

Sir Gawain Is None Dismayed

"Gramercy," quoth Gawain, but ill pleased. "Good fortune be his who wishes me good, and that thou wouldst keep faith with me I well believe; but didst thou keep it never so truly, an I passed here and fled for fear as thou sayest, then were I a coward knight, and might not be held guiltless. So I will to the chapel let chance what may, and talk with that man, even as I may list, whether for weal or for woe as fate may have it. Fierce though he may be in fight, yet God knoweth well how to save His servants."

"Well," quoth the other, "now that ye have said so much that ye will take your own harm on yourself, and ye be pleased to lose your life, I will neither let nor keep ye. Have here your helm and the spear in your hand, and ride down this same road beside the rock till ye come to the bottom of the valley, and there look a little to the left hand, and ye shall see in that vale the chapel, and the grim man who keeps it. Now fare ye well, noble Gawain; for all the gold on earth I would not go with ye nor bear ye fellowship one step further." With that the man turned his bridle into the wood, smote the horse with his spurs as hard as he could, and galloped off, leaving the knight alone.

Quoth Gawain, "I will neither greet nor groan, but commend myself to God, and yield me to His will."

Then the knight spurred Gringalet, and rode adown the path close in by a bank beside a grove. So he rode through the rough thicket, right into the dale, and there he halted, for it seemed him wild enough. No sign of a chapel could he see, but high and burnt banks on either side and rough rugged crags with great stones above. An ill-looking place he thought it.

Then he drew in his horse and looked around to seek the chapel, but he saw none and thought it strange. Then he saw as it were a mound on a level space of land by a bank beside the stream where it ran swiftly, the water bubbled within as if boiling. The knight turned his steed to the mound, and lighted down and tied the rein to the branch of a linden; and he turned to the mound and walked round it, questioning with himself what it might be. It had a hole at the end and at either side, and was overgrown with clumps of grass, and it was hollow within as an old cave or the crevice of a crag; he knew not what it might be.

The Finding of the Chapel

"Ah," quoth Gawain, "can this be the Green Chapel? Here might the devil say his mattins at midnight! Now I wis there is wizardry here. 'Tis an ugly oratory, all overgrown with grass, and 'twould well beseem that fellow in green to say his devotions on devil's wise. By my five wits, 'tis the foul fiend himself who hath set me this tryst, to destroy me here! This is a chapel of mischance: ill-luck betide it, 'tis the cursedest kirk that ever I came in!"

Helmet on head and lance in hand, he came up to the rough dwelling, when he heard over the high hill beyond the brook, as it were in a bank, a wondrous fierce noise, that rang in the cliff as if it would cleave asunder. 'Twas as if one ground a scythe on a grindstone, it whirred and whetted like water on a mill-wheel and rushed and rang, terrible to hear.

"By God," quoth Gawain, "I trow that gear is preparing for the knight who will meet me here. Alas! naught may help me, yet should my life be forfeit, I fear not a jot!" With that he called aloud. "Who waiteth in this place to give me tryst? Now is Gawain come hither: if any man will aught of him let him hasten hither now or never."

The Coming of the Green Knight

"Stay," quoth one on the bank above his head, "and ye shall speedily have that which I promised ye." Yet for a while the noise of whetting went on ere he appeared, and then he came forth from a cave in the crag with a fell weapon, a Danish axe newly dight, wherewith to deal the blow. An evil head it had, four feet large, no less, sharply ground, and bound to the handle by the lace that gleamed brightly. And the knight himself was all green as before, face and foot, locks and beard, but now he was afoot. When he came to the water he would not wade it, but sprang over with the pole of his axe, and strode boldly over the brent that was white with snow.

Sir Gawain went to meet him, but he made no low bow. The other said, "Now, fair sir, one may trust thee to keep tryst. Thou art welcome, Gawain, to my place. Thou hast timed thy coming as befits a true man. Thou knowest the covenant set between us: at this time twelve months agone thou didst take that which fell to thee, and I at this New Year will readily requite thee. We are in this valley, verily alone, here are no knights to sever us, do what we will. Have off thy helm from thine head, and have here thy pay; make me no more talking than I did then when thou didst strike off my head with one blow."

"Nay," quoth Gawain, "by God that gave me life, I shall make no moan whatever befall me, but make thou ready for the blow and I shall stand still and say never a word to thee, do as thou wilt."

With that he bent his head and shewed his neck all bare, and made as if he had no fear, for he would not be thought a-dread.

How Sir Gawain Failed to Stand the Blow

Then the Green Knight made him ready, and grasped his grim weapon to smite Gawain. With all his force he bore it aloft with a mighty feint of slaying him: had it fallen as straight as he aimed he who was ever doughty of deed had been slain by the blow. But Gawain swerved aside as the axe came gliding down to slay him as he stood, and shrank a little with the shoulders, for the sharp iron. The other heaved up the blade and rebuked the prince with many proud words:

Of the Green Knight's Reproaches

"Thou art not Gawain," he said, "who is held so valiant, that never feared he man by hill or vale, but *thou* shrinkest for fear ere thou feelest hurt. Such cowardice did I never hear of Gawain! Neither did *I* flinch from thy blow, or make strife in King Arthur's hall. My head fell to my feet, and yet I fled not, but thou didst wax faint of heart ere any harm befell. Wherefore must I be deemed the braver knight."

Quoth Gawain, "I shrank once, but so will I no more, though an *my* head fall on the stones I cannot replace it. But haste, Sir Knight, by thy faith, and bring me to the point, deal me my destiny, and do it out of hand, for I will stand thee a stroke and move no more till thine axe have hit me – my troth on it."

"Have at thee, then," quoth the other, and heaved aloft the axe with fierce mien, as if he were mad. He struck at him fiercely but wounded him not, withholding his hand ere it might strike him.

Gawain abode the stroke, and flinched in no limb, but stood still as a stone or the stump of a tree that is fast rooted in the rocky ground with a hundred roots.

Then spake gaily the man in green, "So now thou hast thine heart whole it behoves me to smite. Hold aside thy hood that Arthur gave thee, and keep thy neck thus bent lest it cover it again."

Then Gawain said angrily, "Why talk on thus? Thou dost threaten too long. I hope thy heart misgives thee."

How the Green Knight Dealt the Blow

"For sooth," quoth the other, "so fiercely thou speakest I will no longer let thine errand wait its reward." Then he braced himself to strike, frowning with lips and brow, 'twas no marvel that he who hoped for no rescue misliked him. He lifted the axe lightly and let it fall with the edge of the blade on the bare neck. Though he struck swiftly it hurt him no more than on the one side where it severed the skin. The sharp blade cut into the flesh so that the blood ran over his shoulder to the ground. And when the knight saw the blood staining the snow, he sprang forth, swift-foot, more than a spear's length, seized his helmet and set it on his head, cast his shield over his shoulder, drew out his bright sword, and spake boldly (never since he was born was he half so blithe), "Stop, Sir Knight, bid me no more blows. I have stood a stroke here without flinching, and if thou give me another, I shall requite thee, and give thee as good again. By the covenant made betwixt us in Arthur's hall but one blow falls to me here. Halt, therefore."

Of the Three Covenants

Then the Green Knight drew off from him, and leaned on his axe, setting the shaft on the ground, and looked on Gawain as he stood all armed and faced him fearlessly – at heart it pleased him well. Then he spake merrily in a loud voice, and said to the knight, "Bold sir, be not so fierce, no man here hath done thee wrong, nor will do, save by covenant, as we made at Arthur's court. I promised thee a blow and thou hast it – hold thyself well paid! I release thee of all other claims. If I had been so minded I might perchance have given thee a rougher buffet. First I menaced thee with a feigned one, and hurt thee not for the covenant that we made in the first night, and which thou didst hold truly. All the gain didst thou give me as a true man should. The other feint I proffered thee for the morrow: my fair wife kissed thee, and thou didst give me her kisses – for both those days I gave thee two blows without scathe – true man, true return. But the third time thou didst fail, and therefore hadst thou that blow. For 'tis my weed thou wearest, that same woven girdle, my own wife wrought it, that do I wot for sooth. Now know I well thy kisses, and thy conversation, and the wooing of my wife, for 'twas mine own doing. I sent her to try thee, and in sooth I think thou art the most faultless knight that ever trode earth. As a pearl among white peas is of more worth than they, so is Gawain, i' faith, by other knights. But thou didst lack a little, Sir Knight, and wast wanting in loyalty, yet that was for no evil work, nor for wooing neither, but because thou lovedst thy life – therefore I blame thee the less."

The Shame of Sir Gawain

Then the other stood a great while still, sorely angered and vexed within himself; all the blood flew to his face, and he shrank for shame as the Green Knight spake; and the first words he said were, "Cursed be ye, cowardice and covetousness, for in ye is the destruction of virtue." Then he loosed the girdle, and gave it to the knight. "Lo, take there the falsity, may foul befall it! For fear of thy blow cowardice bade me make friends with covetousness and forsake the customs of largess and loyalty, which befit all knights. Now am I faulty and false and have been afeard: from treachery and untruth come sorrow and care. I avow to thee, Sir Knight, that I have ill done; do then thy will. I shall be more wary hereafter."

Then the other laughed and said gaily, "I wot I am whole of the hurt I had, and thou hast made such free confession of thy misdeeds, and hast so borne the penance of mine axe-edge, that I hold thee absolved from that sin, and purged as clean as if thou hadst never sinned since thou wast born. And this girdle that is wrought with gold and green, like my raiment, do I give thee, Sir Gawain, that thou mayest think upon this chance when thou goest forth among princes of renown, and keep this for a token of the adventure of the Green Chapel, as it chanced between chivalrous knights. And thou shalt come again with me to my dwelling and pass the rest of this feast in gladness." Then the lord laid hold of him, and said, "I wot we shall soon make peace with my wife, who was thy bitter enemy."

How Sir Gawain Would Keep the Girdle

"Nay, forsooth," said Sir Gawain and seized his helmet and took it off swiftly, and thanked the knight: "I have fared ill, may bliss betide thee, and may He who rules all things reward thee swiftly. Commend me to that courteous lady, thy fair wife, and to the other my honoured ladies, who have beguiled their knight with skilful craft. But 'tis no marvel if one be made a fool and brought to sorrow by women's wiles, for so was Adam beguiled, and many a mighty man of old, Samson, and David, and Solomon – if one might love a woman and believe her not, 'twere great gain! And since all they were beguiled by women, methinks 'tis the less blame to me that I was misled! But as for thy girdle, that will I take with good will, not for gain of the gold, nor for samite, nor silk, nor the costly pendants, neither for weal nor for worship, but in sign of my frailty. I shall look upon it when I ride in renown and remind myself of the fault and faintness of the flesh; and so when pride uplifts me for prowess of arms, the sight of this lace shall humble my heart. But one thing would I pray, if it displease thee not: since thou art lord of yonder land wherein I have dwelt, tell me what thy rightful name may be, and I will ask no more."

How the Marvel Was Wrought

"That will I truly," quoth the other. "Bernlak de Hautdesert am I called in this land. Morgain le Fay dwelleth in mine house,[11] and through knowledge of clerkly craft hath she taken many. For long time was she the mistress of Merlin, who knew well all you knights of the court. Morgain the goddess is she called therefore, and there is none so haughty but she can bring him low. She sent me in this guise to yon fair hall to test the truth of the renown that is spread abroad of the valour of the Round Table. She taught me this marvel to betray your wits, to vex Guinevere and fright her to death by the man who spake with his head in his hand at the high table. That is she who is at home, that ancient lady, she is even thine aunt, Arthur's half-sister, the daughter of the Duchess of Tintagel, who afterward married King Uther. Therefore I bid thee, knight, come to thine aunt, and make merry in thine house; my folk love thee, and I wish thee as well as any man on earth, by my faith, for thy true dealing."

But Sir Gawain said nay, he would in no wise do so; so they embraced and kissed, and commended each other to the Prince of Paradise, and parted right there, on the cold ground. Gawain on his steed rode swiftly to the king's hall, and the Green Knight got him whithersoever he would.

How Sir Gawain Came Again to Camelot

Sir Gawain, who had thus won grace of his life, rode through wild ways on Gringalet; oft he lodged in a house, and oft without, and many adventures did he have and came off victor full often, as at this time I cannot relate in tale. The hurt that he had in his neck was healed, he bare the shining girdle as a baldric bound by his side, and made fast with a knot 'neath his left arm, in token that he was taken in a fault – and thus he came in safety again to the court.

Then joy awakened in that dwelling when the king knew that the good Sir Gawain was come, for he deemed it gain. King Arthur kissed the knight, and the queen also, and many valiant knights sought to embrace him. They asked him how he had fared, and he told them all that had chanced to him – the adventure of the chapel, the fashion of the knight, the love of the lady – at last of the lace. He showed them the wound in the neck which he won for his disloyalty at the hand of the knight, the blood flew to his face for shame as he told the tale.

Sir Gawain Makes Confession of His Fault

"Lo, lady," he quoth, and handled the lace, "this is the bond of the blame that I bear in my neck, this is the harm and the loss I have suffered, the cowardice and covetousness in which I was caught, the token of my covenant in which I was taken. And I must needs wear it so long as I live, for none may hide his harm, but undone it may not be, for if it hath clung to thee once, it may never be severed."

The Knights Wear the Lace in Honour of Gawain

Then the king comforted the knight, and the court laughed loudly at the tale, and all made accord that the lords and the ladies who belonged to the Round Table, each hero among them, should wear bound about him a baldric of bright green[12] for the sake of Sir Gawain. And to this was agreed all the honour of the Round Table, and he who ware it was honoured the more thereafter, as it is testified in the best book of romance.

The End of the Tale

That in Arthur's days this adventure befell, the book of Brutus bears witness. For since that bold knight came hither first, and the siege and the assault were ceased at Troy, I wis

Many a venture herebefore
Hath fallen such as this:
May He that bare the crown of thorn
Bring us unto His bliss.

Amen

Notes for *Sir Gawain and the Green Knight*

1. *Carol.* Dance accompanied by song. Often mentioned in old romances.

2. *Agravain,* "*à la dure main.*" This characterisation of Gawain's brother seems to indicate that there was a French source at the root of this story. The author distinctly tells us more than once that the tale, as he tells it, was written *in a book.* M. Gaston Paris thinks that the direct source was an Anglo-Norman poem, now lost.

3. *If any in this hall holds himself so hardy.* This, the main incident of the tale, is apparently of very early date. The oldest version we possess is that found in the Irish tale of the *Fled Bricrend* (Bricriu's feast), where the hero of the tale is the Irish champion, Cuchulinn. Two mediaeval romances, the *Mule sans Frein* (French) and *Diu Krône* (German), again attribute it to Gawain; while the continuator of Chrétien de Troye's *Conte del Graal* gives as hero a certain Carados, whom he represents as Arthur's nephew; and the prose *Perceval* has Lancelot. So far as the mediaeval versions are concerned, the original hero is undoubtedly Gawain; and our poem gives the fullest and most complete form of the story we possess. In the Irish version the magician is a *giant*, and the abnormal size and stature of the Green Knight is, in all probability, the survival of a primitive feature. His curious *colour* is a trait found nowhere else. In *Diu Krône* we are told that the challenger changes shapes in a terrifying manner, but no details are given.

4. *For Yule was over-past.* This passage, descriptive of the flight of the year, should be especially noticed. Combined with other passages – the description of Gawain's journey, the early morning hunts, the dawning of New Year's Day, and the ride to the Green Chapel – they indicate a knowledge of Nature, and an observant eye for her moods, uncommon among mediaeval poets. It is usual enough to find graceful and charming descriptions of spring and early summer – an appreciation of *May* in especial, when the summer courts were held, is part of the stock-in-trade of mediaeval romancers – but a sympathy with the year in all its changes is far rarer, and certainly deserves to be specially reckoned to the credit of this nameless writer.

5. *First a rich carpet was stretched on the floor.* The description of the arming of Gawain is rather more detailed in the original, but some of the minor points are not easy to understand, the identification of sundry of the pieces of armour being doubtful.

6. *The pentangle painted thereupon in gleaming gold.* I do not remember that the pentangle is elsewhere attributed to Gawain. He often bears a red shield; but the blazon varies. Indeed, the heraldic devices borne by Arthur's knights are distractingly chaotic – their legends are older than the science of heraldry, and no one has done for them the good office that the compiler of the Thidrek Saga has rendered to his Teutonic heroes.

7. *The Wilderness of Wirral.* This is in Cheshire. Sir F. Madden suggests that the forest which forms the final stage of Gawain's journey is that of Inglewood, in Cumberland. The geography here is far clearer than is often the case in such descriptions.

8. *'Twas the fairest castle that ever a knight owned.* Here, again, I have omitted some of the details of the original, the architectural terms lacking identification.

9. *With blast of the bugle fared forth to the field.* The account of each day's hunting contains a number of obsolete terms and details of woodcraft, not given in full. The meaning of some has been lost, and the minute description of skinning and dismembering the game would be distinctly repulsive to the general reader. They are valuable for a student of the history of the English sport, but interfere with the progress of the story. The fact that the author devotes so much space to them seems to indicate that he lived in the country and was keenly interested in field sports. (Gottfried von Stressbourg's *Tristan* contains a similar and almost more detailed description.)

10. *I will give thee my girdle.* This magic girdle, which confers invulnerability on its owner, is a noticeable feature of our story. It is found nowhere else in this connection, yet in other romances we find that Gawain possesses a girdle with similar powers (cf., my *Legend of Sir Gawain*, Chap. IX.). Such a talisman was also owned by Cuchulinn, the Irish hero, who has many points of contact with Gawain. It seems not improbable that this was also an old feature of the story. I have commented, in the Introduction, on the lady's persistent wooing of Gawain, and need not repeat the remarks here. The Celtic *Lay of the Great Fool* (*Amadan Mor*) presents some curious points of contact with our story, which may, however, well be noted here. In the *Lay* the hero is mysteriously deprived of his legs, through the draught from a cup proffered by a *Gruagach* or magician. He comes to a castle, the lord of which goes out hunting, leaving his wife in the care of the Great Fool, who is to allow no man to enter. He falls asleep, and a young knight arrives and kisses the host's wife. The Great Fool, awaking, refuses to allow the intruder to depart; and, in spite of threats and blandishments, insists on detaining him till the husband returns. Finally, the stranger reveals himself as the host in another shape; he is also the *Gruagach*, who deprived the hero of his limbs, and the Great Fool's brother. He has only intended to test the *Amadan Mor's* fidelity. A curious point in connection with this story is that it possesses a prose opening which shows a marked affinity with the "Perceval" *enfances*. That the Perceval and Gawain stories early became connected is certain, but what is the precise connection between them and the Celtic *Lay* is not clear. *In its present form* the latter is certainly posterior to the Grail romances, but it is quite possible that the matter with which it deals represents a tradition older than the Arthurian story.

11. *Morgain le Fay, who dwelleth in my house.* The enmity between Morgain le Fay and Guinevere, which is here stated to have been the *motif* of the enchantment, is no invention of the author, but is found in the *Merlin*, probably the earliest of the Arthurian *prose* romances. In a later version of our story, a poem, written in ballad form, and contained in the "Percy" MS., Morgain does not appear; her place is taken by an old witch, mother to the lady, but the enchantment is still due to her spells. In this later form the knight bears the curious name of *Sir Bredbeddle*. That given in our romance, *Bernlak de Hautdesert*, seems to point to the original French source of the story. (It is curious that Morgain should here be represented as extremely old, while Arthur is still in his first youth. There is evidently a discrepancy or misunderstanding of the source here.)

12. *A baldric of bright green, for sake of Sir Gawain.* – The later version connects this *lace* with that worn by the knights of the Bath; but this latter was *white*, not *green*. The knights wore it on the left shoulder till they had done some gallant deed, or till some noble lady took it off for them.

The Grene Knight

THE FACT that *SGGK* survives in only one manuscript implies that it was not widely known in its day. Nevertheless, an interesting survival, a romance written about 1500 called *The Grene Knight*, suggests that *SGGK* was not unknown in the later Middle Ages. *The Grene Knight* and several other romances that appear in the great compilation known as the Percy Folio Manuscript also attest to the continuing popularity of Gawain as an English hero. Written in six-line rhyming stanzas rather than alliterative verse, *The Grene Knight* contains many of the motifs of its predecessor, including the beheading contest, the exchange of winnings, hunts and temptations, and the protective girdle or 'lace'. And it is a fascinating example of how a chivalric romance was reworked for a popular audience.

The lord in this poem, called Bredbeddle, is sent in 'transposed likenesse' by his mother-in-law, the sorceress Agostes, because his wife loves Gawain and her mother wants to bring him into her presence and to test his knightly qualities. *The Grene Knight* does not have the elaborate parallels that are found in the alliterative romance. The blow with the axe is repaid with a stroke of a sword. There is only one hunt and one temptation. The poem is interested in narrative economy and gets right to the point – the keeping of the lace that Gawain believes will protect him. Following the one return blow, Bredbeddle and Gawain go back to Arthur's court. The poem ends abruptly with a statement that this (presumably the story of the lace) is why Knights of Bath wear the lace until they have won their spurs, a parallel to the inclusion of the motto of the Order of the Garter at the end of *SGGK* in the Cotton manuscript.

The Grene Knight
In Two Parts

THIS IS A LATE, popular version of the old romance of 'Sir Gawain and the Green Knight', preserved amongst the Cottonian MSS. (Nero A. X. fol. 91) edited by Sir Frederick Madden for the Bannatyne Club in 1839 and by Richard Morris Esq. for the Early English Text Society in 1864. The old romance, written, according to Mr. Morris, about 1320 AD, by the author of the Early English Alliterative Poems also printed by the E.E. Text Society, is lengthy, is written in alliterative metre, and is as difficult as the old alliterative poems usually are.

To dissipate this besetting obscurity, to relieve this apparent tediousness, the present translation and abridgement was made. The form is changed; the language is modernized. In a word, the old romance was adapted to the taste and understanding of the translator's time. Moreover, it was made to explain a custom of that time – a custom followed by an Order that was instituted, according to Selden and Camden, some three-quarters of a century (AD 1399) after the time when, according to Mr. Morris, the poem first appeared. It explains why

> *Knights of the bathe weare the lace*
> *Untill they have wonen their shoen,*
> *Or else a ladye of hye estate*
> *From about his neeke shall it take*
> *For the doughtye deeds hee hath done.*

On this point Somerset Herald has kindly furnished us with the following note:

> *College of Arms, June 8.*
> *It appears to have been the custom of Knights of the Bath, from at least as early as the reign of Henry IV, to wear a lace or*

shoulder knot of white silk on the left shoulder of their mantles or gowns, ("theis xxxii nw knights preceding immediately before the king in theire gownis, and hoodis, and tookins of white silke upon theire shouldeirs as is accustumid att the Bath:" MS. temp. Edw. IV, fragment published by Hearne at the end of Sprott's Chronicle, p. 88). This lace was to be worn till it should be taken off by the hand of the prince or of some noble lady, upon the knight's having performed "some brave and considerable action", vide Anstis's History of the Order. What this custom originated in does not appear, and the writer of the poem has only exercised the allowed privilege of his craft, in attributing the derivation to the adventure of Sir Gawaine and '"the Lady gay" in this legend of 'The Green Knight'.

In the Statutes of the Order, 11th of George I 1725, it is commanded that they shall wear on the left shoulder of their mantle "the lace of white silk antiently worn by the said knights," but there is no mention of its being taken off at any time for any reason.

J.R. Planché.

The recast belongs then to an age which was beginning to study itself, and to enquire into the origin of practices which it found itself observing. It is an infant antiquarian effort. But the poem has lost much of its vigour in the translation. It is in its present shape but a shadow of itself. Moreover, the following copy appears much mutilated. Several half-stanzas have dropped out altogether, probably through the sheer carelessness of the scribe.

The two leading persons of the romance are the well-known Sir Gawain, of King Arthur's court, and Sir Bredbeddle of the West country – the same knight who appears in *King Arthur and the King of Cornwall*, vol. i. p. 67. The main interest rests upon Sir Gawain. His "points three" – his boldness, his courtesy, his hardiness – are all proved. He is eager for adventures; he unshrinkingly pursues them to the end; he bears extreme hardships patiently; his courtesy is shown in his nobly resisting the overtures made him by his host's wife, whom Agostes has brought to his bedside.

The ladye kissed him times three,
Saith, "Without I have the love of thee,
My life standeth in dere."
Sir Gawaine blushed on the Lady bright,
Saith, "Your husband is a gentle Knight,
By Him that bought mee deare!
To me itt were great shame.
If I shold doe him any grame,
That hath beene kind to mee."

All these provings are given much more fully in the original romance.
But enough is given here to uphold the fame of the chivalrous knight. See
the *Turk and Gowin.*

Part I

List! wen Arthur he was King,
he had all att his leadinge
the broad Ile of Brittaine;
England & Scotland one was,
& wales stood in the same case,
the truth itt is not to layne.

[When Arthur lived, he ruled all Britain,]

he drive allyance out of this Ile,
soe Arthur liued in peace a while,
as men of Mickle maine,
knights strong of their degree
[strove] which, of them hyest shold bee;
therof Arthur was not faine;

[and lived, for a time, in peace. To stop his
knights contending for precendency,]

hee made the round table for their behoue,
that none of them shold sitt aboue,
but all shold sitt as one,
the King himselfe in state royall,
Dame Gueneuer our queene withall,
seemlye of body and bone.

[he made the Round Table, that all might be equal.]

itt fell againe the christmase,
many came to that Lords place,
to that worthye one
with helme on head, & brand bright,
all that tooke order knight;
none wold linger att home.

[One Christmas many knights came to Arthur's court.]

there was noe castle nor manour free
that might harbour that companye,
their puissance was soe great,
their tents vp the pight
for to lodge there all that night,
therto were sett to meate.

[No house could hold all of them, so they pitched their tents,]

Messengers there came [&] went
With much victualls verament
both by way & streete;
wine & wild fowle thither was brought,

within they spared nought
for gold, & they might itt gett.

[and food was served to them.]

Now of King Arthur noe more I mell;
but of a venterous knight I will you tell
that dwelled in the west countrye;
Sir Bredbeddle, for sooth he hett;
he was a man of Mickele might,
& Lord of great bewtye.

[But I shall leave Arthur, and tell you about Sir Bredbeddle.]

he had a lady to his wife,
he loued her deerlye as his liffe,
shee was both blyth and blee;
because Sir Gawaine was stiffe in stowre,
shee loued him priuilye paramour,
& shee neuer him see.

[He loved his wife dearly, but she loved Sir Gawaine.]

itt was Agostes that was her mother;
itt was witchcraft & noe other
that shee dealt with all:

[Her mother Agostes dealt in witchcraft,]

shee cold transpose knights & swaine
like as in battaile they were slaine,
wounded both Lim & lightt,
shee taught her sonne the knight alsoe
in transposed likenesse he shold goe
both by fell and frythe;

[could transform men, and told Bredbeddle to go, transformed,]

> shee said, "thou shalt to Arthurs hall;
> for there great aduentures shall befall
> That euer saw King or Knight."
> all was for her daughters sake,
> that which, she soe sadlye spake
> to her sonne-in-law the knight,
> because Sir Gawaine was bold and hardye.
> & therto full of curtesye,
> to bring him into her sight.

[to Arthur's court to see adventures. This was in order
to get Gawaine brought to her daughter.]

> the knight said "soe mote I thee,
> to Arthurs court will I mee hye
> for to praise thee right,
> & to proue Gawaines points 3;
> & that be true that men tell me,
> by Mary Most of Might."

[Bredbeddle agrees to go, and prove whether Gawaine is so good.]

> earlye, soone as itt was day,
> the Knight dressed him full gay,
> vmstrode a full good steede;
> helme and hawberke both he hent,
> a long fauchion verament
> to fend them in his neede.

[Bredbeddle starts next day on horseback.]

> that was a Iolly sight to seene,
> when horsse and armour was all greene,

& weapon that hee bare,
when that burne was harnisht still,
his countenance he became right well,
I dare itt safelye sweare.

[He was a goodly sight, in his green
armour, and on his green horse.]

that time att Carleile lay our King;
att a Castle of flatting was his dwelling,
in the fforrest of delamore.
for sooth he rode, the sooth to say,
to Carleile he came on Christmas day,
into that fayre countrye."

[Arthur is at Carlisle, at Castle Flatting, in Delamere
Forest, Bredbeddle arrives on Christmas day.]

when lie into that place came,
the porter thought him a Maruelous groome:
he saith, "Sir, wither wold yee?"
hee said, "I am a venterous Knight,
& of your King wold haue sight,
& other Lords that heere bee."

[The porter asks him where he's going to.
"To see King Arthur and his lords."]

noe word to him the porter spake,
but left him standing att the gate,
& went forth, as I weene,
& kneeled downe before the King;
saith, "in lifes dayes old or younge,
such a sight I haue not scene!

"for yonder att your gates right;"
he saith, "hee is a venterous Knight
all his vesture is greene."
then spake the King proudest in all,
saith, "bring him into the hall;
let vs see what hee doth meane."

[The porter tells Arthur of the Green Knight's arrival,
and the king orders him to be let in.]

when the greene Knight came before the King,
he stood in his stirrops strechinge,
& spoke with voice cleere,
& saith, "King Arthur, god saue thee
as thou sittest in thy prosperitye,
& Maintaine thine honor!

[Bredbeddle comes, wishes Arthur God speed,]

"why thou wold me nothing but right;
I am come hither a venterous [Knight,]
& kayred thorrow countrye farr,
to proue poynts in thy pallace
that longeth to manhood in euerye case
among thy Lords deere."

[and says he has come to challenge his lords to a trial of manhood.]

the King, he sayd full still
till he had said all his will;
certain thus can he say:
"as I am true knight and King,
thou shalt haue thy askinge!
I will not say thy nay,

"whether thou wilt on foote fighting,
or on steed backe iusting
for loue of Ladyes gay.
If & thine armor be not fine,
I will giue thee part of mine."
"god amercy, Lord!" can he say,

[Arthur consents to let him try on foot, or horseback.]

"here I make a challenging
among the Lords both old and younge
that worthy beene in weede,
which of them will take in hand –
hee that is both stifie and stronge
and full good att need –

[Bredbeddle challenges Arthur's lords: he'll let any one]

"I shall lay my head downe,
strike itt of if he can
with a stroke to garr itt bleed,
for this day 12 monthe another at his:
let me see who will answer this,
a knight that is doughtye of deed;

[cut his head off, for a return cut at his executioner's head a year hence]

"for this day 12 month, the sooth to say,
let him come to me & seicth his praye;
rudlye, or euer hee blin,
whither to come, I shall him tell,
the readie way to the greene chappell,
that place I will be in."

[at the Green Chappell.]

the King att ease sate full still,
& all his lords said but litle
till he had said all his will,
vpp stood Sir Kay thai crabbed knight,
spake mightye words that were of height,
that were both Loud and shrill;

"I shall strike his necke in tooe,
the head away the body froe."
thé bade him all be still,
saith, "Kay, of thy dints make noe rouse,
thou wottest full litle what "thou does;
noe good, but Mickle ill."

[Kay accepts the challenge. The other knights tell Kay
to be quiet: he's always getting into a mess.]

Eche man wold this deed haue done,
vp start Sir Gawaine soone,
vpon his knees can kneele,
he said, "that were great villanye
without you put this deede to me,
my leege, as I haue sayd;

[Sir Gawaine says it will be too bad if Arthur
doesn't let him take the adventure.]

"remember, I am your sisters sonne."
the King said, "I grant thy boone;
but mirth is best att meele;
cheere thy guest, and giue him wine,
& after dinner, to itt fine,
& sett the buffett well!"

[Arthur consents, but not till after dinner.]

now the greene 'Knight is set att meate,
seemlye serued in his seate,
beside the round table,
to talke of his welfare, nothing he needs,
like a Knight himselfe he feeds,
with long time reasnable.

[Bredbeddle dines.]

when the dinner, it was done,
the King said to Sir Gawaine soone,
withouten any fable
he said, "on you will doe this deede,
I pray Iesus be your speede!
this knight is nothing vnstable."

[Arthur wishes Gawaine God speed. Bredbeddle is a stiff one.]

the greene Knight his head downe layd;
Sir Gawaine, to the axe he braid
to strike with eger will;
he stroke the necke bone in twaine,
the blood burst out in euerye vaine,
the head from the body fell.

[Gawaine chops off Bredbeddle's head.]

the greene Knight his head vp hent,
into his saddle wightilye he sprent,
spake words both Lowd & shrill,
saith: "Gawaine! thinke on thy couenant!
this day 12 monthes see thou ne want
to come to the greene chappell!"

[Bredbeddle picks it up, jumps into his saddle, reminds

Gawaine to meet him twelve months hence,]

All had great maruell, that thé see
that he spake so merrilye
& bare his head in his hand,
forth att the hall dore he rode right,
and that saw both King and knight
and Lords that were in land.

without the hall dore, the sooth to saine,
hee sett his head vpon againe,
saies, "Arthur, haue heere my hand!
when-soeuer the Knight cometh to mee,
a better buffett sickerlye
I dare him well warrand."

[rides off, puts his head on again, and promises Gawaine a better buffet.]

the greene Knight away went.
all this was done by enchantment
that the old witch had wrought,
sore sicke fell Arthur the King,
and for him made great mourning
that into such bale was brought.

[Arthur is very sorry for Gawain,]

the Queen, shee weeped for his sake;
sorry was Sir Lancelott dulake,
& other were dreery in thought
because he was brought into great perill;
his mightye manhood will not availe,
that before hath freshlye fought.

[so is Lancelot.]

Sir Gawaine comfort King and Queen,
& all the doughtye there be-deene;
he bade thé shold be still;
said, "of my deede I was neuer feard,
nor yett I am nothing a-dread,
I swere by Saint Michaell;

[Gawaine cheers them up, swears that]

"for when draweth toward my day,
I will dresse me in mine array
my promise to fulfill.
Sir," he saith, "as I haue blis,
I wott not where the greene chappell is,
therfore seeke itt I will."

[he'll keep his pledge, and will seek out the Green Chapel.]

the royall Couett verament
all rought Sir Gawaines intent,
they thought itt was the best.
they went forth into the feild,
knights that ware both speare and sheeld
thé priced forth full prest;

[The court approve, and go forth]

some chuse them to Iustinge,
some to dance, Reuell, and sing;
of mirth the wold not rest.
all they swore together in fere,
that and Sir Gawaine ouer-come were,
the wold bren all the west.

[to joust, revel, and sport, swearing to revenge Gawaine if he's killed.]

Now leaue wee the King in his pallace.
the greene knight come home is
to his owne Castle;
this folke frend when he came home
what doughtye deeds he had done.
nothing he wold them tell;

[Bredbeddle reaches his home, tells no one what he has done,]

full well bee wist in certaine
that his wiffe loued Sir Gawaine
that comelye was vnder kell.
listen, Lords! & yee will sitt,
& yee shall heere the second ffitt,
what adventures Sir Gawaine befell.

[but knows that his wife loves Gawaine.]

Part II

The day is come that Gawaine must gone:
Knights & Ladyes waxed wann
that were without in that place;
the king himselfe siked ill,
ther Queen a swounding almost fell,
to that Iorney when he shold passe.

[The year is up, and Gawaine must go. The king and court grieve.]

When he was in armour bright,
he was one of the goodlyest Knights
that euer in brittaine was borne,

they brought Sir Gawaine a steed,
was dapple gray and good att need,
I tell withouten scorne;

[His steed was dapple-grey,]

his bridle was with stones sett,
with gold & pearle ouerfrett,
& stones of great vertue;
he was of a furley kind;
his stirropps were of silke of ynd;
I tell you this tale for true.

[his bridle jewelled, his stirrups silk]

when he rode ouer the Mold,
his geere glistered as gold.
by the way as he rode,
many furleys he there did see,
fowles by the water did flee,
by brimes & bankes soe broad.

[he glittered like gold.]

many furleys there saw hee
of wolues & wild beasts sikerlye;
on hunting hee tooke most heede.
forth he rode, the sooth to tell,
for to seeke the greene chappell,
he wist not where indeed.

[Gawaine sees wondrous beasts;]

As he rode in an eue[n]ing late,
riding downe a greene gate,

a faire castell saw hee,
that seemed a place of Mickle pride;
thitherward Sir Gawaine can ryde
to gett some harborrowe.

[discerns a castle, rides to it,]

thither he came in the twylight,
he was ware of a gentle Knight,
the lord of the place was hee.
Meekly to him Sir Gawaine can speake,
& asked him, "for King Arthurs sake,
of harborrowe I pray thee!

"I am a far Labordd Knight,
I pray you lodge me all this night."
he sayd him not nay,
hee tooke him by the arme & led him to the hall,
a poore child can hee call,
saith, "dight well this palfrey."

[and asks its lord lodging for the night.
The lord leads him in,]

into a chamber thé went a full great speed;
there thé found all things readye att need,
I dare safelye swere;
fier in chambers burning bright,
candles in chandlers burning light;
to supper thé went full yare.

[and they go to supper.]

he sent after his Ladye bright
to come to supp with that gentle Knight,

& shee came blythe with-all;
forth shee came then anon,
her Maids following her eche one
in robes of rich pall.

as shee sate att her supper,
euer-more the Ladye clere
Sir Gawaine shee looked vpon.
when the supper it was done,
shee tooke her Maids, & to her chamber gone.

[The lord's wife sups with them, and then retires.]

he cheered the Knight & gaue him wine,
& said, "welcome, by St. Martine!
I pray you take itt for none ill;
one thing, Sir, I wold you pray;
what you make soe farr this way?
the truth you wold me tell;

[The lord asks Gawaine what he has come there for.]

"I am a knight, & soe are yee;
Your concell, an you will tell mee,
forsooth keepe itt I will;
for if itt be poynt of any dread,
perchance I may helpe att need
either lowd or still."

[He will keep his counsel.]

for his words that were soe smooth,
had Sir Gawaine wist the soothe,
all he wold not haue told.
for that was the greene Knight

that hee was lodged with that night,
& harbarrowes in his hold.

[Gawaine tells him all, not knowing he was in Bredbeddle's castle.]

he saith, "as to the greene chappell,
thitherward I can you tell,
itt is but furlongs 3.
the Master of it is a venterous Knight,
& workes by witchcraft day & night,
with many a great furley.

[Bredbeddle directs Gawaine to the Green Chapel,
(whose master works witchcraft),]

"if he worke with neuer soe much frauce,
he is curteous as he sees cause.
I tell you sikerlye,
you shall abyde, & take your rest,
& I will into yonder fforrest
vnder the greenwood tree."

[but advises him to stay and rest.]

they plight their truthes to beleeue,
either with other for to deale,
whether it were siluer or gold;
he said, "we 2 both [sworn] wilbe,
what soeuer god sends you & mee,
to be parted on the Mold."

[They agree to share whatever either may get.]

The greene Knight went on hunting;
Sir Gawaine in the castle beinge,

lay sleeping in his bed.
Vprose the old witche with hast throwe,
& to her dauhter can shee goe,
& said, "be not adread!"

to her daughter can shee say,
"the man that thou hast wisht many a day,
of him thou maist be sped;
for Sir Gawaine that curteous knight
is lodged in this hall all night."
shee brought her to his bedd.

[Bredbeddle's witch mother-in-law tell his wife that
Gawaine is in the castle, and takes her to him,]

shee saith, "gentle Knight, awake!
& for this faire Ladies sake
that hath loued thee soe deere,
take her boldly in thine armes,
there is noe man shall doe thee harme;"
now beene they both heere.

[and tells him to embrace her.]

the ladye kissed him times 3,
saith, "without I have the loue of thee,
my life standeth in dere."
Sir Gawaine blushed on the Lady bright,
saith, "your husband is a gentle Knight,
by him that bought mee deare!

[The wife kisses him thrice, and asks his love.]

"to me itt were great shame
if I shold doe him any grame,

that hath beene kind to mee;
for I haue such a deede to doe,
that I can neyther rest nor roe,
att an end till itt bee."

[Gawaine refuses to shame his host.]

then spake that Ladye gay,
saith, "tell me some of your Iourney,
your succour I may bee;
if itt be poynt of any warr,
there shall noe man doe you noe darr
& yee wilbe gouerned by mee;

[The wife offers to help Gawaine in his adventure,]

"for heere I haue a lace of silke,
it is as white as any milke,
& of a great value."
shee saith, "I dare safelye sweare
there shall noe man doe you deere
when you haue it vpon you."

[and will give him a silk lace that will
protect him from all harm.]

Sir Gawaine spake mildlye in the place,
he thanked the Lady & tooke the lace,
& promised her to come againe.
the Knight in the fforrest slew many a hind,
other venison he cold none find
but wild bores on the plaine.

[Gawaine takes the lace.]

plentye of does & wild swine,
foxes & other ravine,
as I hard true men tell.
Sir Gawaine swore sickerlye
"home to your owne, welcome you bee,
by him that harrowes hell!"

[Bredbeddle, after hunting, is welcomed home by Gawaine.]

the greene Knight his venison downe Layd;
then to Sir Gawaine thus hee said,
"tell me anon in heght,
what noueltyes that you haue won,
for heers plenty of venison."
Sir Gawaine said full right,

[He shares his venison with Gawaine,]

Sir Gawaine sware by St. Leonard,
"such as god sends, you shall haue part:"
in his armes he hent the Knight,
& there he kissed him times 3,
saith, "heere is such as god sends mee,
by Mary most of Might."

[and Gawaine gives him his three kisses,]

euer priuilye he held the Lace:
that was all the villanye that euer was
prooued by Sir Gawaine the gay.
then to bed soone thé went,
& sleeped there verament
till morrow itt was day.

[but keeps back the lace.]

then Sir Gawaine soe curteous & free,
his leaue soone taketh hee
att the Lady soe gaye;
Hee thanked her, & tooke the lace,
& rode towards the chappell apace;
he knew noe whitt the way.

[Next day Gawaine takes leave, and
rides towards the chapel.]

euer more in his thought he had
whether he shold worke as the Ladye bade,
that was soe curteous & sheene.
the greene knight rode another way;
he transposed him in another array,
before as it was greene.

[Bredbeddle rides there too.]

as Sir Gawaine rode ouer the plaine,
he hard one high vpon a Mountaine
a horne blowne full lowde.
he looked after the greene chappell,
he saw itt stand vnder a hill
couered with euyes about;

[Gawaine hears a horn, and sees the Green Chapel,]

he looked after the greene Knight,
he hard him wehett a fauchion bright,
that the hills rang about,
the Knight spake with strong cheere,
said, "yee be welcome, S[ir] Gawaine heere,
it behooveth thee to Lowte."
he stroke, & litle perced the skin,

vnneth the flesh within.
then Sir Gawaine had noe doubt;

[and the Green Knight; who calls him to lay down his head,
then strikes, but hardly cuts through the flesh.]

he saith, "thou shontest! why dost thou soe?"
then Sir Gawaine in hart waxed throe;
vpon his ffeete can stand,
& soone he drew out his sword,
& saith, "traitor! if thou speake a word,
thy liffe is in my hand;
I had but one stroke att thee,
& thou hast had another att mee,
noe falshood in me thou found!"

[He reproaches Gawaine for shrinking. Gawaine threatens to kill him.]

the Knight said withouten laine,
"I wend I had Sir Gawaine slaine,
the gentlest Knight in this land;
men told me of great renowne,
of curtesie thou might haue woon the crowne
aboue both free & bound,

"& alsoe of great gentrye;
& now 3 points be put fro thee,
it is the Moe pittye:
Sir Gawaine! thou wast not Leele
when thou didst the lace conceale
that my wiffe gaue to thee!

[Bredbeddle answers that Gawaine has lost his three chief virtues,
of truth, gentleness, and courtesy. He has concealed the lace,]

"ffor wee were both, thou wist full well,
for thou hadst the halfe dale
of my venerye;
if the lace had neuer beene wrought,
to haue slaine thee was neuer my thought,
I swere by god verelye!

[and should have shared it.]

"I wist it well my wiffe loued thee;
thou wold doe me noe villanye,
but nicked her with nay;
but wilt thou doe as I bidd thee,
take me to Arthurs court with thee,
then were all to my pay."

[Yet Bredbeddle will forgive him if he'll take him to Arthur's court.]

now are the Knights accorded thore;
to the castle of hutton can thé fare,
to lodge there all that night.
earlye on the other day
to Arthurs court thé tooke the way
with harts blyth & light.

[Gawaine agrees. They go back to Hutton Castle,
and next day on to Arthur's court.]

all the Court was full faine,
aliue when they saw Sir Gawaine;
they thanked god abone.
that is the matter & the case
why Knights of the bathe weare the lace
vntill they haue wonen their shoen,

[All rejoice at Gawaine's return. This is why knights of
the Bath wear the lace till they've won their spurs,]

or else a ladye of hye estate
from about his necke shall it take,
for the doughtye deeds that hee hath done.
it was confirmed by Arthur the K[ing;]
thorrow Sir Gawaines desiringe
The King granted him his boone.

[or a lady takes the lace off.]

Thus endeth the tale of the greene Knight,
god, that is soe full of might,
to heauen their soules bring
that haue hard this litle storye
that fell some times in the west countrye
in Arthurs days our King!

[God bring all my hearers to heaven! This little
story befell in the West Country.]

The Carle of Carlisle

OTHER POPULAR WORKS in the Percy Folio Manuscript indicate that Gawain remained a figure of interest to general audiences. *The Carle of Carlisle*, written in rhyming couplets in the sixteenth century, reworks *Sir Gawain and the Carle of Carlisle*, a romance from about 1400. Both tell a similar story of an encounter of three knights – Gawain, Kay and Baldwin – with a giant Carl, who in *The Carle of Carlisle* is fifty cubits (seventy-five feet) in height and able to drink fifteen gallons of wine in one gulp.

When the knights seek lodging from the Carl, Kay's and Baldwin's discourtesy is contrasted with Gawain's respect for his sovereignty in his own home. In both poems, the Carl instructs Gawain to thrust at his face with a spear. Obedient to his host, Gawain does so, though the Carl ducks and avoids the blow. Also in both, the Carl commands Gawain to get in bed with his wife, then stops him from having intercourse with her but rewards him for his obedience by letting him sleep with his daughter. In the morning, the Carl tells Gawain that he vowed that anyone who lodged with him and did not do his bidding would be killed. As evidence that he was serious about this vow, he shows Gawain the bones of 1,500 men he has slain because they failed his test.

In *The Carle of Carlisle* (but not in the earlier romance), after Gawain has slept with his daughter, the Carl asks him to cut off his head with a sword. In a variation from other such contests, the Carl will behead Gawain only if he does not comply. Gawain reluctantly beheads his host, whereupon the Carl stands before him as a man of normal height, rather than as the giant he formerly was. He explains that he had been enchanted into his giant form until a knight of the Round Table would cut off his head. Many had failed in the test and were killed by the Carl.

Since Gawain, unlike all the Carl's previous guests, has been courteous and compliant, the Carl promises to end his wicked ways and to welcome all who come to his home. After giving gifts to the three knights, he allows his daughter to become Gawain's wife, does homage to Arthur, and is made a knight of the Round Table. As Thomas Hahn, the most recent editor of these poems, has observed, "Gawain's role is to bring the strange, the threatening, and the resistant within the ambit of the Round Table."

Carle off Carlile
A Curious Song of the Marriage of Sir Gawane, one of King Arthur's Knights

THIS POEM was printed from the Folio by Sir F. Madden in the Appendix to his *Syr Gawayne* for the Bannatyne Club, pp. 256-74. Some of his readings of the MS. differ from mine; and though, if I can trust my eyes, the MS. does not make all the mistakes that Sir F. Madden attributes to it, I have thought it only due to his well-established reputation and great experience in reading MSS., as well as to our readers, who will probably trust him rather than me, to put his readings in the notes. The poem is, as he says, a modernized copy of the *Syre Gawene and the Carle of Carelyle* in the Porkington MS. No. 10, "written in the reign of Edward IV," printed by him (Sir F. Madden) in the Appendix to his *Syr Gawayne*, pp. 187-206.

Though Mrs. Ormsby Gore has kindly lent me this Porkington MS., I have not collated the Folio with it, as its *Syre Gawene* will be printed by Mr. Richard Morris for the Early English Text Society next year, and will there be easily accessible to all readers. The alterations are great in words, small in incidents, and the earlier poem is the better one. Sir F. Madden looks on the occurrence of the present poem and *The Grene Knight* (vol. ii. p. 58) in our Folio as settling the "question of the genuineness and antiquity of the *romance-poems* (as distinguished from the longer and bettor-known *romances*) in this celebrated MS." – that is, that the Folio poems are not abstracts made of the old romances in the seventeenth century, but retellings or adaptations of abstracts made in the fourteenth and fifteenth centuries. "The original of this story must be sought for in the literature of the Continent, and we find it in the beautiful *fabliau* of *Le Chevalier à L'Epée*, printed in Meon's *Recueil*, tome i. p. 127, 8vo, 1823, and previously analysed by Le Grand."

Like the other Gawaine stories in the Folio, this one takes us into weirdland, the region where necromancers have been at work, where Kelts loved specially to range. And, as in *The Turke and Gowin* and *The Marriage of Sir Gawaine*, the counter charm which undoes the fiendly work is Gawaine's courtesy. Though he was not held worthy of the highest honours in Arthur-story, though he kept not the state of the virgin three who alone achieved the Quest of the Holy Graal – Galahad, Percival, Bors, – yet the sweetness of his spirit, his never-failing gentleness to poor as well as rich, to frightful dames as well as beauties, made him the favourite of most of the Arthur-writers, and they sang his praises and his prowess, blessed him with the loveliest wives – the second appears here – and, with Israelitish unction, added many concubines. In contrast with him, here, is not only crabbed Kay, but also the Christian Bishop who has sunk the humility of his religion in the pride of his office, has forgotten that

It ffitteth a clarke to be curteous and ffree,

and gets accordingly a rap on his crown that sends him down. But Gawaine does not fail: what courtesy requires, that he does, all that his host asks; and so, escapes himself, and rescues his friends, from the fate that had befallen 1500 men before who "coude not their curtasye," – death at the hand and mouths of the Carle and his Four Whelps. As of the Turke (vol. i. p. 101, l. 288) so of the Carle, Gawaine strikes off the head; the bale that Necromancy had wrought is turned to bliss, the loathsome giant becomes again a man, and Gawaine weds the lady gay. What is not possible to those sweet souls who sun their world, at whose presence words of wrath and thoughts of evil cease, the remembrance even of whose smile wins us from bitterness and gloom?

* * *

Listen: to me a litle stond,
yee shall heare of one that was sober & sound:
hee was meeke as maid in bower,
stiffe & strong in euery stoure;
certes withouten ffable
he was one of the round table;
the Knights name was Sir Gawaine,

[I'll tell you about Sir Gawaine.]

that much worshipp wan in Brittaine.
the Ile of Brittaine called is
both England & Scottland I-wis;
wales is an angle to that Ile,
where King Arthur soiorned a while;
with him 24 Knights told,
besids Barrens & dukes bold.
the King to his Bishopp gan say,
"wee will have a Masse to-day,
Bishopp Bodwim shall itt done:
after, to the ffairest wee will gone,
ffor now itts grass time of the yeere,
Barrons bold shall breake the deere.
ffaine theroff was Sir Marrocke,
soe was Sir Kay, the Knight stout;
ffaine was Sir Lancelott Dulake,
soe was Sir Perciuall, I vndertake;
ffaine was Sir Ewaine
& Sir Lott of Lothaine,
soe was the Knight of armes greene,
& alsoe Sir Gawaine the sheene.
Sir Gawaine was steward in Arthurs hall,
hee was the curteous Knight amongst them all.
King Arthur & his Cozen Mordred,
& other Knights withouten Lett,
Sir Lybius Disconyus was there
with proud archers lesse & more,
Blanch ffaire & Sir Ironside,
& many Knights that day can ryde.
& Ironside, as I weene,

[Arthur stayed a while in Wales, and one day said he'd hear
Mass, and then go hunting. Murrock was glad. Kay too,
and Lancelot, Percival, Ewaine, Lott, the Green Knight,
Gawaine, Mordred, Lyvius Disconyus, and Ironside,]

gate the Knight of armour greene –
certes as I vnderstand –
of a ffaire Lady of blaunch Land.
hee cold more of honor in warr
then all the Knights that with Arthur weare
burning dragons he slew in Land,
& wilde beasts, as I vnderstand;
wilde beares he slew that stond;
a hardyer Knight was neuer ffound;
he was called in his dayes
one of King Arthurs ffellowes.
why was hee called Ironsyde?
ffor, euer armed wold he ryde;
hee wold allwais arms beare,
ffor Gyants & hee were euer att warr.
dapple coulour was his steede,
his armour and his other weede,
Azure of gold he bare,
with a Griffon lesse or more,
& a difference of a Molatt
he bare in his crest Allgate.
where-soeuer he went, East nor west,
he neuer fforsooke man nor beast.
beagles, keenely away thé ran,
the King ffollowed affter with many a man.
they gray hounds out of the Leashe,
they drew downe the deere of grasse.
ffine tents in the ffeild were sett,
a merry sort there were mett
of comely knights of kind,
vppon the bent there can they lead,

[who was better than any of Arthur's knights, and got
his name because he went always armed, to fight giants.
Beagles ran, greyhounds pulled down the deer,]

& by noone of the same day
a 100d harts on the ground thé Lay.
then Sir Gawaine & Sir Kay,
& Bishopp Bodwin, as I heard say,
after a redd deere thé rode
into a fforrest wyde & brode.
a thicke mist ffell them among,
that caused them all to goe wronge:
great moane made then Sir Kay
that they shold loose the hart that day;
that red hart wold not dwell.
hearken what aduentures them beffell:
ffull sore thé were adread
ere thé any Lodginge had;
then spake Sir Gawaine,
"this Labour wee haue had in vaine;
this red hart is out of sight,
wee meete with him no more this night.
I reede wee of our horsses do light,
& lodge wee heere all this night;
Truly itt is best, as thinketh mee,
to Lodge low vnder this tree."
"nay," said Kay, "goe wee hence anon,
ffor I will lodge whersoere I come;
for there dare no man warne me,
of whatt estate soeuer hee bee."
"yes," said the Bishopp, "that wott I well;
here dwelleth a Carle in a Castele,
the Carle of Carlile is his name,
I know itt well by St. Iame;

[and by noon 100 harts were killed. But Gawaine, Kay, and Bishop Bodwin, lose their way in following a red deer. Gawaine proposes to dismount, and stay all night in the forest. Kay says he'll lodge in somebody's house. No one dare stop him. The Bishop says,]

was there neuer man yett soe bold
that durst lodge within his hold;
but, & if hee scape with his liffe away,
hee ruleth him well, I you say."
then said Kay, "all in ffere,
to goe thither is my desire;
ffor & the Carle be neuer soe bolde,
I thinke to lodge within his hold.
ffor if he iangle & make itt stout,
I shall beate the Carle all about,
& I shall make his bigging bare,
& doe to him mickle Care;
& I shall beate [him,] as I thinke,
till he both sweate and stinke."
then said the Bishopp, "so mote I ffare,
att his bidding I wilbe yare."
Gawaine said "lett be thy bostlye ffare,
ffor thou dost euer waken care.
if thou scape with thy liffe away,
thou ruleth thee well, I dare say."
then said Kay, "that pleaseth mee;
thither Let vs ryde all three.
such as hee bakes, such shall hee brew;
such as hee shapes, such shall hee sew;
such as he breweth, such shall he drinke."
"that is contrary," said Gawaine, "as I thinke;
but if any ffaire speeche will he gaine,
wee shall make him Lord within his owne;
if noe ffaire speech will auayle,
then to karp on Kay wee will not ffaile."
then said the Bishopp, "that senteth mee;

[The Carle of Carlisle will: he never lets any man lodge with him. "If he refuses me, I'll beat him till he stinks," says Kay. Gawaine tells Kay not to brag; they'll try fair speech first; if that's no good, Kay may scold.]

thither lett vs ryde all three."
when they came to the carles gate,
a hammer they ffound hanging theratt:
Gawaine hent the hammer in his hand,
& curteouslye on the gates dange.
fforth came the Porter with still ffare,
saying, "who is soe bold to knocke there?"
Gawaine answered him curteouslye
"man," hee said, "that is I.
wee be 2 Knights of Arthurs inn,
& a Bishopp, no moe to min;
wee haue rydden all day in the fforrest still
till horsse & man beene like to spill;
ffor Arthurs sake, that is our Kinge,
wee desire my Lord of a nights Lodginge,
& harbarrow till the day att Morne,
that wee may scape away without scorne."
Then spake the crabbed Knight Sir Kay:
"Porter, our errand I reede the say,
or else the Castle gate wee shall breake,
& the Keyes thereof to Arthur take."
the Porter sayd with words throe,
"theres no man aliue that dares doe soe!
of a 100d such as thou his death had sworne,
yett he wold ryde on hunting to morne."
then answered Gawain that was curteous aye,
"Porter, our errand I pray thee say."
"yes," said the Porter, "withouten ffayle
I shall say your errand ffull well."
as soone as the Porter the Carle see,

[They ride to the Earl's gate. Gawaine knocks, and tells the Porter that they are tired out with hunting, and ask his lord for a night's lodging. Kay threatens the Porter, but he answers boldly. Gawaine asks him courteously, and the Porter gives his message to the Carle.]

hee kneeled downe vpon his knee:
"Yonder beene 2 Knights of Arthurs in,
& a Bishopp, no more to myn;
they haue roden all day in the fforrest still,
that horsse [&] man is like to spill;
they desire you ffor Arthirs sake, their King,
to grant them one nights Lodginge,
& herberrow till the day att Morne
that they may scape away without scorne."
"noe thing greeues me," sayd the Carle without doubt,
"but that they Knights stand soe long without."
with that they Porter opened the gates wyde,
& the Knights rode in that tyde.
their steeds into the stable are tane,
the Knights into the hall are gone:
heere the Carle sate in his chaire on hye,
with his legg cast ouer the other knee;
his mouth was wyde, & his beard was gray,
his lockes on his shoulders lay;
betweene his browes, certaine
itt was large there a spann,
with 2 great eyen brening as ffyer.
Lord! hee was a Lodlye syer!
ouer his sholders he bare a bread
3 taylors yards, as clarkes doe reade;
his ffingars were like to teddar stakes,
& his hands like breads that wiues may bake;
50 Cubitts he was in height;
Lord, he was a Lothesome wight!
when Sir Gawaine that carle see,
he halched him ffull curteouslye,

[The Carle regrets that they have been kept so long waiting.
Gawaine &c. ride in, go to the hall, and see the Carle, a loathly
man, with fingers like stakes and hands like leaves.]

& saith, "carle of Carlile, god saue thee
as thou sitteth in thy prosperitye!"
the carle said, "as christ me saue,
yee shall be welcome ffor Arthurs sake.
yet is itt not my part to doe soe,
ffor Arthur hath beene euer my ffoe;
he hath beaten my Knights, & done them bale,
& send them wounded to my owne hall,
yett the truth to tell I will not Leane,
I haue quitt him the same againe."
"that is a kind of a knaue," said Kay, "without Leasing,
soe to reuile a Noble King."
Gawaine heard, & made answere,
"Kay, thou sayst more then meete weere."
with that they went ffurther into the hall,
where bords were spredd, & couered with pall;
4 welpes of great Ire
they ffound Lying by the ffire.
there was a beare that did rome,
& a bore that did whett his tushes ffome,
alsoe a bull that did rore,
& a Lyon that did both gape & rore;
the Lyon did both gape and gren.
"O peace, whelpes!" said the carle then:
ffor that word that they carle did speake,
the 4 whelpes vnder they bord did creepe.
downe came a Lady ffaire & ffree,
& sett her on the carles knee;
one whiles shee harped, another whiles song,
both of Paramours & louinge amonge.

[Gawaine salutes him courteously, and the Carle welcomes them
for Arthur's sake, though Arthur and he have long been foes.
They go to the tables, and see 4 whelps, a bear, a boar, a bull,
and a lion. A fair lady seats herself on the Carle's knee,]

"well were that man," said Gawaine, "that ere were borne
that might Lye with that Lady till day att morne.
"that were great shame," said the carle ffree,
"that thou sholdest doe me such villanye."
"Sir," said Gawaine, "I sayd nought."
"no, man," said the carle; "more thou thought."
Then start Kay to the fflore,
& said hee wold see how his palfrey ffore.
both corne & hay he ffound Lyand,
& the carles palfrey by his steed did stand.
Kay tooke the carles palfrey by the necke,
& soone hee thrust him out att the hecke:
thus Kay put the carles ffole out,
& on his backe he sett a clout.
then the carle himselfe hee stood there by,
and sayd, "this buffett, man, thou shalt abuy."
The carle raught Kay such a rapp
that backward he ffell fflatt;
had itt not beene ffor a ffeald of straw.
Kayes backe had gone in 2.
then said Kay, "& thow were without thy hold,
Man! this buffett shold be deere sold."
"what," sayd the carle, "dost thou menace me?
I swere by all soules sicerlye!
Man! I swere ffurther thore,
if I heere any malice more,
ffor this one word that thou hast spoken
itt is but ernest thou hast gotten."
then went Kay into the hall,

[and Gawaine says her bedfellow will be a happy man.
The Carle reproves him. Kay goes to the stable, finds the
Carle's palfrey next to his, turns it out, and gives it a clout.
The Carle knocks Kay down. Kay threatens him, and he tells
Kay that if he says any more he'll get more knocks.]

& the Bishopp to him can call,
saith: Brother Kay, where you haue beene?"
"to Looke my palffrey, as I weene."
then said the Bishopp, "itt ffalleth me
that my palfrey I must see."
both corne & hay he ffound Lyand,
& the carles palffrey, as I vnderstand.
the Bishopp tooke the carles horsse by the necke,
& soone hee thrust him out att the hecke;
thus he turned the carles ffole out,
& on his backe he sett a clout;
sais, "wend forth, ffole, in the devills way!
who made thee soe bold with my palfrey?"
the carle himselfe he stood there by:
"man! this buffett thou shalt abuy."
he hitt the Bishopp vpon the crowne,
that his miter & he ffell downe.
"Mercy!" said the Bishopp, "I am a clarke!
somewhatt I can of chr[i]sts werke."
he saith, "by the Clergye I sett nothing,
nor yett by thy Miter nor by thy ringe.
It ffitteth a clarke to be curteous & ffree,
by the conning of his clergy."
with that the Bishopp went into the hall,
& Sir Gawaine to him can call,
saith, "brother Bishopp where haue you beene?"
"to looke my palfrey, as I weene."
then sayd Sir Gawaine, "itt ffalleth mee
that my palfreye I must needs see."
corne & hay he ffound enoughe Lyand,

[Then the Bishop goes to look at his palfrey. He finds the
Carle's there, and turns it out with a cut to go to the devil.
The Carle knocks the Bishop over, he cares nothing for
mitre or ring. Then Gawaine goes to see his palfrey.]

& the carles ffole by his did stand.
the carles ffole had beene fforth in the raine;
therof Sir Gawaine was not ffaine;
hee tooke his mantle that was of greene,
& couered the ffole, as I weene;
sayth, "stand vp, ffole, & eate thy meate;
thy Master payeth ffor all that wee heere gett."
they carle himselfe stood thereby,
& thanked him of his curtesye;
they carle tooke Gawaine by the hand,
& both together in they hall they wend.
the carles called ffor a bowle of wine,
& soone they settled them to dine;
70 bowles in that bowle were, –
he was not weake that did itt beare, –
then they carle sett itt to his Chin,
& said, "to you I will begin!"
15 gallons he dranke that tyde,
& raught to his men on euery side.
then they carle said to them anon,
"Sirrs, to supper gett you gone!"
Gawaine answered the carle then,
"Sir, att your bidding we will be ben."
"if you be bayne att my bidding,
you honor me without Leasinge."
they washed all, & went to meate,
& dranke the wine that was soe sweete.
the carle said to Gawaine anon,
"a long speare see thou take in thy hand,
att the buttrye dore take thou thy race,

[He finds the Carle's foal by it, wet with rain. Gawaine covers the foal
with his mantle and tells it to eat away. The Carle thanks Gawaine, takes
him in, calls for a bowl of wine, and drinks 15 gallons at one draught.
Then they all have supper. After it, the Carle tells Gawaine]

& marke me well in middest the face.
"a!" thought Sir Kay, "that that were I!
then his buffett he sold deere abuy."
"well," quoth the carle, "when thou wilt, thou may,
when thou wilt thy strength assay." –
"well Sir," said Kay, "I said nought."
"Noe," said the carle, "but more thou thought."
then Gawaine was ffull glad of that,
& a long spere in his hand he gatt;
att the buttery dore he tooke his race,
& marked the carle in the middst the fface.
the carle saw Sir Gawaine come in ire,
& cast his head vnder his speare,
Gawaine raught the wall such a rapp,
the flyer fllew out, & the speare brake;
he stroke a ffoote into the wall of stone,
a bolder Barren was there neuer none.
"soft," said the carle, "thow was tó radd."
"I did but, Sir, as you me bade."
"if thou had hitt me as thou had ment,
thou had raught me a ffell dint."
they carle tooke Gawaine by the hand,
& both into a Chamber they wend;
a ffull ffaire bed there was spred,
the carles wiffe therin was laid:
the carles said, "Gawaine, of curtesye
gett into this bedd with this ffaire Ladye.
kisse thou her 3se before mine eye;
looke thou doe no other villanye."
the carle opened the sheetes wyde;

[to take a spear and to mark him in his face. Gawaine takes the
spear, charges at the Carle (who doges his head), runs the spear
into the wall, and breaks it off. Then the Carle takes Gawaine to his
wife's bed, and bids him get in and kiss her, but do nothing more]

Gawaine gott in by the Laydes syde;
Gawaine ouer her put his arme;
with that his fflesh began to warme:
Gawaine had thought to haue made in ffare,
"hold," quoth the carle, "man, stopp there!
itt were great shame," quoth they carle, "for me
that thou sholdest doe me such villanye;
but arise vp, Gawaine, & goe with me,
I shall bring thee to a ffairer Lady then euer was shee."
they carle tooke Gawaine by the hand;
both into another Chamber they wend;
a ffaire bedd there found they spred,
and the Carles daughter therin Laid:
saith, "Gawaine, now for thy curtesye
gett thee to bedd to this ffaire Lady."
the carle opened the sheetes wyde,
Sir Gawaine gott in by the Ladyes side.
Gawaine put his arme ouer that sweet thing;
"sleepe, daughter," sais the carle, "on my blessing."
they carle turned his backe & went his way,
& lockt the dore with a siluer Kaye.
on the other morning when the carles rose
vnto his daughters chamber he goes:
"rise vp, Sir Gawaine, & goe with mee,
a maruelous sight I shall lett thee see."
they carle tooke him by the hand,
& both into another chamber they wend,
& there they found many a bloody serke
which were wrought with curyous werke:
1500 dead mens bones

[Gawaine does so, and thinks to do more, but the Carle stops him, and takes him to his daughter's bed, and tells him to get into it. Gawaine does so, and the Carle goes away, locking the door. Next morning he calls Gawaine, and shows him bloody shirts]

they found vpon a rooke att once,
"alacke!" quoth Sir Gawaine, "what haue been here?"
saith, "I & my welpes haue slaine all there."
then Sir Gawaine curteous and kind,
he tooke his leaue away to wend,
& thanked they carle & the Ladyes there,
right as they worthy were.
"nay," said the carle, "wee will first dine,
& then thou shalt goe with blessing mine."
after dinner, the sooth to say,
the carle tooke Gawaine to a Chamber gay
where were hanginge swords towe;
the Carle soone tooke one of tho,
& sayd to the Knight then,
"Gawaine, as thou art a man,
take this sword & stryke of my head."
"Nay," said Gawaine, "I had rather be dead;
ffor I had rather suffer pine & woe
or euer I wold that deede doe."
the carle sayd to Sir Gawaine,
"looke thou doe as I thee saine,
& therof be not adread;
but shortly smite of my head,
ffor if thou wilt not doe itt tyte,
ffor-ssooth thy head I will of smyte."
To the carle said Sir Gawaine,
"Sir, your bidding shall be done:"
he stroke the head the body ffroe,
& he stood vp a man thoe

[and 1500 dead men's bones, slain by him, the Carle. Gawaine
wants to take leave, but the Carle makes him stop to dinner. After
it he shows Gawaine a sword, and begs him to cut his (the Carle's)
head off. Gawaine refuses, whereupon the Carle says he'll cut his
head off if he don't do it. So Gawaine cuts the Carle's head off,]

of the height of Sir Gawaine,
the certaine soothe withouten Laine.
the carle sayd, "Gawaine, god blese thee,
ffor thou hast deliuered mee!
ffrom all ffalse witchcrafft
I am deliuerd att the Last;
by Nigromance thus was I shapen
till a Knight of the round table
had with a sword smitten of my head,
if he had grace to doe that deede.
itt is 40 winters agoe
since I was transformed soe;
since then, none Lodged within this wooun,
but I & my whelpes driuen them downe;
& but if hee did my bidding soone,
I killed him & drew him downe,
euery one but only thee.
Christ grant thee of his mercye!
he that the world made, reward thee this!
ffor all my bale thou hast turned to blisse.
now will I leaue that Lawe;
there shall no man ffor me be slawe,
& I purpose ffor their sake
a chantrey in this place to make,
& 5 preists to sing ffor aye
vntill itt be doomes day.
& Gawaine, for the loue of thee
euery one shall bee welcome to me."
Sir Gawaine & the young Lady clere,
the Bishopp weded them in ffere;

[and he stands up a proper man, and thanks Gawaine for delivering him from the witchcraft that 40 years ago transformed him, so to be till a Knight of the Round Table should cut his head off. "Christ reward you! Henceforth I'll kill no one; but everybody shall be welcome to me.]

the carle gaue him for his wedding
a staffe, miter, & a ringe.
he gaue Sir Kay, that angry Knight,
a blood red steede, & a wight.
he gaue his daughter, the sooth to say,
an ambling white palfrey,
the ffairest hee was on the mold;
her palfrey was charged with gold;
shee was soe gorgeous & soe gay,
no man cold tell her array.
the carle commanded Sir Gawaine to wend
& "say vnto Arthur our King,
& pray him that hee wold –
ffor his loue that Iudas sold,
& for his sake that in Bethelem was borne, –
that hee wold dine with him to morne."
Sir Gawaine sayd the carle vnto,
"fforssooth I shall your message doe."
then they rode singing by the way
with the Ladye that was gay;
they were as glad of that Lady bright
as euer was ffowle of the day-Lyght.
they told King Arthur where they had beene,
& what aduentures they had seene.
"I thanke god," sayd the King, "cozen Kay,
that thou didst on liue part away."
"Marry," sayd Sir Kay againe,
"of my liffe I may be ffaine.
ffor his loue that was in Bethlem borne,
you must dine with the carle to-morne."

[The Bishop marries Gawaine and the Carle's daughter. The Carle gives Kay a blood-red steed, and Gawaine's lady a white palfrey. Then he bids Gawaine go to Arthur and ask him to dine with him next day. Gawaine goes singing with his lady, and tells Arthur his adventures.]

in the dawning of the day thé rode;
a merryer meeting was neuer made.
when they together were mett,
itt was a good thing, I you hett;
the trumpetts plaid att the gate,
with trumpetts of siluer theratt;
there [was] all manner of Minstrelsye,
harpe, Gyttorne, and sowtrye.
into the hall the King was ffett,
& royallye in seat was sett.
by then the dinner was readye dight,
tables were couered all on height;
then to wash they wold not blinn,
& the ffeast they can beginn.
there they were mached arright,
euery Lady against a Knight;
And Minstrells sate in windowes ffaire,
& playd on their instruments cleere;
"Minstrells ffor worshipp att euery messe
ffull Lowd they cry Largnesse!"
the carle bade the King "doe gladlye,
ffor heere yee gett great curtesye."
the Kinq said "by Saint Michaell
this dinner Liketh me ffull well."
he dubd the carle a Knight anon,
he gaue him the county of carlile soone,
& made him Erle of all that Land,
& after, Knight of the table round.
the King said, "Knight, I tell thee,

[Kay gives Arthur the Carle's invitation. Arthur and his company
ride off, are received at the Carle's with sound of trumpet, harp,
gittern, and psaltery; tables are laid, and the feast begins, minstrels
playing the while. Arthur likes his dinner, knights the Carle, gives
him Carlisle, makes him an Earl, and a Knight of the Round Table,]

Carlile shall thy name bee."
when the dinner was all done,
euery Knight tooke his leaue soone,
to wend forward soberlye
home into their owne countrye.
he that made vs all with his hand,
both the sea and the Land,
grant vs all ffor his sake
this ffalse world to fforsake,
& out of this world when wee shall wend,
to heauens blisse our soules bringe!
god grant vs grace itt may soe bee!
Amen, say all, ffor Charitye!

[and christens him Carlisle. After dinner the guests go
home. May God bring our souls to heaven! Amen!]

The Turke and Sir Gawain

GAWAIN PLAYS a similar role to that in *The Carle of Carlisle* in *The Turke and Sir Gawain*, a romance written about 1500 in six-line rhyming stanzas. The Turke of the title comes to Arthur's court and proposes an exchange of blows (perhaps punches rather than beheadings). After he endures Gawain's blow, the Turke takes Gawain with him, first to a strange castle and then to the Isle of Man, where a heathen sultan rules. The Turke helps Gawain survive several trials at the castle and kills the sultan. Then, in a scene that has similarities to the beheading in *The Carle of Carlisle*, he asks Gawain to cut off his head, an act that transforms the Turke into the knight Sir Gromer. Gromer proposes that Arthur make Gawain King of Man, but the knight refuses and recommends that the Turke be rewarded with that title.

In the English romances, Gawain often has his valour tested. He endures tests of his virtue and beheading contests that other knights do not dare to undertake, and by his courtesy he breaks enchantments and brings about peace and alliances with those outside Arthur's control. Though he is not always without flaw, he is generally the hero against whom all others are measured.

The Turke & Gowin

THIS FRAGMENT is printed from the Percy Folio in Sir Frederick Madden's 'Sir Gawayne'. The commencement of it strongly resembles the opening scene of the 'Green Knight' (see below, vol. ii. and 'Sir Gawayne and the Green Knight' in Madden's 'Sir Gawayne', and among the Early English Text Society's Publications). Indeed, the commencement is probably borrowed from that poem, and imperfectly amalgamated with the main story. The proposed exchange of buffets is apparently forgotten altogether as the story proceeds. Instead of Sir Gawain's receiving in his turn a blow, the Turk implores and persuades him to give another – he offers him the other cheek.

The scene of the terrible competition to which Sir Gawain is challenged is the Isle of Man. Superstition firmly believed for many a century that that island was tenanted by a population of giants. Even when Waldron visited it about the middle of the last century, that belief prevailed. He intitules his book 'The History and Description of the Isle of Man, its antiquity, curious and authentick Relations of Apparitions of giants that have lived under the castle, time immemorial. Likewise many comical and entertaining stories of the pranks play'd by fairies, &c.' Giants had overpowered the primitive population – the fairies – said the common account, and been themselves in course of time overpowered and spell-bound by Merlin; and spell-bound they were still lying in huge subterranean chambers. "They say," says Waldron, who is himself not quite untouched by the infirmities of the islanders, "there are a great number of fine apartments underground, exceeding in magnificence any of the upper rooms [of the Castle, at Castleton]. Several men of more than ordinary courage have in former times ventured down to explore the secrets of this subterraneous dwelling-place, but none of them ever returned to give an account of what they saw." And then he tells a story current amongst the natives how at one time an uncommonly bold fellow, well fortified with brandy, penetrated these dark regions, and at last reached light and a magnificent house, with a monster, fourteen feet long and ten or eleven round, recumbent in it, at the sight of whom he judiciously retraced his steps. So of Douglas Fort he tells us "there is certainly a very strong and secret apartment underground in it, having no passage to it but a hole, which is covered with a large stone, and is called to this day 'The great man's chamber'." The island abounds with ancient stone circles, to some account of which a small pamphlet is devoted by Mr. Halliwell. So it was naturally enough made the scene of Sir Gawain's encounter with the giant brood.

The sports in which the monsters indulge are those, on a huge scale, which were generally in vogue at the time of the composition of the romance. The old writers could not conceive an age with different fashions from those of their own. Alexander was even as Arthur. So the giants sport after the manner of the knights. Hand-tennis (eu de paume, pila palmaria our 'fives') was a popular game at a very early period. Strutt quotes from the 'Romance of the Three Kings' sons and the King of Sicily' (MS. Harl. 326): "The king for to assaie him made justes and tournies, and no man did so well as he; in runnyng, *playing at the pame*, shotyng, and *castyng of the barre*, ne found he his maister." Tennis-courts were common in France in Charles V's time (1364–80). Our Henry VII was a tennis-player. "Item," runs a MS. Register of his expenses in the Remembrancer's Office, "for the king's loss at tennis I2d., for the loss of balls 5d." In MSS. Harl. 2248 and 6271 (*apud* Strutt) we find mentioned "tenes coats" and "drawers" and "slippers" for his son. The other sports – the flinging of the axletree, and of the huge chimney or fire-place (Cf. "Than was then on a chymenay a gret fyr that brente rede," MS. Ashmole, 33 f. 29 *apud* Halliwell s. v.) – are of one and the same kind, and a kind extremely popular in Old England, as still in the North, and in Scotland. Fitzstephen's 'Description of London' informs us that such sports were in great favour in the twelfth century. In Edward III's time they were so much so as to endanger the practice of archery. The objects thrown or hurled were stones, darts, bars of wood and iron, and similar things. Cf. Barclay's 'Ecloges' (1508), quoted by Strutt:

> *I can dance the raye; I can both pipe and sing,*
> *If I were merry; I can both hurle and fling;*
> *I runne, I wrestle, I can well throw the barre,*

No shepherd threweth the axeltree so farre;
If I were merry, I could well leape and spring;
I were a man mete to serve a prince or king.

Verses 154-165 inclusive would seem to be an interpolation made at one of the many periods when there was felt a general disgust with the clergy – probably in the fifteenth century.

The contrast between Sir Kay and Sir Gawain – the crabbed knight and the courteous – is one often brought out. See the next piece.

* * *

Listen, lords great & small,
what aduentures did befall
in England, where hath beene
of knights that held the round table
which were doughty & profittable,
of kempys cruell & keene.

All England both East & west,
lords & ladyes of the best,
they busked & made them bowne,
& when the king sate in seate, –
lords serued him att his meate, –
into the hall a burne there cane:

[While the lords and ladies of the court were
feasting, there entered the hall a man,]

He was not hye, but he was broad,
& like a turke he was made
both legg & thye,
& said, "is there any will, as a brother,
to giue a buffett & take another,
giff any soe hardy bee?"

[short, broad, Turk-like, and offered
to exchange buffets with any one.]

Then spake sir Kay, that crabbed knight,
& said "man, thou seemest not soe wight,
if thou be not adread,
for there beene knights within this hall
with a buffett will garr thee fall,
& grope thee to the ground.

[Sir Kay derides him.]

"Giue thou be neuer soe stalworth of hand
I shall bring thee to the ground,
that dare I safely sweare."
then spake sir Gawaine, that worthy knight,
saith, "cozen Kay, thou speakest not right,
lewd is thy answere;

[Sir Gawain reproves Sir Kay]

"What & that man want of his witt,
then litle worshipp were to thee pitt
if thou shold him forefore."

[The Turk challenges the better of them.]

then spake the turke with word[e]s thraw,
saith, "come the better of your tow
though ye be breme as bore"
[half a page missing]

"this buffett thou hast …
well quitt that it shall be,
And yett I shall make thee 3ise as feard

as euer was man on middlearth,
this court againe ere thou see."

["I shall scare you before you get back here."]

Then said Gawaine, "my truth I plight,
I dare goe with thee full right,
& neuer from thee flye;
I will neuer flee from noe aduenture,
Iusting nor noe other turnament,
whilest I may liue on lee."

[Gawain declares himself bold
to go with the Turk]

The turke tooke leaue of King with crowne,
Sir Gawaine made him ready bowne,
his armor & his steed,
they rode northwards 2 dayes and more;
by then Sir Gawaine hungred sore,
of meate & drinke he had great need.

[They ride off together northwards for more
than two days. Gawain gets hungry.]

The turke wist Gawaine had need of meate,
& spake to him with word[e]s great,
hawtinge vppon hee;
says "Gawaine, where is all thy plenty?
yesterday thou wast serued with dainty,
& noe part thou wold giue me,
"but with buffett thou did me sore
therefore thou shalt haue mickle care,
& aduentures shalt thou see.
I wold I had king Arthur heere,

64 & many of thy fellowes in fere
that behaues to try mastery."

[The Turk taunts him, and promises him trouble.]

He led Sir Gawaine to a hill soe plaine;
the earth opened & closed againe,
then Gawaine was adread;
the Merke was comen & the light is gone;
thundering, lightning, snow & raine,
therof enough they had.

[They enter a hall full of darkness, and
thunder, lightning, snow, and rain.]

Then spake Sir Gawaine & sighed sore,
"such wether saw I neuer afore
in noe stead where I haue beene stood"
[half a page missing]
"... made them noe answere
but only vnto mee."

[Gawain had never known such weather.]

To the Castle they then yode:
Sir Gawaine light beside his steed,
for horsse the turke had none;
there they found chamber, bower, & hall,
richly rayled about with pale,
seemly to look vppon;

[They go up to the castle, and find fair chambers, and bowers and a hall,]

A Bord was spred within that place,
all manner of meates & drinkes there was

for groomes that might it againe:
Sir Gawaine wold haue fallen to that fare,
the turke bad him leaue for care;
then waxt he vnfaine;

[and a board spread with viands; wherefrom
the Turk warns Gawain to abstain.]

Gawaine said, "man, I maruell haue
that thou may none of these v[i]ttells spare,
& here is soe great plentye;
yett haue I more mervaile, by my fay,
that I see neither man nor maid,
woman nor child soe free;

"I had leuer now att mine owne will
of this fayre meate to eate my fill
then all the gold in christenty."
the turke went forth, & tarryed nought;
Meate & drinke he forth brought,
was seemly for to see;

[The Turk goes forth and brings him meat and drink.]

He said, "eate, Gawaine, & make thee yare,
infaith or thou gett victalls more
thou shalt both swinke & sweat;
eate, Gawaine, & spare thee nought!"
Sir Gawaine eate as him good thought,
& well he liked his meate;

He dranke ale, & after, wine,
he saith, "I will be att thy bidding baine
without bost or threat;
but one thing I wold thee pray,

giue me my bufiett & let me goe my way,
I wold not longer be hereatt.
[half a page gone]

[He asks that he may have his
buffet and go his way.]

There stood a bote and ...
Sir Gawaine left behind his steed,
he might noe other doe.

The turke said to Sir Gawaine,
"he shalbe here when thou comes againe, –
I plight my troth to thee, –
within an bower, as men tell me."
they were sailed over the sea;
the turke said, "Gawaine, hee!

[He and the Turk sail over the sea.]

"Heere are we withouten scath;
but now beginneth the great othe.
when he shall aduentures doe."
he lett him see a castle faire,
such a one he neuer saw yare,
noe wher in noe country.
The turke said to Sir Gawaine
"yonder dwells the King of Man,
a heathen soldan is hee,

[The Turk shows him a castle.
"There dwells the King of Man,"]

"With him he hath a hideous rout
of giants strong & stout

& vglie to looke vppon;
who-so-euer had sought farr & neere
as wide as the world were,
such a companye he cold find none.

[with his giants, a rare company."]

"Many auentures thou shalt see there,
such as thou neuer saw yare
in all the world about:
thou shalt see a tenisse ball
that neuer knight in Arthurs hall
is able to giue it a lout;
& other aduentures there are moe:
wee shall be assayled ere we goe,
therof haue thou noe doute;

[And tells him of adventures at hand.]

"But & yee will take to me good heed,
I shall helpe you in time of need;
for ought I can see
there shall be none soe strong in stower
but I shall bring thee againe to hi …
[half a page missing]

["But heed me, and I will help you."]

… *"Sir Gawaine stifle & stowre,*
how fareth thy vnckle King Arthur,
& all his company,
& that Bishopp Sir Bodwine
that will not let my goods alone,
but spiteth them euery day?

["How do your uncle King Arthur and all his
society, and that Bishop Bodwin?]

"He preached much of a crowne of thorne;
he shall ban the time that he was borne
& euer I catch him may;
I anger more att the spiritually
in England nor att the temporaltie,
they goe soe in theire array;

[I hate all the clergy, burn them all!]

And I purpose in full great ire
to brenn their clergy in a fire
& punish them to my pay:
sitt downe, Sir Gawaine, at the bord."
Sir Gawaine answered at that word,
saith, "nay, that may not be,

[But pray sit down at our table."
"No," answers Gawain,]

"I trow not a venturous knight shall
sitt downe in a kings hall
aduentures or you see."
the King said, "Gawaine, faire mot then fall!
goe feitch me forth my tennisse ball;
for play will I and see."

["not before I see adventures."
The king sends for his tennis ball.]

They brought it out with-out doubt;
with it came a hideous rout
of Gyants great & plenty;

all the giants were there then
heire by the halfe then Sir Gawaine,
I tell you withouten nay.

[The ball comes; with a hideous mob of giants.]

There were 17 giants bold of blood,
& all thought Gawaine but litle good.
when they thought with him to play,
all the giants thoughten then
to haue strucke out Sir Gawaines braine.
help him god that best may!

The ball of brasse was made for the giants hand,
There was noe man in all england
were able to carry it ...
[half a page missing]

[The ball is made for giants' play.]

and sticked a giant in the hall
that grysly can hee grone.
The King sayd, "bray away this axeltree,
for such a boy I neuer see;
yett he shalbe assayd better ere he goe;

["Take away this axle-tree. This boy (*i.e.* the Turk)
is a rare one; but he shall be tried yet."]

"I told you, soe Mote I tho,
with the 3 aduenture, & then no more
befor me at this tide."
Then there stood amongst them all
a chimney in they Kings hall
with barres mickle of pride;

there was laid on in that stond
coales & wood that cost a pound,
that vpon it did abide.

[There stood in their midst a fireplace with huge bars,
and a pounds-worth of coals and wood on it.]

A giant bad gawaine assay,
& said, "Gawaine, begin the play!
thou knowest best how it shold be;
& afterwards when thou hast done,
I trow you shalbe answered soone
either with boy or me.
A great giant, I vnderstand,
lift vp the chimney with his hand
& sett it downe againe fairly."

[A giant bids Gawain lift the huge fireplace with his hand.]

Sir Gawaine was neuer soe adread
sith he was man on middle earth,
& cryd on god in his thought.
Gawaine vnto his boy can say
"lift this chimney – if you may –
that is soe worthily wrought."

[He bids his boy (the Turk) lift it.]

Gawaines boy to it did leape,
& gatt itt by the bowles great,
& about his head he it flang;
3is about his head he it swang
that the coals & the red brands
[half a page missing]

... saw of mickle might
& strong were in battell.

[The boy seizes it and swings it thrice round his head.]

"I haue slaine them thorrow my mastery,
& now, Gawaine, I will slay thee,
& then I haue slaine all the flower;
there went neuer none againe no tale to tell,
nor more shalt thou, thoe thou be fell,
nor none that longeth to King Arthur."

["I have slain them, and now I will slay thee."]

The turke was clad inuissible gay,
no man cold see him withouten nay,
he was cladd in such a weede;
he heard their talking lesse & more,
& yet he thought they shold find him there
when they shold do that deed.

[The Turk, invisible, hears.]

Then he led him into steddie
werhas was a boyling leade,
& welling vppon hie:
& before it a giant did stand
with an Iron forke in his hand
thai hideous was to see.

[Gawain is conducted to a boiling cauldron, before
which stands a giant with an iron fork.]

The giant that looked soe keene
that before Sir Gawaine had neuer scene

noe where in noe country:
the King saide to the giant thoe,
"here is none but wee tow;
let see how best may bee."

[The king and the giant conspire.]

when the giant saw Gawaines boy there was,
he leapt & threw, & cryed "alas
that he came in that stead!"
Sir Gawaines boy to him lept,
& with strenght vp him gett,
& cast him in the lead;

[The giant discovers Gawain's boy,
who throws him into the lead]

with, an Iron forke made of steele
he held him downe wondorous weele
till he was scalded to the dead,
then Sir Gawaine vnto the K.ing can say,
"with-out thou wilt agree vnto our law,
eatein is all thy bread."

[amd holds him down with the fork.]

The King spitt on Gawaine the knight:
with that the turke hent him vpright
& into the fyer him flang,
& saide to Sir Gawaine at the last,
"Noe force, Master, all the perill is past!
thinke not we tarrie too longe,"
[half a page missing]

[The king spits on Gawain –

is thrown into the fire by the Turk.]

be tooke forth a bason of gold
as an Emperour washe shold,
as fell for his degree:

He tooke a sword of Mettle free,
saies "if euer I did any thing for thee,
doe for me in this stead;
take here this sword of steele
that in battell will bite weele,
therwith strike of my head."

[He brings a basin and a sword, and entreats
Gawain to strike off his (the Turk's) head.]

"that I forefend!" said Sir Gawaine,
"for I wold not haue thee slaine
for all the gold soe red."
"haue done, Sir Gawaine, I haue no dread,
but in this bason let me bleed
that standeth here in this steed,

[Gawain says "Nay." The Turk urges him.]

"And thou shalt see a new play,
with helpe of Mary that mild mayd
that saued vs from all dread."
he drew forth the brand of steele
that in battell bite wold weele,
& there stroke of his head.

And when the blood in the bason light,
he stood vp a stalwortht Knight
that day, I vndertake,

& song "Te deum laudam[u]s,
worshipp be to our lord Iesus
that saued vs from all wracke!

[He does as he is asked, and up stands a stalwart
knight, who sings the Te Deum,]

"A! Sir Gawaine! blesed thou be!
for all the service I haue don thee,
thou hast well quitt it me."
then he tooke him by the hand,
& many a worthy man they fand
that before they neue[r] see.

[and blesses Sir Gawain. They release many
worthy captives, ladies and men.]

He said, "Sir Gawaine, withouten threat
sitt downe boldly at thy meate,
& I will eate with thee;
Ladyes all, be of good cheere,
eche ane shall wend to his owne dee.
in all hast that may be;

"first we will to King Arthurs hall,
& soone after your husbands send we shall
in country where they beene;
There they wold ... abide
[half a page missing]

"Thus we haue brought 17 ladys cleere
that there were left in great danger,
& we haue brought them out."
then sent they for theire husbands swithe,
& euery one tooke his oune wife,

& lowlye can they lowte,
And thanked the 2 knights & the King
& said the wold be at theire bidding
in all england about.

[The ladies are restored to their thankful husbands.]

Sir Gromer kneeld vpon his knee,
saith "Sir King, and your wilbe,
crowne Gawaine King of man."
Sir Gawaine kneeled downe by,
& said "lord, nay, not I;
giue it him, for he it wan,

[Sir Gromer asks Arthur to make Gawain King
of Man. Gawain declines the honour.]

"for I neuer purposed to be noe King,
neuer in all my liuinge,
whilest I am a liuing man."
he said, "Sir Gromer, take it thee,
for Gawaine will neuer King bee
for no craft that I can."

[The king confers it on Sir Gromer himself,]

Thus endeth the tale that I of meane,
of Arthur & his knight[e]s keene
that hardy were & free,
god give them good life far & neere
that such talking loues to heere!
Amen for Charity!

[and thus ends the tale. The Lord
love all that enjoy such tale-telling!]

'Sir Gawain and the Lady of Lys' and 'Castle Orguellous'

THE TALE of Gawain and the Lady of Lys and the story of the adventures at Castle Orguellous are two episodes from the much longer *First Continuation* of Chrétien de Troyes's *Percival*. The former episode tells of Gawain's encounter with the family of a woman with whom he has slept and had a child and his battle with her brother Bran de Lis. As they fight, Gawain gets the upper hand, and the Lady of Lys tells the child sired by Gawain to plead with him to spare her brother. When the child is endangered by the clashing swords, the onlookers ask Arthur to stop the combat. He does so and makes peace between Gawain and Bran.

These events stem from Gawain's liaison with the Lady of Lys; and they call attention to what is sometimes a feature of Gawain's character. In some tales, he is said to be a champion of women. At the end of Malory's *Morte d'Arthur*, for example, when the ghost of Gawain returns to warn Arthur, he is accompanied by the spirits of ladies for whom he fought in righteous quarrels. Gawain is also depicted as something of a ladies' man. There are a number of medieval works in which he fathers children, as in the Lady of Lys episode, or in which events leading to his marriage are recounted. The comment of Bernlak's wife in *SGGK* that the Gawain she has heard of would not have spent time with a lady without asking for a kiss is a reflection of how his relationship to women is perceived.

The Lady of Lys episode is also interesting to students of English literature because a fifteenth-century stanzaic romance called *The Jeaste of Sir Gawain* has its source in this scene from the *First Continuation*. The author of the *Jeaste* narrates Gawain's defeat of the father of the lady and two of her brothers. Brandles, the third and oldest brother, challenges Gawain, and they fight a fierce battle that must be postponed because of darkness. The two swear to fight to the death when next they encounter each other, but they never meet again. Gawain returns to court without having won a victory over the fiercest of the brothers and without even protecting his mistress from Brandles, who calls his sister a 'harlot' and beats her, after which she leaves and is never seen again. Gawain thus seems, in this work, less than perfect both in valour and in love, and less courteous and courtly than he is portrayed in most other works.

Another parallel to an English work is found in a scene prior to the combat of Gawain and Bran. When Arthur and his knights set out for Castle Orguellous, Kay attempts to obtain food from a castle on their route by rudely demanding it, and he is rebuffed and humiliated by the castle's lord. Gawain then approaches the lord courteously and acquires the needed provisions. The same scenario is played out in the alliterative romance *Golagros and Gawain*. The echoes of the French text in two very different English works suggest some of the ways in which literary texts could be adapted and repurposed by medieval authors.

Sir Gawain and the Lady of Lys

HEARKEN TO ME and ye shall hear how the good King Arthur and his knights went forth to the wood for archery, and how at vesper-tide they gat them homeward right joyfully.

The knights rode gaily ahead, holding converse the one with the other, and behind them came the king, on a tall and prancing steed. He ware no robe of state, but a short coat, which became him right well.

Behind all his men he rode, pensive and frowning, as one lost in thought. And as he thus lagged behind Sir Gawain looked back, and saw the king riding alone and pensive, and he bade his comrades draw rein and wait for their lord. And as the king came anigh he drew his steed beside him, and stretched out his hand, laughing, and laid hold on the bridle, and said, "Sire, tell us, for the love of God, of what ye may now be thinking? Sire, your thoughts should be of naught but good, for there is no prince in this world equal to ye in valour or in honour, therefore should ye be very joyful!"

The king made answer courteously, "Fair nephew, an I may be joyful I will tell ye truly that whereon I thought. There is no king living on earth who hath had such good and such great service from his men as I; it seemeth to me now right and fitting that I should give to them that which they have deserved for the toil they have suffered for me, whereby I be come to such high estate. Fair nephew, I bethought me that my riches would avail little if through sloth I failed to reward the good service of these my knights, who have made me everywhere to be obeyed and honoured. Now without delay will I tell ye that I am minded to hold, at Pentecost, a far greater court than is my wont, and to give to each and all such gifts as shall be well pleasing to them, so that each may be glad and joyful, and ever hereafter of good will towards me."

Swiftly, and before all the others, Sir Gawain made answer, "Fair Sire, blessed be the thought into which ye have fallen, for 'tis so fair and so good that neither kaiser nor king nor count might think a better."

And the king asked, "Nephew, tell me straightway where do ye counsel that this my court be held?"

"Sire, at Carnarvon; there let all your knighthood assemble, for there is not in all your kingdom a fairer place, nor nobler halls, and it lieth in the marches of Wales, and of the land of Britain."

The king and all his company rode back joyfully, and that selfsame night did the king Arthur give command that all the knights and all the barons throughout the land should be summoned by letter to come to him at Pentecost.

That great knighthood came thither, that famous knighthood came thither, even so have I heard, and assembled for this court at Carnarvon.

Ah God! from what far-off lands did they come. Thither were come the men of Ireland, and of Scotland, of Iceland, of Wales, and of Galvoie (a land where many a man goeth astray). From Logres they came, and from Escavalon; men of Norway, Bretons, Danes, and they of Orcanie. Never was so great a knighthood assembled at any court as that which the good king Arthur summoned to him.

The day of the Holy Feast, when he had worn his crown at the high procession, knights and barons conducted him with joy to his palace; and therewith Kay, the seneschal, bade them sound the trumpets and bring water. First the king washed, and thereafter sat down aloft, on the high daïs, so that all who sat there at meat might see him. Four hundred knights, save three, sat themselves down at the Round Table; at the second were seated the thirty peers. Crowded were the ranks of the other knights who were seated throughout the hall, as was fitting, on daïs, and at tables on the ground. Then quickly Kay the seneschal bare the first meat, and the service was made throughout the hall, in joyful wise, as befitted such high festivity.

Now as the king ate, he looked towards the Round Table, even as one who would take knowledge of all, and by hap his eye fell on the seat of a knight good and true, which was void and lacking its rightful lord. Then so great a pity and tenderness took him that the tears rose from his heart to his eyes, and thence welled forth, and he sighed a great and piteous sigh when he remembered him of that knight. He took a knife which Yones held (nephew was he to king Ydier, and carved before Arthur), and, frowning and thoughtful, smote the blade through the bread which lay on the board. Then he rested his head on the one hand, even as one whose thoughts are troubled by anger or grief, and unheeding, ran the palm of the other adown the sharp knife, so that he was somewhat wounded. At sight of the blood he bethought himself, and left hold of the knife and taking the napkin, wrapped it swiftly around his hand, so that they who ate in the hall below might not see. And with that he fell once more into thought and bowed down his head, and as he mused the tears came again to his eyes.

When Sir Gawain beheld this he marvelled much, and therein was he right, for to all who were in the hall it seemed but folly. Then he rose up straightway, and passed between the ranks till that he came before the daïs, and saw that the king was again lost in thought. He hasted not to speak till that he saw him raise his head, but so soon as he lifted up his face Sir Gawain spake right courteously; "Sire, Sire, 'tis neither right nor fitting that ye should have such wrath or displeasure as should make ye thus moody in the sight of so many high and noble barons as ye may see here around ye; rather should their solace and their company please and rejoice ye."

"Gawain, will ye that I tell ye whence came the thought which has made me thus sad and silent?"

"Yea, Sire, that do I pray of ye."

"Fair nephew, know of a truth that I will tell ye willingly, in the hearing of all these good knights. My thoughts were of ye, and of many another whom I see here, of the wickedness of which ye are full, and of the envy and the treason long time hid, and now made manifest." With that the king held his peace, and said no more.

Sir Gawain grew crimson with anger and shame, and throughout the palace all held their peace, for much they marvelled that the king spake thus evilly to his nephew, calling him in the hearing of all a traitor proven, and all were wroth therefor. Then he to whom the ill words were said answered as best he might, "Sire, that was an ugly word; for your honour bethink ye of what ye have said in the hearing of all who be here within."

"Gawain," answered the king, "'tis no empty word, thus of a truth do I repeat it, and Ywain may well take heed and know that I thought of him but now, when I sat silent and pensive, here within have I not one single comrade whom I do not accuse of treason and too great felony!"

With that I know not how many sprang to their feet, and a great clamour filled the hall. "Lords," cried Tor fis Ares, "I conjure ye by the oath which ye and I alike sware to king Arthur that ye restrain yourselves, and act as is befitting; he accuses ye all of treason – these be right evil tidings!" In like wise also spake Sir Ywain. "Ah God," quoth Sir Gawain, "with what joy was all this great court summoned and assembled, and in what grief shall it be broken up!"

The king heard, and, sighing, spake, "Gawain, I have spoken but the truth!"

"Fair Sire, for the love of God, and for honesty, tell us after what manner and in what fashion we be felon and traitorous?"

Quoth the king, "An ye will I will tell ye; now hearken. Ye know of a truth that aforetime there reigned in this land a folk who built castles and cities, strong towers and fortresses, and the great Chastel Orguellous did they fortify against us. When we heard tell thereof ye, my knights, delayed not to go thither, not with my will! There did I lose so many of my folk that the thought thereof yet grieveth my heart; the greater part were slain, but some among them were made captive. They took one of my companions, three years long have they held him in prison, and thereof have I great grief at heart. Here within do I see no better knight; he was beyond measure valiant, fair of face and form, and very wise was he in counsel. But now, when all this great lordship was set down here to meat, I beheld that knight's seat void and lacking its lord, and for sorrow and grief was my heart heavy and troubled when I saw him not in his place in your ranks; it lacked but little that I were distraught. Therefore, my lords, do I arraign ye all of treason; Giflet fis Do is he named that good and gentle knight, three whole years have gone by since he was imprisoned in that tower, and ye be all traitors who have left your comrade three years and have not sought for or freed him! Yea, and I who have blamed ye, I be even more the traitor in that I ever ware crown, or made joy, or held high feast before I knew if he might be restored to me, or where he now may be, whether dead or living! Now on this have I set my heart, – by the faith I owe to that Heavenly Lord who hath bestowed on me earthly honour, and kingdom, and lands, that for no hap that may befall me will I delay to set forth in search of him, be it in never so distant a land. For verily I tell ye all that the king who loseth so good a knight by wrongful deed or by sloth, he hath right neither to lands nor to honour, nor should he live a day longer, an he deliver not that knight who for his honour suffered toil and was made captive. In the ears of ye all do I make a vow that I will lie not more than one night in any place till that I know whether he be dead, or may be freed."

Then all cried with one voice, "Shame upon him, Sire, who will not plead guilty to this treason, for ye speak with right and reason; by overmuch sloth have we delayed to ride forth and seek him far hence, even at the Chastel Orguellous."

"Lords," quoth the king, "I tell ye here and at once that I shall set forth to-morrow, but by the faith that I owe to Saint Germain I must needs proceed with wisdom, for here is force of no avail."

"True, fair Sire," answered Sir Gawain. "Know for sooth that the roads 'twixt here and the Chastel Orguellous be passing hard and difficult; 'tis a good fifteen days ere ye be come thither; longer days have ye never ridden! 'Tis best that one tell ye the truth! And when ye be come thither, fair Sire, then shall ye have each day battle, as I know right well, one knight against the other, a hundred against a hundred, that shall ye find truly. Now take good counsel for the journey, what folk ye may best take with ye."

"Lords," said the king, "now let us to meat, and afterward will I see by aid of your counsel whom I take with me, and whom I leave to guard my land and my folk."

With that all in the palace, great and small, ate as quickly as might be; and so soon as the king saw that 'twas time and place to speak he bade remove the cloths, which they did without delay. Thereafter they brought water, and bare round the wine in cups of fine gold. Then, it seemeth me, there sprang to their feet at once more than three thousand knights, who cried the king mercy, and prayed that he would take them with him on this adventure, for right willingly would they go.

"Lords," quoth the king, "they whom my barons elect, those will I take, and the others shall remain to keep my kingdom in peace."

Then first, before all others, spake king Urien, a very wise knight was he. "My Lord king, ye have no need to take with ye too great a force; take with ye rather a few, but good, men, so to my thinking will ye more swiftly free Giflet, our good comrade, from his prison. Take with ye the best of your knights, 'twill be for your greater honour, and your foes will be the more speedily vanquished; knight against knight must ye fight there, and I think me that such of their men shall there be worsted that they shall that same day yield ye Giflet the good and valiant knight. Have no doubt for the when or how, but bid them make ready. I can but praise the folk who shall go with ye."

Then quoth the king, "What say ye, Lords? I await your counsel!"

King Ydier spake. "Sire, none of us should give ye praise, or speak other than the best he knoweth. Shamed be he who should give ye counsel wherein ye may find no honour. I know full well that the more part of your folk would gladly go with ye, but if ye take them, Sire, 'twill not be for your honour, but believe king Urien, for he hath given good counsel so I tell ye of a truth."

"Certes," saith Sir Gawain, "he would be false and foolish who should give other rede!" And all said, "Let it be as the king will; let him take those whom he please, and leave the others in the land."

"Ye have said well," said the king; "now go ye to your lodging, and prepare to depart, and I will cause to be made ready a pennon of silk for each of those whom I shall lead with me." As he said, so it was done, and all betook them to their lodging.

The king forthwith sent the pennons, and bade them without fail be armed and ahorse at dawn.

What more shall I tell ye? At sunrise were all the knights armed, even as the king commanded, all they who had received the pennons came together ahorse before the hall.

Now will I tell ye their names: there were Sir Gawain, king Ydier, Guengasoains, Kay, and Lucains, the butler. The sixth was Tors. Then Saigremors, and Mabonagrain, who was nephew unto king Urien. Eight have I now named unto ye, counting the kinsman of king Urien. The ninth was Lancelot du Lac; the tenth Ider, son of Nut; the Laid Hardi, the eleventh; with Doon l'Aiglain have we twelve, all very courteous knights.

Galegantins the Galois, and the brave Carados Briefbras, who was a right cheery comrade, made fourteen, and the fifteenth was the good Taulas de Rogemont: so many were they, nor more, nor less.

All ready armed were they before the hall the while they awaited the king, ere he came forth armed from his chamber. Then he mounted his steed, and I tell ye that, to my knowledge, was never king so richly armed afore, nor ever hereafter shall there be such. The queen bare him company even to the entrance of the palace, then she turned her back.

Then the king bade his companions march, and they began to move as swiftly as might be on the highway, but so great a folk convoyed them that hardly might they depart or go forth from the burg. And when the king had ridden three miles he drew rein in the midst of a meadow, and there he bade farewell to his folk, who, sad and sorrowful, gat them back to the burg. And the king and his fifteen comrades rode on their way; they passed even through the land of Britain, so I think me, and hasted them much to ride quickly.

One day the king, fasting, came forth from a very great forest, on to a heath of broom; the sun was hot, and burning, and the country over large and waste. The king was so wearied by the heat, in that he rode fasting, that he had much need of rest, could he but find a fitting spot. By chance they found a great tree, where they drew bridle; beneath was a spring, and for heat and for weariness they bared their heads and their hands, and washed their faces and their mouths. I know well that one and all had much need of food, but they had naught with them, and all were sore vexed for the king, who suffered over much from the fast.

Sir Gawain gazed into the plain, far below, 'neath the forest, and he showed unto the seneschal a house of thatch, well fenced about; "Kay," quoth he, "methinks under that roof there must be folk!"

"'Tis true," said Kay; "I will go and see if I may find victual, and ye shall await me here." With that he departed from them, and went straightway to the house; within he found an old woman, but nothing of what he sought; food was there none.

The crone spake and said, "Sir, so God help me, for twenty miles round about are naught but waste lands, know that well, save only that the king of Meliolant has built there below 'neath the trees a forest lodge. He cometh thither ofttimes privately with his hounds. There, Sir, will ye be well lodged, an ye find him; from that tree yonder may ye see the house on the hill."

The seneschal straightway went even as the crone had said, and he saw the dwelling, right well enclosed with orchards, vineyards and meadows. Ponds were there, lands, and fish-tanks, all well fenced about. In the midst was a tower; ye might ask no better, no defence was lacking to it. Beholding it the seneschal stayed not, but passed the roadway, and the gate, and the chief drawbridge, and thus came to the foot of the tower. There did he dismount, but he found no living soul of whom he might ask concerning the dwelling and who might be within. Then he entered a hall, very high and long and wide. On a great hearth he saw a goodly fire alight, but he found no man save a dwarf, who was roasting a fat peacock ('twere hard to find a better!), well larded, on a spit of apple-wood, which the dwarf knew right well how to turn.

Kay came forward quickly, and the dwarf beheld him with evil countenance. "Dwarf," quoth the seneschal, "tell me if there be any here within save thyself?" But the wretch would not speak a word.

Kay would have slain him there and then, if he had not thought to be shamed thereby, but he knew right well that twere too great villainy.

"Miserable hunchback," quoth he, "I see none here in this house save thee and this peacock, which I will now have for my dinner; I will share it as shall seem me good."

"By the King Who lieth not," quoth the dwarf, "ye shall neither eat thereof yourself nor share it with others; I counsel you to quit this hostel, or know ye well, and without doubt, that ye shall be right shamefully thrust out!"

This vexed Kay mightily, and he sprang forward to smite him; with his foot he thrust him against the pillar of the hearth so that the stone thereof became bloody. The dwarf bled freely for the heat, and made loud lament, for he feared lest he should be slain.

Then on the left the seneschal heard a door shut-to sharply, and there came forth a knight, tall and strong, and of proud countenance, and very fair and goodly to look upon; he might not be above thirty years old. He ware a vest of new samite, furred with ermine for warmth; 'twas not long, but wide, and of ample folds. Thus was he well clad and cunningly shod; and I tell ye truly that he ware a fair girdle of golden links; no treasury hath a richer. All uncovered he came forth, in guise of a man greatly wroth, leading two greyhounds by a fair leash of silk which he held in his hand. When he saw that his dwarf bled, he spake, "Ye who be come all armed into this hall, wherefore have ye slain this my servant?"

"A curse upon such a servant," quoth Kay, "from this day on, for in all the world is there not one so evil, so small, or so misshapen!"

Then the knight answered, "By all the saints, but ye say ill, and I challenge ye for it, fair sir."

Quoth the seneschal, "Many a goodly knight have I seen, to the full as noble as ye may be, and ye be evil and vexatious, even if I have smitten this servant who roasted here this peacock, to speak thus concerning the matter."

The knight answered frankly, "Sir, ye speak not courteously, but for God's sake I would ask ye a mere nothing, even that ye vouchsafe to tell me your name."

Kay spake in great wrath, "I will tell ye willingly, so help me God I have told it ere this to five hundred knights better than ye be; know of a truth that my name is Kay."

"Certes, sir, I may well believe that ye speak truly; by your speech alone may one quickly know ye. This lad refused ye the peacock; 'tis not the custom of my house that meat be refused to any who may ask for it; ye shall have your share of the peacock, and that right swiftly, so God help me!" With that he seized the spit, and raised it aloft, and with great strength and force smote Sir Kay therewith, so that he well nigh slew him, and know that he smote him on the neck so that he must needs fall, he had no foot so firm that it might keep him upright. And as the peacock burst asunder, the hot blood thereof ran between the links of his hauberk in such wise that Sir Kay bare the mark thereof all the days of his life. Then the knight threw the peacock to his two hounds, and spake, "Sir Kay, rise, that be your share, ye shall have no more; now get out of my sight quickly, I am over wroth when I behold ye!"

With that came quickly two sergeants, fully armed, and led the seneschal forth from the hall. He mounted his steed, and turned him back, passing the bridge and the plain, and came to where the king had dismounted.

Then his comrades asked him, "Seneschal, have ye found nothing of that which ye went to seek?"

"Not I, my lords; 'tis a right evil land here wherein to seek for food; it behoveth us to ride far, for here may we find nor hostelry, nor victual – so hath it been told to me."

Quoth Sir Gawain, laughing, "Certes, he with whom ye spake lives by meat, even as we; without meat might he not dwell in this great and well wooded land."

"By my faith, no," answered Kay, "but I tell ye truly, 'tis so proud a vassal that for naught that we may say will he give us shelter."

The king said, "Then is he right discourteous, and I counsel that we send Gawain to him. Fair nephew, go, and we will wait ye here."

Sir Gawain mounted forthwith. What more shall I tell ye save that he came straight to the dwelling, and when the knight saw him he made marvellous joy of him, and asked his name, and he answered that men called him Gawain, and straightway the knight knew him.

Then he told him his errand, saying, "The king is not far distant, and would fain lodge with ye." This was well pleasing to the knight, and he said, "Fair Sir, go, bring the king hither."

Then Sir Gawain rode swiftly back, and brought Arthur with him to the hostel; but ere they might enter all the waters were set free and the fountains 'gan to play. For joy and in honour of the king the knight had assembled all his folk, and received him with very great honour, and led him into the tower. The hounds were yet there, devouring the flesh of the peacock. The king looked at Taulas, and quoth, "Body of Saint Thomas, these two hounds have fared better than we to-day!" The knight heard, and laughed to himself. Kay saw that, but said naught.

From thence they passed into the hall, and when they had disarmed the meat was made ready, the knight bade bring white napkins, and pasties. After dinner he made them wash their heads, and their necks, and their feet, which were sorely bruised. Then he caused them to rest in fair beds, covered with cloth of samite, and they slept even to the morrow without stirring. But when they were awakened the host had prepared for them a right plenteous meal, this he did of his good will. They sat them down joyfully, and were richly served. I would weary ye if I told all the dishes. The knights made much mirth of the seneschal's burn, for the dwarf would not keep the tale secret from them, but began to speak thereof. Never would it have been known through Kay, if the dwarf had not brought it to mind, for he was over bent on hiding it, and the host even more than he; all that night his comrades mocked and made sport of him even till they betook them to rest.

Next morn, without delay, the king arose at daybreak, and likewise did all the others, and armed themselves. Then the king thanked his host for the good lodging he had given them.

Why should I make long telling thereof? The king saith, "Hide not from me how ye be called."

"Sire, my name is Ydier the fair, and, Sire, this castle is mine own."

Then Ydier prayed the king that of his kindness he would take him with him, but Arthur said he might not lead with him other save those whom he had brought from his own land; and he took leave of the knight since he might no longer abide in his hostelry, and went forth with his companions.

The tale is here over long, but I will shorten it for ye. Two days did they ride without food, for they might not sooner find place where they might win food or seek lodging. Thus must they needs ride till they came to the Orchard of the Sepulchres, where adventures be found oft and perilous. There they ate with the hermits, of whom there were a hundred and more. Here 'tis not fitting to tell of the marvels of the cemetery, so diverse they be, and so great that there is no man living on earth who could think, or believe, that the tale be true. Since 'twas made and established never has the tale been told whence came those graves, nor the custom which the hermits observed; to my mind 'twould take too long did I tell it ye ere the fitting time and place be come. But this will I tell ye of a truth, when the king had sojourned two days, and beheld the Orchard, on the third, after meat, he departed, and took the road once more.

On the morrow he came to a wondrous fair land; small need to seek a richer in meadows, forests, or orchards planted with rare and diverse trees. In the forest ways the grass grew green and tall, reaching even to the horses' girths. Towards even-tide they came to a trodden way, where the tall grass was beaten to earth, and trampled down by horses, even for the length of a bowshot. "A hundred and more have passed this way," quoth the king's men.

Sir Gawain spake to the king, "Fair Sire, follow me gently with these my comrades on this wide road. I will ride on ahead, and seek out, and ask whether there be near at hand hostel where we may lodge this night, for of lodging have we great need. Yet, Sire, I pray that ye leave not the road for word of any."

With that he set spurs to his steed, and rode swiftly on his way; nor had he ridden long ere he was free of the forest, and saw before him a hill, and a company of well-nigh a hundred horsemen, who rode in knightly guise; 'twas on their track he followed.

Sir Gawain pressed on his steed, but when he had crossed the valley and mounted the hill there was never a man in sight. But he saw before him a castle; none so fair had he beheld afore, which stood on the bank of a broad river; 'twould take me over long to tell the fashion thereof, but this and no more will I say, 'twas the fairest ever seen.

Then Sir Gawain looked toward the river, and beheld two maidens, in very fair vesture of purple, bearing pitchers of fine gold, wherein they had drawn water, and he quoth, "Maidens, God save ye, and give ye good speed!" and they answered, as was fitting, "Fair sir, God bless ye!"

"Maidens, by the faith ye owe me answer me, and hide it not, what bear ye in those pitchers?"

Quoth the one, "No need have we to hide aught; 'tis but water, wherewith the good knight shall wash his hands."

"Of a faith," quoth Sir Gawain, "courteously have ye named him; great honour is there in such a name!"

The second maiden answered, "Sir, she hath spoken truth; ye will not lightly find a fairer, or a better, knight. See, but now doth he enter within his burg."

Then Sir Gawain hasted, and spake no more with the maidens, but rode over the bridge, and entered the castle by the gateway. Since the hour of his birth never had he seen one so fair, nor, I think me, so long as he live shall he see a fairer. All the way by which he passed was hung with curtains richly wrought, whereat he marvelled strangely. 'Twas closed all along with fair buildings of diverse fashions. In long rows adown the street Sir Gawain beheld rich booths of changers, wherein on many-coloured carpets were set forth vessels of gold and silver (no treasury ever held richer), cups, tankards, and dishes, the fairest ever seen, with money of all lands: esterlins, besants, deniers of Africa, and treasure trove. Every kind of money was there, and much the good knight marvelled thereat.

Stuffs there were too, of all colours, the cost whereof was past his telling. All the doors stood open; but one thing troubled Sir Gawain sore: there was never a living soul to be seen.

Then he said within himself, "Of a sooth, for love and kindness do they bear their lord, who but now hath entered the burg, company to the little castle yonder." Thus he went his way straight to that castle, and came within a goodly hall, both high and wide, and in length equal to a bowshot. On every daïs a linen cloth was spread, and sure never king nor count might eat off fairer or better wrought. All was made ready for meat, and the bread and wine set in readiness on the tables; but never a living soul was there. In a side chamber he beheld on grails of silver more than a hundred boars' heads, with pepper beside them, dressed for the serving. Sir Gawain beheld, and crossed himself with lifted hand, but would no longer abide, finding no man with whom he might have speech.

He turned him again through the castle, thinking to find at the bridgehead the maidens of whom I told but now, whom he had left bearing the water in golden pitchers, but nowhere might he find them, and it vexed him sore that he saw them not, since he thought within himself that they would surely have told him the truth concerning their lord, whom he had seen but now enter the burg.

Much he mused thereon, repenting him that he had not longer spoken with them, but now would he make no more abiding, but set him speedily on his way, to meet the king. Nor did he draw bridle till he came unto him.

"Fair nephew," quoth Arthur, "shall we to-day find hostel where we may take rest, for we have sore need thereof?"

"Fair Sire, be at rest; food shall ye have now," answered Sir Gawain.

"'Tis a good word," quoth Kay; "right gladly will I serve the first course unto the king, and to my comrades after!"

"Kay," saith Sir Gawain "not for all the world might ye guess the marvels I have found!" Then he told unto them the adventure, even as it had fallen out, the while he guided them to the burg. As they rode adown the street the king marvelled greatly at the riches he beheld, and Kay spake a courteous word,

"Castle, he who hence might bear yeWould do ill an he should spare ye!"

Thus came they all into the inner burg, and, still ahorse, into the great hall, but they found no man to whom they might speak, or to whose care they might give their steeds. Then they said to each other, "'Twere ill to let them fast," and the king spake, "I counsel that after supper we go forth into yonder fair meadow."

This they held for good rede, and dismounted, making fast their steeds to the stag's antlers on the wall. Then they washed their faces and their hands in a bowl of silver, and the king sat himself down first, and his knights after.

With no delay Kay set the first course before the king; 'twas a great boar's head, and he bare it joyfully, and thereafter swiftly served the rest, saying an any found cause for plaint, there was no lack, he could have at his will. "The food hath cost me naught and I give it freely; nay, of a verity we might, an we were so minded, feed our steeds on boars' heads; this is no niggard hostelry! See ye the fair couches in yonder chamber?" And he pointed to an open doorway.

Sir Gawain looked, and saw a shield hanging on the wall, and within the shield yet stood the fragment of a mighty lance, with a silken pennon hanging from it. I tell ye of a truth, so soon as he was ware thereof the blood stirred in his veins; he spake no word, but swiftly as might be he sprang up from meat, casting aside the knife he held, and gat him to his steed, and girthed him tightly, and set his helmet on his head, and sat him down again on a bench near by the daïs, his shield beside him.

The king marvelled greatly, and the knights said the one to the other, "Ha, God, what aileth Sir Gawain?" Each would fain know wherefore he had armed himself thus swiftly; they thought of a surety his head had grown light through over much fasting and the great heat of the day. They were sore dismayed thereat, for they had seen and heard naught that might give occasion for arming, and they might not guess the cause.

The king spake simply, "Fair nephew, say, wherefore have ye ceased to eat? And wherefore thus arm in haste? Ye make us much to marvel; tell me, I pray, doth aught ail ye?"

"Naught, Sire, save that I pray ye to eat quickly, an ye love me!"

"How," quoth Arthur, "without ye, who have fasted even as we? Methinks that were ill done!"

"By God and Saint Thomas, to eat here will profit me naught; ye are wrong, Sire!" Thus answered Sir Gawain, swearing that for naught in the world would he eat in this hostelry, neither might he be joyful or at ease so long as they abode therein. "But I pray ye, Sire, hasten and eat."

Then the king in the hearing of all sware straitly by Him who lieth not, that he would eat naught till that he knew wherefore his nephew had thus donned his helmet.

"Sire," quoth Sir Gawain, "ill and falsely should I have wrought if for the telling of so slight a matter I should make ye fast this day; certes I will tell ye, and lie not. Ye know well how five years agone ye led an army great and strong against the city of Branlant; many a king, many a baron, with twenty thousand men all told, with ye laid siege to the city. Within were many of great valour to aid the lord who held the seignorie of that land. One morn, at break of day, they made a sortie on our host; the cry and clamour were so great that I took no leisure to arm me, but mounted my steed and rode forth, even as I was, to learn the cause of the tumult, bearing with me but shield and lance. Thus I rode forth from the camp, and came straightway on the men of the city, who were hasting to return with their spoil. I followed them, wherein I did foolishly, since I came near to lose my life thereby, for I was wounded by a spear in the shoulder, as ye know, so that I was like to die, and must needs lie sick four months and more ere that I was whole and sound.

"One morning, as I lay in my tent, I bade them raise the hangings around that I might look on the land, and I beheld one of my squires, mounted on the Gringalet, making his way from the stream where he had watered the steed. I called him, and he came to me, and I bade him without delay saddle the good horse, and he did my bidding. I clad me swiftly the while, and bade them bring me my armour secretly, and when I had armed me I mounted, and rode alone out of the camp. Fair Sire, ye followed me, ere I came beyond the tents, praying me straitly to return, but I entreated ye gently that since I had lain overlong sick ye would grant me to go forth into the fields to disport myself, and to test if I were in very truth healed of my wound, promising to return speedily to camp. By this covenant, Sire, ye granted me to ride forth.

"Thus I went my way till I came to a leafy grove, beset with flowers, and abounding in birds, which sang loud and clear. I stayed my steed to hearken, and for the sweetness of the song my heart grew light, and I felt nor pain nor ill. Then I set spurs to my steed, and galloped adown the glade. I found myself hale and strong, and feared no longer for my wound.

"Thus I hearkened to the sweet song of the birds till that I forgat myself, and passed a second grove, and a third, and a fourth, ere that I bethought me of returning. Thus I rode till I came to a clearing fair and wide, where I saw beside a fountain a pavilion, richly fashioned. I rode even to the doorway, and looked within, and there on a couch I beheld so wondrous fair a maiden that I was abashed for her great beauty. Sire, I dismounted, and fastened my steed without the tent and entered and saluted the maiden; but, Sire, first she greeted Sir Gawain ere that she made answer to me.

"Then I asked her wherefore she did thus, and she answered that she held Sir Gawain in honour above all knights, and therefore she first gave him greeting. And when I heard this I spake saying that I was indeed Sir Gawain, and her most true knight, but scarce would the maiden believe me. I must needs unhelm, and from an inner chamber she brought forth a silken ribbon, whereon a Saracen maiden of the queen's household had wrought my semblance. And when she had looked thereon, and beheld me disarmed, and knew of a verity that I was he whom she desired, then she threw her arms around me, and kissed me more than a hundred times, saying that she was mine even as long as she might live.

"Then I took that fair gift right joyfully, and we spake together long, and had our will the one of the other. And this I tell ye that ere we parted I sware to her that other love would I never have. Then when I had armed me again, and mounted my steed, I took leave of the maid right lovingly, and turned me again for the camp, joyful of this my fair adventure.

"Thus I rode swiftly through one grove, but had gone scarce a bowshot beyond when a knight came fast behind me, marvellous well armed, and bearing a lance with a fair pennon. He cried loudly upon me, 'Traitor, ye may go no further; ye must pay dearly for my brother, whom ye slew, and for this my daughter, whom ye have now dishonoured.' Then I answered him, 'Sir Knight, ye might speak more courteously, for I have done ye neither shame nor evil; an I had, I were ready to give ye what amends might seem good to ye and to my lady; treason have I not done.'

"With that I set spurs to my steed, and he likewise, and we came fast the one against the other, and his lance was shivered on my shield, but my blade pierced him through shield and hauberk, so that he fell to the ground sore wounded. Sire, I pray ye eat, for an I tell ye more it may turn to evil." And the king quoth, "Nephew, say on speedily, and delay not."

Then spake Sir Gawain, "Sire, I left the knight lying, and went my way, but ere I had gone far I heard one cry upon me, 'Traitor, stay; ye must pay for my uncle and this my father, whom ye have wrongfully slain, and for my sister, whom ye have dishonoured!' Then I stayed my steed, and prayed him to speak more courteously, for that I was ready to make amends an I had done wrong, but that I was no traitor.

"Then we set ourselves to joust, and I tell ye, Sire, we came so hard together that we were borne both of us to the earth. Then we betook us to our swords, and dealt many a blow the one to the other; but in the end, in that I was scarce healed of my wound, he dealt me more harm than I might deal him; in this I lie not, I was well-nigh worn down, and put to the worse. Then I bethought me, Sire, and prayed him to tell me his name since I was fain to know it; and he told me he was Bran de Lis. Ider de Lis, the good and valiant, was his father, and Melians de Lis his uncle, and he said did I get the better of him, then had I slain the three best knights in any land, yet he deemed well, an God would help him, that he might even avenge the twain; for he quoth, 'I know well that a combat betwixt us may not endure over long, but that one of us must needs be slain.' And I answered, 'Sir, let us do otherwise, for an ye put me to the worse but few will believe the tale, for in this land it were not lightly held that any man may vanquish me. Methinks 'twere better that our combat be fought in the sight of many, who shall bear true witness as to the which of us comes off the better.' Thus, Sire, we made covenant together by token that in what place soever he should find me, whether armed or unarmed, there we should fight. This we sware, the one to the other. By the love I bear ye, Sire, never since that day have I heard aught of him in any land where I might be. Thus was our combat ended, as I tell ye, and of a truth I saw him no more.

"But even now, Sire, as I sat at meat, from which I arose in wrath and misease (willingly would I have eaten an I might), this is what chanced: I saw in yonder chamber the selfsame shield which Bran de Lis bare the day we did combat together; full well I remember it, and there it hangeth on the wall. Fair lord king, an God help me 'tis no lie; there in the shield standeth fast my pennon, and a great splinter of my lance; by that token, Sire, Bran de Lis doth haunt this country, since his shield be here. Therefore am I vexed and wrathful, and therefore I arose from meat, since I feared to be taken at a loss; in sooth, I somewhat fear him, for so good a knight I never saw! Sire, now have I told ye the truth, and wherefore I have donned my helmet, ye need press me no further, since not for the kingdom of Logres would I be found unarmed in such place as he may be. Fair Sire, I pray ye hasten, otherwise, an there be long abiding, I may chance to pay over dear for my meat."

Quoth the king, "Fair nephew, sit ye down again, nor have fear of any foe. He cometh not."

But Sir Gawain answered, "Sire, for naught that ye may say will I eat in this hostel!"

"So be it," quoth the king, "an ye will do naught for my prayer." With that all the others betook them to meat in good fellowship.

After no long time they beheld a little brachet, which ran out from a side chamber and came into the hall. A long leash trailed behind it, and round its neck was a collar of gold, wherein were many precious stones, red, and green as ivy leaves. The brachet was white as snow, and smoother than any ermine. I tell ye of a truth 'twas not ugly, but very fair and well shapen, and the king gazed long at it. It barked loudly at the knights on the daïs, and made small joy of them, I tell ye. Then Kay the seneschal coveted it, and spake to the king, "Sire, I will keep this brachet, and take it hence, an ye grant me this gift; 'twill be a comrade for Huden." And the king said, "Take it, seneschal, and bear it hence."

With that the brachet turned tail, and Kay with no delay sprang up and thought to seize it, but the dog would not await him, but fled on through a chamber wrought in marble, and the leash which was long fell about the feet of Kay, who would fain have caught it but might not come at it. Might he set foot on the leash he could have held it, but he failed to catch it.

Thus the chase went from chamber to chamber till five were passed, and the seneschal came into a fair garden set with olive trees and pines, wherein were more folk than in a city. They were playing at diverse games, and making such joy and festivity as 'twere overlong to recount, for that day they were keeping the feast of a saint of that land.

Beneath the shade of a laurel in the midst of an orchard a knight was disarming; tall he was and strong, valiant and proud, and to serve him and honour him the best and most renowned of the folk stood and knelt around waiting on his disarming. The brachet which Kay was chasing stayed not till it came to the knight, and took shelter betwixt his legs, barking loudly at the pursuer.

Kay stayed his steps, abashed at the sight and sound of this folk, and thought to return swiftly, and with no delay; but the knight looked on his people and said, "There is a stranger among us, whoever he may be!" Then beholding Kay, who would turn him again whence he came, he spake, "See him there, take him, and bring him hither!"

This they did swiftly, and brought Kay before him, and when the knight beheld him he said joyfully, "Sir Kay, ye are right welcome as my friend and comrade; where is the king, your master?"

"Sir, he is within, on the daïs, and with him many a valiant knight; they are even now at meat!"

"And is the king's nephew, Gawain, there? Fain would I be assured thereof." And Kay answered, "The best knight in the world is in the king's company; without him would he go nowhither!"

Now when the knight heard this he was like to fly for joy. Half armed as he was he sprang to his feet, and for very gladness stayed not to finish his disarming. A rich mantle had they hung on his shoulders, but the neck was yet unfastened, nor would he tarry to clasp it, for haste and joy. And know that one leg was still shod with iron, which hung downward, half unlaced, nor would he stay to rid himself thereof. Thus he sped in all haste to the hall, and his folk after him, and without slacking speed he ran into the hall, followed by so great a crowd that the king was sore abashed when he heard the tumult.

The knight went forward even to the daïs, and saluted the king courteously, and commanded the folk to bring torches, for 'twas scarce light therein, and they did at his pleasures, and he bade bring other meats, so that Arthur, the valiant and courteous, was well served as befitting a king.

The knight was very joyous, and quoth, "Sire, now hath God done me great honour, for never before might I do ye service; now am I right glad and joyful that ye be lodged here! I have greeted ye in all fair friendship without thought of ill, ye and this goodly company, save one whom as yet I see not!"

With that there entered men bearing torches and tapers, so that the hall, which before was dark and dim, became light and clear. The folk who had come thither that they might look upon the king, of whom they had oft heard tell, made such haste to see him that there was no space to sit down, and all the palace was but a sea of heads.

The lord was sore vexed. He held in his hand a little round staff, short and heavy, and being chafed with anger in that he saw not Sir Gawain, and knew not where he might be, began laying about him to part the crowd, making them by force to mount on the daïs, and sills of the windows, and buttresses of the walls, since he might not drive them from the hall.

When Sir Gawain saw that the folk was thus parted asunder, without delaying he mounted him on his steed. Then first the lord of the castle beheld him, and was sore vexed that he had not come upon him disarmed. Scowling for very anger, he threw his staff aside, and when he had somewhat bethought him he lifted his head, and gat him to Sir Gawain, and laid hold of his bridle, saying, "Fair sir, hearken, are ye ready to keep the covenant ye made with me? It vexeth me that ye are so far quit that I have failed to find ye disarmed, as I fain had done; I had better have been slain the day I made this compact, for then, verily, ye too had died, had I not granted the respite, but now I deem our battle shall last the longer!"

Sir Gawain straightway granted him his battle, and the knight bade bring more torches, for the stars already shone forth. Then they brought them in great plenty, and he told off folk to hold them by the fist full, so that one might see far and near, as clearly as might be. Then the lord of the castle seated himself in the midst of the hall, on a great carpet, which a squire spread swiftly at his bidding, and he bade them bring thither all that was needful to the rightful arming of a knight desirous of battle rather than of aught beside. He donned a greave of iron, and relaced that which hung loose; then he bade them bring armpieces, and he laced them on his arms, and when he had done this he came before the king and said, "Eat joyfully, and be not dismayed; behold me, that I am strong and bold, hale and swift. Your nephew on his part is even as I am; I know not if he hath told ye how the matter be come to this point that the one of us must needs die ere we be parted. 'Twere hard to think this morn that the one of us was so nigh unto his end!"

Then the king's eyes filled with tears, and the knight, beholding, spake in his pride: "Certes, Sire, I prize ye less than afore; ye are but half-hearted who are thus compassionate for naught; by all the Saints in the calendar, ye be like unto him who crieth out afore he be hurt! Never before did I set eyes on a king who wept, and knew not wherefore! By my faith, this cometh of a cowardly heart!"

He turned him again without further word, and armed him swiftly, and did on his harness, and when he was armed he mounted his steed, and bade bring a lance, stout and strong, with shining blade. Then he hung his shield on his neck by a broidered band, and settled him well in his saddle, and called unto Sir Gawain, and quoth, "Here in this house is the lordship mine by right of heritage, yet would I do no outrage nor take vantage thereof; the rather do I bid and conjure ye to take that part of the hall which seemeth best; now look well where ye will make your stand."

Sir Gawain hearkened, but stirred not, save that he drew somewhat back, and lowered his lance, and his foe, on his part, did likewise. I testify of a truth, and tell ye, that they rode over hard a joust, for as they came together at their horses' full speed the one smote the other so fiercely on the shield that both alike were split asunder, so that the sharp blade passed right through, yet they harmed not the hauberks which clung close and tight. Thus as they sped on the lances bent and brake, yet the steeds stayed not, and the knights who bestrode them were naught dismayed, but when they would have passed each other in their course they came together with such weight of body and shield, and full front of the horses, that they smote each other to the ground, and all four fell on a heap, the good steeds undermost. But the knights lightly sprang to their feet, and threw aside their lances, and drew their good swords, and dealt each the other so mighty a blow on the shining helm that it was well indented. The king and they who looked on were sore anguished and afraid, but the twain, 'twixt whom there was such enmity, ran again on each other in such fashion that, I tell ye and lie not, never was so fierce a mêlée of two knights beheld. They made sparks to spring from the helmet and smote the circlets asunder as those who make no feint to fight. When the good swords smote the shields they made the splinters to fly apace: so eager was each to put the other to the worse that they ceased not nor slackened this the first assault till that both were covered with blood. Then the heat which vexed them mightily made them perforce draw asunder, to recover breath. Too heavy and too sore had been their combat for those who loved them to behold; never day of his life had King Arthur so feared for his nephew.

Now at the head of the master daïs was a door, opening into an inner chamber, and, as the tale telleth, in a little space there came forth a damosel, so fair of face and form that Christendom might not show her peer. She was clad in fair and fitting fashion, in a vesture richly broidered in gold, and had seen, perchance, some twenty summers. She was so fair, so tall and gracious, that no woman born might equal her, and all marvelled at her beauty.

She leant awhile on the head of the daïs, beholding the two knights, who strove hard to slay each the other. They had returned to the onslaught in such pride and wrath that verily I tell ye they might not long endure. Such blows they dealt on helm and shield with their naked blades that they made the splinters fly, and the crimson blood welled from their wounds and streamed through the mail of their hauberk down on to the pavement. Nor was the fight equal, for Sir Gawain had broken the laces of his helm, so that 'twas no longer on his head, but lay on the ground at his feet. Yet he covered himself full well with his shield, as one who was no child in sword play. But his foeman pressed him sore, and oft he smote him with hard and angry blows; Sir Gawain defended himself right valiantly, but it went too ill with him in that he had lost his helm, therefore as much as might be he held himself on the defensive. But once, as he made attack, Bran de Lis smote him so fierce and heavy a blow at his head that, but that it fell first on the shield, it had then and there ended the matter, and all said that without fail he had been a dead man. Bran de Lis spake wrathfully, "Take this blow for mine uncle; ye shall have one anon for my father; if I may, it shall be the last!"

Sir Gawain struck back, but he was sore hindered by the blood which ran down into his eyes ('twas that which vexed him the most); he would fain have drawn him back, but Bran de Lis left him no space, so wrathfully did he run upon him, and Sir Gawain withstood him sturdily, yet so hardly was he pressed that whether he would or no he must needs yield ground.

Then the damosel of whom I spake but now turned her, and ran swiftly into the inner chamber, and in a short space came forth with a little child, whom she set upon the daïs. He wore a little coat of red samite, furred with ermine, cut to his measure; and of his age no fairer child might be seen. His face was oval and fair, his eyes bright and laughing; he was marvellous tall and strong for his age, which might not be more than four years; and by the richness of his clothing 'twas clear that there were those who held him dear.

The knights who fought below still dealt each other such mighty blows that all who beheld them had dole and wrath. I can tell ye each was weak and weary enow, but verily Sir Gawain had yielded ground somewhat, and would fain have wiped away the blood which ran adown his face and into his eyes, but he might in no wise do so, since Bran de Lis held him so close, doing what he might to slay or wound him.

Then without delay the damosel took her child, there where he stood before her, and said very softly, "Fair little son, go quickly to yonder tall knight, 'tis thine uncle, doubt it not, fall at his feet, little son, and kiss them, and pray for God's sake the life of thy father that he slay him not!"

Straightway she set him on the ground, and the child ran, and clasped his uncle by the right leg, and kissed his foot, and said, "My mother prays ye for the love of God, that ye slay not my father, fair sweet uncle; she will die of grief an ye do!"

Great pity fell upon the king when he heard the child speak thus, and all who hearkened and beheld were filled with wrath and anguish. All had compassion on the child, save Bran de Lis alone, for he quoth in wrath and anger, "Get thee hence, son of a light woman!" and he withdrew his foot so swiftly from the child's clasp that, whether he would or no, he fell, and smote face and forehead hard on the stone of the pavement, so that he grazed mouth and face, and lay senseless and bleeding on the floor.

Then King Arthur sprang from the daïs, and caught the child to him, and kissed it twenty times on face and eyes and mouth, and wept for very anger; nor for the blood on the child's face would he cease to caress it, so great love had he towards it, for he thought of a truth that he held again Gawain, whom he now counted for lost. He quoth, "Sir Bran de Lis, this little child is very fair; never in your life did ye do such villainy as to go near to slay so sweet a child, nor ought ye to have denied the request he made, for he asked naught outrageous. Nor will I have him slain, for he is my joy and my solace; henceforward know well that for naught will I leave him in your care!"

Quoth Bran de Lis, "Sire, ye are less courteous than I had heard tell, and ye make overmuch dole and plaint for the life of a single knight; ye should not so be dismayed, this is naught but feebleness of heart."

As Bran de Lis thus spake to the king Sir Gawain wiped off the blood which ran down his face, and bound up his wounds, the while he had respite; the king, who was wise enow, held his foeman the longer in speech that his nephew might be the more refreshed, for the strength and valour of that good knight doubled as midnight passed. For this was the custom of Sir Gawain: when as ever midnight had struck his strength was redoubled and he waxed in force even until noon.

Now so soon as his strength came again, and he saw the king, and his love, and the great folk who beheld them, then a mighty shame overtook him, and he ran in wrath on his foe, and assailed him straitly, but the other yielded not, crying, "Honour to ye that ye thus seek me!"

Then might ye see them smite blows great and fierce, with the swords they wielded, so that they were well nigh beaten down. Sir Bran de Lis smote a mighty blow, thinking to catch Sir Gawain on the head, but that good knight, who knew right well how to cover himself, held his shield in such wise that the stroke fell upon it, and split it adown the midst; so hard had he smitten that the blade entered even to the hilt, and his body following the blow he bent him forwards, and ere he might recover him Sir Gawain smote him full on the helm, so that the laces brake, and it flew off adown the hall, leaving the head bare. And ere Sir Bran de Lis was well aware he followed up the blow with one above the ventaille so that he bled right freely. Now were they again on a par, so that one might scarce tell the which of them had the better. In great pride and wrath they ran each on the other, so that in short space of time they had lost overmuch blood. Mightily each strove to put his foe to the worse, and all who looked upon them waxed strangely pitiful, and would fain have parted them asunder had they dared.

Now might ye have seen that gentle knight, who full oft had made offering of good deeds and alms, right well acquit himself, for so sorely he vexed his foeman that he hacked his shield all to pieces, and he might no longer hold his ground, but whether he would or no he must yield place, and wavered backward adown the hall. Then he smote him again, so that he tottered upon his feet, and Sir Gawain hasted, and threw himself upon him with such weight of body and of shield that he well nigh bare him to earth, so he drave him staggering adown the hall till he fell against a daïs.

When the damosel saw this she tare her child from the king's arms, and ran swiftly, and threw herself right valiantly betwixt the two, so that she came nigh to be cut in pieces, and cried, "Son, pray thy father that he have pity on thy mother, and stay his hand ere he slay my brother, whom I love more than mine own life!" But the child spake no word, but looked up at the glancing sword blades, and laughed blithely. And all were moved to pity and wrath who saw him anon bleeding and now laughing for very joy.

Then Sir Gawain, of right good will, drew himself aback, but he whom he had thus hard pressed drave forward at him, like one reft of his senses, and came nigh to doing him a mischief in that Sir Gawain was off his guard. Then she who held the child sprang swiftly betwixt them, and cried, "Now by God I will see the which of ye twain will slay him, for he shall be cloven asunder ere that I take him hence."

The swords clashed together aloft, but wrought no ill, for neither might come at the other for fear of the child whom they were loth to harm, and for fear of her who held him. And the child laughed gaily at the glancing swords, and stretched up his hands to his own shadow, which he saw on the shining blade, and showed it with his finger to his father when he saw it come anear, and had fain sprung up and caught the blades, sharp though they might be. And many a man wept, and there arose within the hall a great cry, as of one voice, "Good lord king, stay the fight; we will all aid thee thereto, for no man should longer suffer this!"

Then Arthur sprang up swiftly, and seized his sword and shield, and came unto the twain, and parted them asunder, whether they would or no, and said to the knight ye have heard me praise, "Sir, take the amends offered, and I tell ye truly I will add thereto, for I myself will do ye honour, and become your man, for the sake of peace." And all cried with one voice, "Sir, by God and by the True Cross, ye shall not refuse this, for the king has spoken as right valiant man." Then the knight held his hand, hearing that which pleased him.

Thus was peace made, and the battle parted asunder, and Sir Bran de Lis did right sagely, for he spake, "Sire, it were nor right nor reason that ye should become my man, hence will I do ye true homage, but for hostage will I ask the knights of the Round Table, who are the most valiant in the world; also shall your nephew do other amends, even as he promised me, in abbey and nuns, for the repose of my father's soul, and ye shall free one hundred serfs with your own hand." And the king answered, "Know of a truth that all shall be done at my charges."

Then Bran de Lis did homage to the king, and kissed him in all good faith, and then came forward Sir Gawain, and he humbled himself before him, kneeling at his feet, and praying that he would pardon his ill will; and Sir Gawain took him by the hand, and raised him up, and quoth, "I pardon thee all, and henceforth will I be your friend in all good faith and courage, nor will I fail ye for any harm ye may aforetime have done me."

Both were sore faint and feeble, and void of strength by reason of the blood they had lost, so that scarce might they stand on their feet without falling to the ground. They bare them to an inner chamber; never knight nor maiden entered within a fairer, for I tell of a truth there was no good herb in Christendom with which it was not strewn. 'Twas richly garnished, and four great tapers, cunningly placed, gave fitting light. Then leeches searched their wounds and said there was no need for dismay, for neither was wounded to the death, and within fifteen days both might well be healed, and all were joyful at the tidings.

The king and his barons abode the fifteen days at the castle of Lys, nor departed therefrom; in all the world was neither fish nor fowl, fruit nor venison, of which the king might not each day eat in plenty if he so willed. But he was loth to part from Sir Bran de Lis, by reason of the good tales which he told concerning the folk of the Castle Orguellous, whereat the king rejoiced greatly.

"Sire," quoth Bran de Lis, "I myself will go with ye, and we will take with us squires and footmen. My pavilion is large and fair, and by faith, we will carry that too along with us; and also a pack of hounds, the best we may find, for there be thick forests all around, where we may hunt at our will, and go a-shooting too, an it please us, for we shall find great plenty of deer and other game."

Sir Gawain took little heed of all he said, so wholly was he taken up with his lady, and she forgat him not, but was ever at his service, at any hour that might please him; 'twas all gladness, and no ill thought. Nor did Sir Gawain mislike his fair son, whom he caressed right often. Fain would he have tarried long time with them. Nor marvel at that, my masters, for he was there at ease, and he who hath whatsoever he may desire doeth ill methinks to make over haste to change, nor will he make plaint, since he suffereth nor pain nor ill.

But when the fifteen days came to an end, then did the king bid make ready, for he had no mind to tarry longer; well I know 'twas a Tuesday morn that they set them on their way, and with them went that good knight, Sir Bran de Lis.

Castle Orguellous

FOR SEVEN FULL DAYS King Arthur and his men journeyed, and passed through many a forest ere they came into the open land and saw before their eyes the rich Castle Orguellous, the

**which they had greatly desired to behold. They who had gone
ahead had already pitched the king's pavilion in a fair meadow
nigh unto a grove of branching olive trees, very fair and full of
leaf. There the king, and they who were with him, dismounted
gladly; they might go no further, since 'twas well known in the
land that they came to make war on the castle.**

They had made no long abiding when they heard a great bell toll – no
man had ever heard a greater – five leagues around might the sound be
heard, and all the earth trembled. Then the king asked of him who knew
the customs of the castle wherefore the bell tolled thus.

Quoth Bran de Lis, "Of a truth, 'tis that all the country round may know
that the castle is besieged, till that the bell be tolled nor shield nor spear
may be set on the walls, the towers, or battlements." As he spake thus they
saw to the right more than five thousand banners wave from the walls, the
towers, and donjon, and as many shields hung forth from the battlements.
Then they saw issue forth from the forest on to the plain knights mounted
on palfreys and war-horses, who made their way by many roads to the
castles; right gladly did the king and his comrades behold them.

I will not devise unto ye all the fashion of the castle, I must needs
spend overmuch time thereon, but since the birth of Christ no man ever
saw one more fairly placed, nor richer, nor better garnished with tall
towers and donjon.

Now was meat made ready in the king's tent, and all sat them down
to supper in right merry mood; they said among themselves that enough
knights were entered into the castle to give work to each and all. Thus
they spake and made sport concerning those within.

So soon as the king had sat him down Lucains the butler poured the
wine into a golden cup, and spake unto the king, "I pray the right of the
first joust that be ridden to-morrow morn, for it pertaineth unto mine
office!" Quoth the king, "I were loth to refuse the first gift prayed of me
here in this land." "'Tis well said," quoth the lord of Lys. And the king said
to the butler, "Go, eat with my nephew," and he did so right gladly.

So soon as supper was done, and they had washed, swiftly they
commanded their arms to be brought, nor will I lie to ye; thereafter

might ye have seen a great testing, many greaves of iron laced on, limbs outstretched, feet bent; squires were bidden don the hauberks that they might look well to them, and add straps or take away – all were fain to see that naught was lacking, but all in fair and knightly order. Ye never saw a folk thus busy themselves. They made merry with the king the while, and prayed of him in sport to say the day he would allot to each, that their pain might be the sooner ended. "Nay, lords," quoth Arthur, "I would fain keep ye the longer in dread." Thus when they had made sport enow, and it was nightfall, they drank, and betook them to rest.

On the morrow, without delay, they arose at sunrise, and betook them to a chapel in a wood, nigh to a meadow where were buried all the good knights slain before the castle, whether strangers or men of the land. And so soon as the priest had said the Mass of the Holy Ghost, and the service was ended, they turned them again, and made ready for meat in the king's pavilion, and the king and all his knights ate together right joyfully. When they had eaten they arose, and armed Lucains the butler well and courteously. The vest he ware under his hauberk was of purple broidered with gold. Then they brought him his horse and his shield, and he mounted right glad and joyful, and they brought unto him his pennon. Thus he departed from the king and his comrades, and set spurs to his steed, and stayed not till he came unto the field of battle, whither they betook them and demanded joust of those of the castle.

Masters, at the four corners of the meadow were planted four olive trees, to show the bounds of the field, and he was held for vanquished who should first pass the boundary of the olives. Since he had come thither armed, it befell not Lucains to await long, but short space after he had entered the field he saw ride proudly forth from the castle a great knight, mounted on a roan steed, right well appointed of arms and accoutrements. He came at full speed to the meadow, and swiftly, as befitted, each lowered his lance, and set spurs to his steed, and rode the one against the other. Great blows they dealt on each other's shield, and the knight smote Lucains so fiercely that he brake his lance all to shivers, and the butler smote back in such wise that he bare him out of the saddle on to the ground. Then he took the steed, and turned him, leaving his foeman afoot, and came gladly and blithely again to the pavilion. Quoth

Bran de Lis, "Certes, butler, the siege had been raised had ye brought yon knight captive, nor would ye have had further travail, for the quest on which ye came hither had been achieved, and ere nightfall Sir Giflet had been delivered up, for yonder is so good a knight they had gladly made the exchange!"

When the butler heard this he was ill-pleased, and he tarried no longer at the pavilion, but leaving the steed gat him back to the meadow, nor turned again for the king, who many a time called upon him. Then from the gateway rode forth a great knight bearing his pennon, and came spurring into the meadow, and when the butler saw him he rode against him, and smote him so fiercely on the shield that the shaft of apple-wood brake, and the knight smote him back with so strong a lance that he bare him to the ground. Lucains sprang up swiftly, and thought to take the splinters from his arm without delaying, but the knight ran upon him fiercely, and he defended himself as best he might, though wounded, but since the blade was yet in him, whether he would or no, he must needs yield himself prisoner, as one who might do no more. Thus he yielded up his sword to the knight, who led him with him to the castle, but first he drew out the blade carefully, stanching the blood, and binding up the wound.

Very wrathful was the king when he saw his butler thus led thence; then quoth Sir Gawain, "Certes, an Lucains were whole I should rejoice in that he is captive, for now will our comrade Giflet, the brave and valiant, who hath been there in durance four years, learn such tidings of us as shall make him glad and joyful. The butler is a right gallant knight, and it may chance to any that he be overthrown and wounded. I have no mind to blame him for such ill hap." Sir Bran de Lis answered, "Fair Sir, an God help me, he hath overthrown one of their men, and I know no better among their ten thousand knights." So spake Sir Bran de Lis, but for all that was he somewhat vexed concerning the butler, in that he had reproached him for not having taken the knight captive, for he thought in his heart that for these words of his, and for naught else, had Lucains been taken.

Then he came unto the king, and besought him for the great love he bare him to grant him the morrow's joust; but though he prayed him straitly the king was loth to yield, but answered that in no wise would he grant his request save that he was fain not to anger him by reason of the true faith that he bare unto him. "So God help me, fair friend; I have it in my mind that I were but ill sped did I chance to lose ye!"

"Sire, think not of that; 'tis ill done to summon evil, an God will this shall not befall so long as I live; doubt ye not, Sire, but grant me the fight freely, ere others ask it!"

Then the king quoth, "Have your desire, since ye so will." With that they gat them to meat in the tent, but that day a butler was lacking to them.

Into that selfsame chamber where that good knight, Giflet fis Do, had long lain, they led Lucains prisoner, and Giflet when he beheld him failed not to know him, but sprang up, and embraced him, and asked straightway, "Tell me, gentle friend, in what land were ye made captive?" Then Lucains told him the truth from beginning to end, how the king had set siege to the castle, and was lodged without, "And he hath sworn he will not depart hence, nor lift the siege, till that he hath freed ye." Giflet was right joyful when he heard this, and he spake again, "Sir Lucains, greatly do I desire to hear from ye tidings of the best knights in the world, even the companions of the Round Table; 'tis over long since I saw them, or heard speak of them." And the butler made answer, "Sir, by all the Saints in the calendar, such an one is dead, such an one made captive, this and that knight are hale and whole, and to the places of the dead many a good knight and true hath been elect." And Giflet cried, "Ah, God, how minished is that goodly company; I know not the half of them who yet live!"

Quoth Lucains, "Know of a truth that all greatly desire to have ye again, nor will they know joy in their hearts till that ye be once more of their fellowship."

At these words they brought them food, and they washed, and ate, and when 'twas time they gat them to rest, and passed the night in great joy of each other's company. But the night was short, since Pentecost was past, and the feast of S. John, when the days are the longest in the year.

On the morrow the sun rose fine and fair, for the weather was calm and clear, and the king arose betimes with his comrades. First they gat them to the chapel and heard Mass, and then dinner was made ready, since to eat ere noon is healthful for the brain. The dinner was rich and plentiful, they sat them down gaily and ate with speed, they had larded venison (for of deer was there no lack), and so soon as they had dined the chamberlain armed the lord of Lys right richly, on a fair flowered carpet, and the king himself laced his helmet. Then Sir Bran de Lis mounted and hung the shield about his neck, and took his lance whereon was a pennon, and spurred straight for the meadow, which he knew full well.

Then from the gates of the castle he beheld issue forth a knight on a gallant steed, right fittingly armed, who rode at full speed to the meadow where Sir Bran de Lis awaited his coming. And so soon as each beheld the other they spurred swiftly forward, and I tell ye of a truth that they smote each other on the shield so that their lances brake, and they came together with such force that they hurled each other to the ground; but they lay not there for long, but sprang up anon, and laid to with their swords, dealing each other mighty blows on the gleaming helmets, for the worser of the twain was a gallant knight. But he of the castle was sore vexed, in that he was wounded while Bran de Lis was yet whole, and passing light on his feet, so that he pressed him sore, in so much that he might not abide in any place. By force Sir Bran de Lis brought his foeman to his knees, and ere he might rise he must perforce yield himself captive. Thus he led him to the pavilion, and made gift of him to Arthur, who received him well, and thanked the lord of Lis right heartily.

Then the king bade them make a lodge of boughs, with curtains round about, whereto they led the wounded knight to rest, for much need had he of repose. King Arthur and his men disarmed Sir Bran de Lis gaily, and he washed himself, and they made great sport all day long. And when it came to the freshness of the evening they went forth to disport themselves; many a valiant knight sat there, round about the king, in the shade of an olive tree.

Then they heard the sound of those who blew loudly on the horn and played upon the flageolet; there was no instrument befitting a watch the music of which was not to be heard within the castle, and much joy they made therein. The king was the more wakeful by night in that he took pleasure in the fair melody which the watchmen who sounded the horn made in answering the one the other.

Beside the lord of Lys sat Kay, who hearkened to the music, nor might he long keep silence, but must needs speak his mind. "Sire," quoth he, "by Saint Denis, meseemeth the joust be forgotten, for this eve none hath demanded it; the king hath neither companion nor peer who hath so far prayed it, I wot none be desirous thereof!"

"Kay," quoth the King, "I grant thee the joust."

"Sire," quoth Kay, "by Saint Martin, I were liever to handle a spit than a spear to-morrow; I thank ye for naught! Nevertheless, Sire, an such be your pleasure I will do it, by the faith I owe to my lord Sir Gawain." Then all laughed at Kay's words, and when they had made sport enow of him they gat them back to the tent.

Thus the night passed, and on the morrow at dawn, ere prime had rung, the king hearkened Mass, and when they had dined they armed the seneschal, and he mounted, and took his shield, and departed from them swiftly. No sooner had he come to the meadow when a knight, right well armed, came forth from the castle, and rode on to the field. They smote each other on the shields so that they fell to the ground, and springing up lightly they fell to with their sharp swords; right dourly they pressed on each other, and smote sounding blows on the helms. He of the castle struck wrathfully at Kay, and the seneschal caught the blow, and the knight smote again on the boss of the shield so that the blade brake, notwithstanding he had so pressed on the seneschal that he made him by force to pass the boundary of the four olives, which stood at the corners of the field.

There the knight stayed him, and turned him back to his steed which was in the midst of the meadow, and remounted, and took Kay's horse, for he saw well 'twas a good steed, and led it away, none gainsaying him. Kay went his way back, and knew not that he had been deceived, but deemed he had won the day, though in sooth he was vanquished.

Then the knights spake unto the king, "Sire, let us go to meet Kay, and make merry over him; 'twill be rare sport to mislead him!" The king was right willing, so they went in company towards the seneschal.

The king went ahead, as one wise and courteous, and spake gently, "Kay, hast thou come from far? Has mischance befallen thee?" and Kay, who was ever sharp and ready of tongue, answered, "Sire, let me be;

ye have naught wherewith to reproach me. I have vanquished one of their knights, but he hath taken my horse; the field is mine, for I have conquered it; and he who hath ridden hence hath the worse!" All held their peace, and laughed not.

"Sir, are ye in need of help?" quoth Tor fis Ares. And then the others spake; "Seneschal, are ye wounded?" "Methinks ye limp somewhat," quoth Sir Gawain.

"Kay, hand me your shield," said Sir Ywain. "Right valiantly have ye approved yourself, marvellous were the blows I saw ye deal! God be thanked that ye did thus well!" With that he took the shield, and hung it around his own neck. Each joined in the sport as best he might, and Kay was right well aware thereof.

Then he spake to Sir Ywain, "Sir, I will grant ye to-morrow so much as I have won to-day, the joust and the field shall ye have in exchange for my shield which ye bear. Ye can do well, an ye will, and I were fain to repay ye in such wise as I may."

Those who heard might not refrain their mirth, and in merry mood they led him to the tent, and disarmed him, and the lord of Lys said, "Sir Kay, ye passed the boundary of the four olive trees, and he who first passes betwixt them is held for vanquished." And Kay answered, "May be, Sir, by the faith I owe the King of Heaven an ye know the differ 'twixt entry and exit 'tis more than I may do; sure, 'tis all one, for there where one cometh in the other goeth out!"

Suddenly there rang forth from the castle and the minster a peal so great and glad that ye might scarce hear God thunder, and the king asked wherefore the bells rang thus.

Then Bran de Lis spake, "I will tell ye, Sire: 'tis Saturday to-day, and now that noon be past they within will do naught against ye, come what may. In this land is the Mother of God more honoured than elsewhere in Christendom; know of a truth that ye shall presently see knights and ladies, burgesses and other folk, clad in their best, betake them to the minster; they go to hear Vespers, and do honour to Our Lady. Thus it is from noon on Saturday till Tierce on Monday, when Mass is sung, and the bells chimed throughout the burg, then they get them to their tasks again; the minstrels and other folk. I tell ye without fail till then shall no joust be ridden; to-morrow, an ye will, ye may go forth to hunt in the forest."

The king praised the custom much, and spent the night with a light heart until the morn, when he arose, and with his knights betook him to the woods, and all day long the forest rang to the sound of the huntsman's horn.

Now it chanced that Sir Gawain beheld a great stag, which two of his hounds had severed from the rest of the herd, and he followed hard after the chase till that the quarry was pulled down in a clearing. There he slew and quartered it, and gave their portion to the dogs, but would take with him naught save the back and sides. So he rode on fairly, and without annoy, the hounds running ahead, till, as he went his way, he heard nigh at hand a hawk cry loudly. Then he turned him quickly towards the sound, and came on to a wide and dusky path, and followed it speedily to a dwelling, the fairest he had found in any land wherein he had sojourned.

'Twas set in the midst of a clearing, and no wish or thought of man might devise aught that was lacking unto it. There was a fair hall and a strong tower, 'twas set round about with palisades, and there was a good drawbridge over the moat, which was wide enow, and full of running water. At the entry of the bridge was a pine-tree, and beneath, on a fair carpet, sat a knight; never had ye seen one so tall, or so proud of bearing.

Sir Gawain rode straight and fast to him, but he stirred no whit for his coming, but sat still, frowning and thoughtful. Sir Gawain marvelled at his stature, and spake very courteously, "Sir, God save ye!" But the stranger answered nor loud nor low, having no mind for speech. Thrice Sir Gawain greeted him, but he answered not, and the good knight stayed his steed full before him, but he made no semblance of seeing him.

Quoth Sir Gawain, "Ha, God, who hath made man with Thine own hand, wherefore didst Thou make this man so fair if he be deaf and dumb? So tall is he, and so well fashioned he is like unto a giant. An I had a comrade with me I would lead him hence, even unto the king; methinks he would thank me well, for he would look on him as a marvel!" And he bethought him that he would even bear the knight hence with him on his steed. Thus he laid his venison beneath a tree, and bent him downwards from his saddlebow, and took the other by the shoulders, and raised him a little.

Then the knight clapped hand to his side, but his sword was lacking, and he cried, "Who may ye be? It lacked but little and I had slain ye with my fist, since ye have snatched me from death; had I my sword here 'twere red with your blood! Get ye hence, vassal, and leave me to my death."

Then he sat him again under the tree, and fell a-musing, even as when Sir Gawain found him. And that good knight, without more ado, reloaded his venison and turned him back, leaving the knight sad and sorrowful.

Scarce had Sir Gawain ridden half a league when he saw coming towards him a maiden, fair and courteous, on a great Norman palfrey; nor king nor count had been better horsed. The bridle, the harness, the trappings of her steed were beyond price, nor might I tell ye how richly the maiden was clad. Her vesture was of cloth of gold, the buttons of Moorish work, wrought in silk with golden pendants. The lady smote her steed oft and again, and rode past Sir Gawain with never a word of greeting.

Sir Gawain marvelled much at her haste, and that she had failed to speak with him, and he turned him about, and rode after, crying "Stay a little, Lady!" but she answered not, but made the more haste.

Then Sir Gawain overtook her, and rode alongside, saying, "Lady, stay, and tell me whither ye be bound." Then she made answer, "Sir, for God's sake, hinder me not, for an ye do I tell ye of a truth I shall have slain the best and the fairest knight in any castle of Christendom!"

"What," quoth Sir Gawain, "have ye slain him with your own hands?"

"I, sir? God forbid, but I made covenant with him yesterday that I would be with him ere noon, and now have I failed of my compact. He awaiteth me at a tower near by, mine own true love, the best knight in the world!"

"Certes, Lady, he is yet alive, of that am I true witness; 'twas but now he well nigh dealt me a buffet with his fist! Make not such haste!"

"Fair sir, are ye sure and certain?"

"Yea, Lady, but he was sore bemused."

"Then know of a truth, Sir Knight, that he may no longer be alive, and I may not tarry." With that she struck her steed and rode off apace. Sir Gawain gazed after her, and it vexed him much that he had not asked more concerning the knight, whence he came, his land and his name, but knew neither beginning nor end of his story.

Thus he went on his way, and came again to the pavilion where his companions awaited him, sore perplexed at his delay, and were right joyful when they beheld him. Then straightway he told them the adventure, even as it had chanced, and when the lord of Lys heard it he said unto the King, "Sire, the knight is the Rich Soudoier, he who maintaineth all this goodly following and seignorie; and so much doth he love the maiden whom he calleth his lady and his love, that all men say he will die an he win her not."

As he spake they beheld a great cloud of dust arise toward the forest, and there rode past so great a company of folk there cannot have been less than twenty thousand; there was left in the city not a soul who might well stir thence who went not forth of right good will toward the forest. 'Twas nigh unto nightfall ere all had entered therein.

Then the king asked whither all this folk were bound, and Bran de Lis answered, "Sire, they go to meet their lord, and to do him honour, for never before this hath he led his lady hither. I tell ye of a truth that each one of his barons will dub three new knights, to honour and pleasure him, for so have they sworn, and for that doth he owe them right good will."

What more may I tell ye? All night they held great feast through the city, with many lights in castle, tower, and hall. They blazed upon the walls, the trees, and round about the meadows, till that the great burg seemed all aflame, and all night long they heard the sound of song and loud rejoicing.

Then the king betook him to rest, and at dawn Sir Ywain prayed as gift the joust which Kay had given unto him. The king made no gainsaying, but after meat they armed their comrade well and fittingly, and he mounted quickly, and took shield and lance; nor did he long await a foe, for there rode forth from the castle one well armed, on a strong and swift steed, and spurred upon Sir Ywain. He smote him so that his lance brake, and Sir Ywain smote him again with such force that he bare him to earth ere that his lance failed. Then he rode upon him with unsheathed sword, and by weight of his steed bare him to earth when he had fain arisen, and trod him underfoot so hardly that, whether he would or no, he must needs yield. Then Sir Ywain took his pledge, and led him without more ado to the pavilion, and delivered him to the king.

Such was the day's gain, but know that 'twas one of the new made knights, not of the mesnie of the Rich Soudoier. And when he was disarmed the king spake unto him in the hearing of all his men, and said, "Fair friend, whence do ye come, and of what land may ye be?"

Then he answered, "Sire, I am of Ireland, and son to the Count Brangelis, and ever have I served the lady of the Rich Soudoier. She bade me carve before her, and my lord for love of her yestermorn made me knight, and as guerdon for my service they granted me the joust; yet, but for my lady who prayed for me this grace, they had not given it to me, since within the walls there be many a good man and true who was sore vexed thereat."

"Friend," quoth Sir Gawain, "know ye, perchance, the which of them shall joust on the morrow?"

"Certes, Sir, I should know right well; 'tis the lord of the castle himself who shall be first on the field, and I will tell ye how I know this. 'Tis the custom therein that each morn the maidens mount the walls, and she who first beholds the armed knight take the field, 'tis her knight who shall ride forth against him. Yestereven my lady assembled all the maidens and prayed of them that they would let her alone mount the wall – thus shall the joust be as I tell ye."

Straightway Sir Gawain sprang to his feet, and went before the king, and demanded the joust, but Arthur forbade him saying, "Fair nephew, ye shall not go to-morrow, but later, ere it be my turn, 'tis for us twain to ride the last jousts; ye shall have it when all save I have proved themselves."

"Sire, Sire, I shall be sore shamed an ye deny me this gift; never more shall I be joyful, nor will I ride joust in this land, but will get me hence alone!"

Quoth the king, "An it be thus ye may have it." And Sir Gawain answered, "I thank ye, Sire."

Thus they passed the night, and at daybreak, when the dew lay thick upon the grass, Sir Gawain arose, and Sir Ywain with him. Know that the morning was so fine, so fair and clear, as if 'twere made to be gazed on. Then he who was no coward washed face and hands and feet in the dew, and gat him back to the pavilion. There they brought him a wadded vest, of purple, bordered with samite, and he donned it, and fastened on his armlets deftly.

And ere he was fully armed the king his uncle had risen, and they gat them to Mass, and when Mass was said, to meat. When they had well dined they bade bring thither the armour, and Sir Gawain sat him on a rich carpet, spread on the ground in the midst of the tent, and there was never a knight but stood around uncovered, till that he had armed him at his leisure with all that pertaineth to assault and defence, so that he had naught to do save but to set forth.

Then they led unto him his steed, all covered with a rich trapping, and he mounted, and sat thereon, so goodly to look upon that never might ye hear speak of a fairer knight. Excalibur, his good sword, did King Arthur hand to him, and he girt it round him as he sat on the saddle, lightly, so that it vexed him not. Then he took shield and lance, and departed from them, making great speed for the meadow.

Now the adventure telleth that he had been there but short space when from the master tower of the castle a horn was sounded long and clear, so that for a league around the earth quivered by reason of the echo of the blast, and Sir Bran de Lis spake to the king, "Sire, in short space shall ye see the Rich Soudoier come forth armed on his steed, for they sound not the horn thus save for his arming. I know well by the long blast that he laceth on his spurs."

Then the horn sounded a second time, and he said, "By my faith, now hath he donned and laced his greaves."

For a long space there was silence, and again the horn rang forth so loudly that all the castle re-echoed, and the lord of Lys said, "Sire, now hath he donned his hauberk and laced his helm." With that the horn sounded once again, "Now, Sire, he is mounted, and the horn will be blown no more to-day."

This had the good knight told them truly, for the burg was all astir: he who bare lordship therein rode proudly down from the castle, and after him so many of his folk that they of the pavilion heard the sound of their tread, though they might not behold them. Even to the gate they bare him company, and as he issued forth the king's men beheld him covered with a silken robe, even to his spurs, his banner in his hand. Then they saw a great crowd mount to the battlements to watch the combat of the twain; the walls were covered even to the gateways, so that 'twas a marvel to behold.

Thus the lord of the castle came proudly to the meadow where Sir Gawain awaited him, and when he saw him he gripped his shield tightly, and made ready for the onslaught. Then they laid their lances in rest, and shook forth their blazons, and smote their spurs into their steeds; nor did the joust fail, for they came together with such force of steed and shield and body that, an they would or no, both came to the ground in mid meadow and the good steeds fell over them. But the twain were full of valour, and arose up lightly, and drew their swords, and ran boldly on each other. Then might ye behold a dour combat, and a sight for many folk, for with great wrath they dealt each other mighty blows, so that all who beheld were astonied, and the king was in sore dread for his nephew, and they of the castle for their lord.

From either side many a prayer went up to Heaven that their champion might return safe and whole. And the twain spared not themselves, but each with shining blade smote the other, so that their strength waned apace. For know that that day there was so great a heat that never since hath the like been known, and that heat vexed and weakened them sore.

Now know ye of a certain truth that my lord Sir Gawain waxed ever in strength, doubling his force from midnight, and even till noon was past and the day waned did his strength endure, but then he somewhat weakened till 'twas midnight again. This I tell ye of a truth, 'twas early morn that they fought thus in the meadow, and greatly did this gift aid him, and great evil it wrought to the Rich Soudoier. Neither had conquered aught on the other till it waxed high noon. If the one dealt mighty blows the other knew right well how to return them with wrath and vigour; 'twas hard to say the which were the better, and all marvelled much that neither was as yet or slain or put to the worse.

'Twas the Soudoier who first gave ground; by reason of the over great heat so sore a thirst seized him that he might no longer endure the heavy blows, and well nigh fell to the earth. When Sir Gawain felt his foe thus weakening he pressed him the more, till that he staggered on his feet, and Sir Gawain ran on him with such force that both fell to the ground. But the king's nephew sprang to his feet lightly and cried, "Vassal, yield ye prisoner ere I slay ye!" but his foe was so dazed that for a space he might speak no word.

When he gat breath and speech he sighed forth, "Ah, God, who will slay me? Since she be dead I care naught for my life."

Sir Gawain wondered much what the words might mean, and he shook him by the vizor, and when he saw that he took no heed he spake again, "Sir Knight, yield to me!" And he sighed, "Suddenly was she slain who was fairest in the world; I loved her with a passing great love!"

When Sir Gawain saw that he would answer none otherwise, conjure him as he might, he cut the laces of his helmet, and saw that he lay with his eyes closed as one in a swoon; by reason of the great heat and his sore thirst he had lost all colour, and was senseless. Sir Gawain was vexed in that he might not win from him speech, neither by word nor by blow, yet was he loth to slay him; nor would he leave him lying; for he thought an he slew him he might lose all he would gain by his victory, and should he get him back to the pavilion to seek aid to bear his prisoner hence, on his return he would surely find him gone. Thus was he much perplexed in mind. Then he doffed his helm, and sat him down beside the knight, sheathing Excalibur, and taking the sword of his foe. In a short space the Soudoier came again to himself, and seeing him sit thus, asked of him his name. Then he answered straightway, and when the other knew 'twas Gawain, he said, "Sir, now know I for a certainty that ye be the best knight in the world." Then he held his peace, and spake no further, and Sir Gawain looked upon him, and said, "Fair Sir Knight, bear me no ill will for aught ye may have heard me say, but come with me, an ye will, to yonder pavilion, and we will take your pledge."

Then the Rich Soudoier answered, "I have a lady I love more than my life, and if she die then must I needs die too, so soon as I hear tell thereof. I pray ye, sir, for God's sake, for love's sake, for gentleness, for courtesy, save me my love that she die not, by covenant that, whether for right or for wrong, no man of the Castle Orguellous shall henceforth be against ye. Fair sir, an ye will do for me that which I now pray, I will pledge my faith to do all the king's will, nor shall there be therein man of arms whom I will not make swear the same. But an if my lady knew thereof, as God be my witness, she would die straightway, for never would she believe that ye had conquered me; 'tis truth I tell ye! Now of your courtesy, Sir Knight, I pray of ye this great service, that ye come back with me to the castle, that ye there do me honour, and kneeling to my lady declare ye her prisoner; an ye will thus make feint and say I have vanquished ye in fair field, then shall ye save my life, and that of my most sweet lady, and if ye will not do thus, then slay me here and now!"

Then that gentle knight, Sir Gawain, remembered him of how he had found him aforetime in the forest beneath the tower, and how the maiden who rode to keep tryst feared for his life, and he knew that he loved his lady with so great a love that he would die an she knew him to be shamed, and he thought within himself 'twas over much cruelty to slay so good a knight, and he answered. "Fair sir, certes will I go with ye to the Castle Orguellous, and there yield me captive, nor will I forbear for any doubt or misgiving. It might well turn to my shame, but even if I should die thereby, I would not, Sir Knight, that ye or your lady be wronged or aggrieved."

Then the knight spake frankly, "Sir, I am your liege man all the days of my life." And he gave him his hand, and sware straitly that he would do all the king's pleasure. And when Sir Gawain had taken his oath, straightway the two mounted their steeds and betook them to the Castle Orguellous.

Well nigh did King Arthur die of wrath when he saw his nephew ride hence, and he cried, "Now am I indeed bereft if my nephew be led therein; now will they hold him prisoner! Think ye, my lords, that he be of a truth captive?"

"Yea, Sire, of a faith, so it seemeth, yet are we greatly in marvel thereat, for we know certainly that he had vanquished and overthrown his adversary. Never so great an ill hap hath befallen any knight, for ere the knight of the castle rose we said surely that he was conquered!"

The king had no heart to hearken longer, but betook him straightway to his bed; cause enow had he for woe, or so it seemed him!

But they of the castle sped joyously to meet their lord, whom they thought to have lost, and ran to bear the tidings to the lady, who was well nigh distraught with grief, and anger, and they told her that her lord came again. "And he leadeth by the bridle, as one conquered, Sir Gawain!"

Even at these words came the knights unto the gateway, and dismounted, and Sir Gawain speedily yielded him prisoner to the maiden, saying, "Lady, take here my sword, and know of a proven truth that this good knight, your true lover, hath vanquished me by force of arms."

Never since the hour ye were born did ye see such rejoicing as the maiden made, and the Rich Soudoier spake, saying, "Ride ye to my castle of Bouvies with five hundred knights, and make ready the chambers. I will be with ye to-morrow, and would fain sojourn there; we will have but few folk with us. Marvel not at this, for to-day have I been over much wearied."

And the maiden answered, "Ye have well said; the castle is very fair and pleasant." With that she was mounted, and the knights set forth to convoy her to the castle. And know ye why he sent her hence? 'Twas that he might tell his men the truth of what had passed.

When the lady had departed 'twas made known throughout the castle how the matter had in very truth fallen out, and the lord bade release the son of Do, and the butler, and they did his bidding. But when Sir Gawain saw Giflet he ran towards him, and kissed him more than a hundred times, and made marvellous great joy of him. Then they sat them down on a bench, side by side, and held converse together. And when the twain who had fought were disarmed they brought for the four very fair robes of rich and royal cloth; never had ye seen such. Then the Soudoier bade saddle four steeds, and they mounted, and rode thus adown the street.

Thus they four alone took their way to the pavilion, and the king's men beheld them, even as they came forth from the castle gateway, and Sir Ywain cried, "By my faith, and no lie, I see four men come hither, and all four be knights, so it seemeth me!" And Kay answered, "I see them too!"

And when they came so near to the pavilion that their faces might be seen, Sir Ywain ran joyfully to the king. "Sire, Sire, an God help me, here cometh Sir Gawain, and with him three others, all hand in hand: there be the son of Do, and Sir Lucains, and for the fourth a great knight!"

The king answered no word, but made semblance as if he heard not, and rose not from his couch, save that he raised himself somewhat higher thereon.

In a little space he spake to his knights, "Be not over dismayed, but make as fair a countenance as ye may; methinks they come thither to bid us return with them to prison, but I go not hence ere that I be vanquished, or have freed my comrades." And all answered, "Well spoken, Sire!"

But now had the four come so nigh that they had dismounted, and come before the king; never was seen such rejoicing as his lord made of

Giflet, but now was he in sore distress, and, lo! his sorrow was turned to joy! Why should I lie to ye? The Rich Soudoier told him how Sir Gawain had conquered him, and how, by his courtesy, he had given life to him and to his fair lady; and the king hearkened to the tale right willingly.

Now will I leave speaking of them, but this much will I say, that well might the lord of the castle love and cherish him who first overcame him by arms and then did him so great honour as to yield him to his lady so that his life might thereby be saved. So here will I hold my peace, no, nor speak further, save to tell ye that now was the king lord alike of the Castle Orguellous and the lands around; never in all his days did he make so great a conquest, as Bleheris doth witness to us.

Sir Gawain at the Grail Castle

T HE EPISODES that Jessie Weston gathered together in her volume *Sir Gawain at the Grail Castle* represent a different side of Gawain from the epitome of chivalry and courtesy that he is most often portrayed as in English verse romances and many continental romances. In these episodes, Gawain's adventures are part of the Grail quest, in which even the best of knights can be found wanting.

In the story of 'The Unknown Knight' from the *First Continuation* to Chrétien's *Perceval*, Gawain takes up the quest of a knight who was killed while under his protection. He is led by the knight's horse, which seems to have a preternatural knowledge of its master's mission, to the Grail castle. When Gawain witnesses the Grail procession, he asks about the bleeding spear of Longinus but not about other things he has seen. As in Chrétien's romance, the asking of questions is the key to success on the quest. Since Gawain does not ask all the appropriate questions, the quest remains unfulfilled.

The account of 'The Achieving of the Quest' is taken from the German romance *Diu Crône* (*The Crown*) by Heinrich von dem Türlin. This is the only medieval work in which Gawain not only is a model of chivalry and courtesy, but also has the character necessary for success in the great spiritual undertaking. As a result, he asks the appropriate questions and so achieves the Grail quest.

By contrast, in the 'Castle Corbenic' episode from the prose *Lancelot*, the Grail-seeking Gawain is spiritually more like his counterpart in Malory's *Morte d'Arthur*. At Corbenic, where the Grail resides, he is unable to free the lord's daughter from a burning bath, a sign that he is not the best knight. Later, he is told by a hermit that he saw the Grail but did not know what he saw. His spiritual blindness explains why, when others were served food, he was given none. His failure is due, as a dwarf tells him, to the fact that there is 'too great villainy' in him.

Thus, in these three episodes, there are examples of Gawain succeeding in the Grail quest, not asking all the appropriate questions and therefore falling short of success, and failing completely. These Grail episodes and the other stories in this volume are a tribute to the great variety with which Gawain, like other characters from the Arthurian legends, has been treated.

Part I
The Unknown Knight

NOW IT CAME TO PASS that the tale went about throughout the land of Britain how that King Arthur had achieved the emprise he had laid upon him for the sake of that good knight, Sir Griffet, who was held in durance by the folk of the Castle Orguellous. For in sooth he had set him free, and would return in all haste to his own land by a set day.

Then the Queen bade carry her pavilion, and many another, to the glade of the Crossways, and said she would go thither to disport herself, nor would she in anywise depart thence till she had there kept tryst with her lord the King. With her went counts and barons enow; many a tent, many a bower, many a pavilion, did they cause to be set up in that glade, for there would they sojourn, and await as was fitting the coming of their lord. At the meeting of the Crossways was the royal tent set up where the Queen, with many a valiant knight, would keep her tryst with the King. 'Twas a fair sojourning in the greenwood, and the huntsmen took many a wild beast, there was no lack of such in the thickets!

As they abode there, even as I tell ye, it fell out on a Tuesday that 'twas a wondrous fair eventide. The Queen sat at chess with King Urien, 'twas the game she best loved, and around, to watch the play, sat Sir Gawain and many another good knight. Even as twilight fell they saw an armed knight come riding upon a gallant steed, who passed before them, and spake word to none. The Queen was vexed thereat, and spake saying, "That knight holdeth me in small account, for he looked not on me nor proffered me greeting. I were fain to know his name, and in sooth to know himself." She spake to Kay, the seneschal, "Kay, mount quickly, and go, bring him hither to me."

"Right willingly, lady" – and with that the seneschal went to arm himself, for know that ever, an he could, he would do the commandment of the Queen. He did off his rich surcoat, furred with ermine, and armed himself in haste, arid mounted, riding in pursuit swiftly, as one who is not well assured. Such haste did he make that he came up with him whom he followed, and cried, "Vassal, ye did great folly in that ye rode past the pavilion without praying leave of the Queen and her folk, turn about quickly!"

The knight answered, "So may God help me, I withheld not my greeting through pride, but never man rode on more urgent quest than that on which I ride, nor may I turn me again.

And Kay quoth, "So may God help me, but ye speak vainly, an ye turn not again, vassal, I will slay your steed!"

The knight made answer, in fashion of a man much troubled, "That would hinder me much, for afoot I may not go, nor may any so come thither; fair Sir, it behoves me to ride far ere this night be ended, say ye to the Queen that so surely as I return will I gladly speak with her, and yield me to her mercy in that I have failed to obey her now."

Kay took no heed of his words, but rode swiftly toward him, as if to joust; and even as the knight saw him coming he spurred his steed, and smote him so fiercely that Kay bent backward over his saddlebow, and fell to the ground, feet in air, but little more an he had been slain, so hard did he fall! The knight rode to Kay's steed, took it by the bridle, and went his way.

Then Kay turned him about, sore ashamed, and took his way to the tents afoot. A good hundred were they who at heart were right joyful for his shaming, but durst speak no word openly.

Forthwith he began to tell them the greatest lies, such as none other would have bethought him of – "Lady," quoth he, "'tis a proud and ribald knight, never man heard greater folly than that which he bath spoken of you!"

Sir Gawain made answer, "Sir Kay, by all the Saints that be, never did valiant knight miscall my lady! Say ye not so, but let the knight be, an he bath taken thy steed 'tis no cause that ye should talk foolishly, that were villainy indeed!"

Quoth the Queen, "pair nephew, go ye, and bring the knight again."

"Right willingly, lady," quoth Sir Gawain.

Then they brought unto him his steed, and he mounted thereon, all unarmed as he was, clad in a purple mantle, and bearing in his hand a painted wand. He followed the knight swiftly, nor would spare haste; 'twas wellnigh nightfall when he came up with him. Then he greeted him fairly, and the knight drew rein courteously when he heard Sir Gawain speak.

He said, "Sir, I pray ye, and the Queen to whom all Britain and Ireland do belong giveth command, that ye come straight-way unto her, so shall ye do well and courteously."

The knight made answer, "Sir, so God help me, that may I not do; but tell me I pray ye, and hide it not, how do men call ye?"

"Sir," saith he, "I am called Gawain."

"Ha, Sir, be ye right certain, that by Saint Peter of Rome, an I might turn again for any man I would do so more gladly for ye than for any other! But I have taken upon me a matter that demandeth haste, nor may I turn back for any. I wot not what I may tell ye further, save that none but I may achieve the quest; nevertheless I deem well ye might achieve it, yet should ye have great pain and travail therewith."

"Sir," saith Sir Gawain, "I pray ye frankly, with joined hands, that ye turn again with me, and come unto the Queen, since for a proud and ribald knight, felon and outrageous, doth the seneschal miscall ye, he who came to ye but now; evilly did he slander ye in the Queen's bower, in the hearing of many barons, yet there were those who laid the blame on him."

Quoth the knight, "What care I for Kay, or for any words that he may speak? But for you, right dear Sir, will I do whatsoever may please ye; yet this my quest must perforce be delayed, an ye do it not for me."

Then Sir Gawain made answer to him, who was in no wise discourteous, despite Kay's words, "Sir, I thank ye right heartily, and loyally do I here make covenant that I will aid ye in any way I may, were I the sole knight in the world. By Christ, Who seeth all, an' I rightly acquit me of this errand ye shall have no damage therefrom, so God preserve mine honour!"

The knight spake forthwith, "Great trust and great assurance, fair Sir, have I in your company; see ye, I am ready to go whithersoever ye shall lead me."

With that they turned them about; Kay's charge; methinks, they let stray as it would, nor deigned to lead it with them.

Thus they came again swiftly, but I tell ye verily and of a truth, that even as they drew nigh unto the tents, ere they had well passed the first, the knight uttered a great plaint suddenly, and cried with a loud voice, "Ha, Sir Gawain! I am a dead man forsooth 'tis a shame and a dishonour that I be slain in your safe-conduct! An God will I think me ye will do that which ye have covenanted with me. But now straightway take this mine armour, and arm yourself therewith, and mount this my steed, which will carry ye surely, and without fail, on the great quest which 1 had thought to achieve."

Then he gave forth a great cry, "Lord God, wherefore have they slain me? For never had I done them harm!"

Sir Gawain looked upon him, marvelling greatly that he thus made plaint, for naught had he seen or heard, and he knew not that any had smitten him. And as he looked, he saw him fall forward upon the neck of his charger, and therewith the blood gushed forth, for he was smitten through the body with the cast of a javelin, so that the iron thereof might be seen.

Quoth Sir Gawain, weeping, "Sir! Sir! heavily hath he shamed me who hath thus smitten ye!"

But the knight fell dead, and spake never word more; nor might any ask his name, whose man he was, nor whence he came, nor whither he went. Then there came together a great folk, who lamented him sorely, but they knew not who had slain him, nor whether 'twere well or ill done. Yet many put the blame on Kay, and said surely Kay had slain him; but he denied it straitly, and made complaint that they so charged him.

Sir Gawain waxed red with wrath and anger, and thrust him from him so that he staggered and had well nigh fallen; but the knights set themselves 'twixt the twain; of a sooth, had they not separated them the one from the other, Sir Gawain had done him a mischief. He spake in great anger, in the hearing of all, "Yet will I make ye pay dearly for his death, proven traitor that ye be! For sure and certain am I that ye slew him with your own hand." Kay hid himself as quickly as might be among the press, and made no answer to that which be heard him speak.

Sir Gawain bade them lay the body of the knight upon his shield, and bear it thus unto the Queen's pavilion; weeping, he bowed him low, and said, "Lady, see here the knight whom ye bade me bring into your presence; he came without word of refusal, great or small. Now is he dead in your safe-conduct, and thereby are ye dishonoured in the sight of all. Behold his corpse! 'Tis great pity, for 'twas a very wise and courteous knight. And I, I think me, am shamed thereby, for never in the sight or hearing of man did such dishonour befall any as today hath befallen me, since it seemeth that 'twas I betrayed him to his death: that I tell ye of a truth!"

With that he bade them disarm the body, and the knights and the barons looked upon the dead knight, and made lamentation, beholding the fashion of the man, and said, "Christ! Where was he born, this man who was so fair to look upon?" Nor might any of them know him, nor the land from whence he came.

Wherefore should I make a long tale thereof? Sir Gawain straightway tookthe harness of the slain knight, and therewith did he arm himself, and he mounted the steed which he aforetime bestrode, who now lay dead within the pavilion. The Queen, who wept for anger and bitter sorrow, said unto him, "Fair nephew, what would ye do? Hide naught from me, but tell me, I pray ye." Sir Gawain made answer, "Certes, lady, I may not tell ye, in that I scarce know myself, but this much may I say in all truth, that even should I die therein I must needs achieve the quest whereto I made covenant with this knight. I know naught that I may tell ye aforehand, save that this steed will surely carry me the road that it behoves me to travel: but whither I know not, nor to what land I know not, nor know I what may be the quest which I have taken upon me. Lady, I pray ye, make inquest into the death of this knight, that I may know the truth thereof at my returning, for never shall I be truly joyful till that I have avenged him."

With that Sir Gawain took leave, and would depart, nor would he remain the night for any prayer, though barons and knights besought him straitly; greatly did they lament for the good nephew of their or the King, for they knew not, nor might think of, the land whither he was bound. Thus Sir Gawain departed from among them, and the stranger knight lay dead in their midst.

Now as the writing doth us to wit the night was black, and of great darkness, for long time it thundered, and it rained, and there was so mighty a wind that the trees were split asunder. So swift and so oft were the lightning flashes that it was a marvel that gentle knight Sir Gawain died not ere the morning; but this I tell ye, that never was he in so strait a place but he was saved through his great loyalty, and his true courtesy, and this very night that we now tell of did God, Who lieth not, protect him. Know ye then verily, that throughout the night the good knight rode, even as the steed would carry him, until he came unto a great and fair chapel, that stood at a crossways in the midst of the forest. Since that he was sore pressed for the thunder and the lightning, that beset him as it were on every side, Sir Gawain made for the door, and found it open, and saw within where the altar stood all bare, with neither cloth nor covering thereon, but a great candlestick, wrought of gold, that stood alone, and therein a tall taper that burned clearly, and shed a great light around. When the knight beheld this he bethought him that he would enter therein, and rest awhile, till that the weather was somewhat cleared, and the great wind abated. Thus he passed the doorway, a horse as he was, and looked round about, up and down, to right and to left, and was ware of a window, right there behind the altar, and even as he looked, lo! a hand black and hideous, naught so marvellous had he beheld afore, came through the window, and took the taper, and extinguished the flame. With that came a voice that made lament, so loud and so dire, that it seemed as if the chapel itself rocked therefrom. This so affrighted the steed that it made a spring, and Sir Gawain was well nigh thrown to earth. Then did he raise his hand and signed him with the sign of the cross, and gat him forth from the chapel. With that the storm abated and the great wind was stayed so that thereafter it blew not nor rained a drop, but the night became clear and calm. Sir Gawain rode on his way swiftly, nor made delay, but many a time was he afeared for the marvels he had seen, yet of them durst no man speak for dread of wrath, for in sooth they appertain unto the high secrets of the Grail, and he bringeth on himself toil and tribulation who undertaketh to recount them, save in that place which is right and fitting. But I tell ye of a truth that that good knight rode all night nor drew bridle, in sorrow, in wrath, and in dread, till that the morn came and he saw the day dawn.

Sir Gawain looked around him on the land and marvelled much, for in that one night had he outridden Britain and all that country, and entered within a great forest which endured even from the morning unto the setting of the sun. Then did he issue forth on to a plain, and beheld the sea, and thither did the good steed bear him at a swift pace. Sir Gawain had held vigil through the night and journeyed far through the day, wind and rain had beaten upon him, neither had he eaten or drunk, so that he was marvellous weary and rode right heavily. Such desire of sleep came upon him that scarce might he sit upright. The good steed knew that well and dragged at the bridle, and Sir Gawain slackened his hand somewhat, and let it go as it willed.

Thus did it bear him till at nightfall he came unto the seashore, nor might he ride further. With that was Sir Gawain troubled in mind and somewhat wroth, but the good steed turned towards a path which he beheld afar off and stayed not till he came to the entering in thereof. On either side the way was planted with cypress, pine, and laurel; 'twas so narrow that the branches met overhead, and Sir Gawain must needs bend him low. Then he looked before him and saw afar off a light as it were of a kindled fire. Thither would the steed carry him, but it might scarce do so for the torment of the sea, which dashed against the pathway as it would wash it away and tear up the trees, which were thrown against each other, groaning for the violence of the wind. Sore afraid, and that of good reason, was Sir Gawain, and he said within himself that he would wait even unto the dawning ere he would adventure himself therein. But I tell ye truly that the good steed reared and strained at the bridle, and made such ado that the knight might in no wise hold it, but the rein was wrenched from his hand, and the horse took the bit in its teeth and entered the pathway, whether its rider would or no. Then the good knight bade it go at its will, and yielded the rein, yea, and spurred it on, so that with great bounds, many and oft, it went swiftly on its way.

Thus they rode even until midnight, but came not unto the light, but went ever on the causeway, and held it until they came I unto a great hail, high, and long, and wide. In the durance of a bowshot came a marvellous great folk (so I tell ye verily), and among them must Sir Gawain dismount; with great honour was he received, and all spake saying, "Fair Sir, blessed and honoured be your coming, for long time have we desired it."

Thus they led their guest within, even unto the fire, and when they had disarmed him a squire brought unto him a furred mantle, and wrapped it around him, and he I sat him down beside the fire. And it came to pass after a while, as they beheld his countenance, the folk began to marvel greatly, and to take counsel the one with the other, saying, "Lord, what may thisbe? 'Tis not he whom we awaited!" How shall I tell ye? Swiftly, in the closing of an eye, did all that great folk vanish, so that Sir Gawain might see them no more.

At this that gentle knight marvelled much, and greatly was he troubled for that not one of the folk remained behind. Angry was he and wroth in that they had so left him alone, and moreover he was troubled in that he had seen them take counsel together. Nor should any man marvel if he were afeard or in doubt. He looked adown the hail, as one ill at ease, and in no wise assured, and there in the midst he beheld a bier, wondrous long, and so soon as Sir Gawain saw it he raised his hand and made the sign of the cross, for know ye that he misdoubted him.

Now he beheld and saw that on the bier there lay a dead body, and above it was spread for honour a fair red samite, with cross of gold work, which covered the bier all round about. At the four corners stood four great tapers that burned in four fair candlesticks, worth a great treasure, at the least would they have weighed a hundred golden marks; and on each candlestick hung a censer of fine gold, richly wrought, wherein were spices which gave forth a most sweet smell. I tell ye truly that never man smelt a sweeter odour. On the samite of which I tell ye was the half and no more, of a sword broken midway below the hilt, as the writing telleth, it lay above and upon the breast of the dead.

Sir Gawain knit his brows, for wroth was he, and in dread, in that he was there alone: so troubled was he, so ill pleased and misdoubtful, that he knew not what it behoved him to do, for much he misliked the bier and the dead knight that lay thereon.

As he stood thus he raised his eyes and beheld a wondrous rich cross of silver, set about with precious stones of manifold virtue, borne by a tall clerk, who had much ado to carry it: he was vested in an alb and tunicle of a rare stuff of Constantinople. After him there came a great procession of canons, robed in silken copes, who stared them around the bier, and began with a loud voice to chant the Vigil of the Dead. As they chanted four clerks censed the bier with the censers that hung upon the golden candlesticks.

When they had ended the service they turned them again whence they came, and lo! the hail was once more filled with folk, and I tell ye verily that since the hour ye were born never might ye hear such wailing and lamentation as arose there above the dead. Sir Gawain commended him unto God, that He would keep him from harm, and made good countenance and sat him down again, for he had stood awhile, covering his eyes with his hand as he were in thought.

Anon he heard a great tumult that drew nigh unto him, and he lifted his head and beheld the great folk that he saw at the first, and he saw how they held cloths and napkins, whiter than lilies or than snow, and spread them upon the daïs. With that there came forth from a chamber a knight, tall and strong of limb, one who might well be a great man and a wise: nor was he of great age, yet was he somewhat bald. He was nobly vested, and bare a sceptre in his hand, and on his head a crown wrought of fine red gold: nor was there in Christendom a fairer man, nor a more courteous.

The King bade them bring water and he washed, and bade Sir Gawain do likewise; then he took him by the hand gently and seated him beside him at meat, even as a friend, and strove much to do him honour. When all were seated, on every daïs bread was set, 'twas the rich Grail that served them, yet no hand held it, but it served them right well, and came and went swiftly amid the knights. But know ye 'twas the butlers who served the wine, in cups of silver and fine gold, and the Grail went and came again the while, though none might know who held it. Full seven courses had those good knights, well and richly did the Grail serve them, on every dais so soon as the one meat was lifted was the other set, all in great dishes of silver – most fair and fitting was the service. Sir Gawain gazed and greatly marvelled, for now was the Grail here and anon was it there, and he knew not what to make of its coming and going, and the fashion of their service.

When they had eaten at leisure the King bade take away the tables, and this I tell ye of a truth that scarce had he spoken the word when the hall was left empty, and the das void, for all had departed, and the King himself first of all.

Think ye that Sir Gawain was in no wise troubled when he found himself thus left alone? I tell ye he was much in doubt and right wrathful that he should be in such case. He commended himself humbly unto God, praying that He would guard him from mischance, sorrow, and enchantment, even as He had power to do. Right suddenly he beheld there a lance, the blade of which was white as snow, 'twas fixed upright at the head of the master-dais, in a rich vessel of silver, and before it burned two tapers which shed a bright light around. From the point of the lance issued a stream of blood, which ran down into the vessel, even unto the brim rose the drops of blood, which fell not save into the silver cup. Yet might it not be filled for a fair mouthpiece, wrought of a verdant emerald, through which the blood fell into a channel of gold, which by great wisdom and artifice ran forth without the hall, but Gawain might not see whither it led. Then he marveled greatly within himself; thinking that never had he seen so great a wonder as this lance, which was of wood and yet bled without stanching. And as he mused thus he heard the door of a chamber open, and he saw come forth the lord of the castle, holding in his hand a sword and know verily that 'twas none other than the sword of the knight of whom I have told ye afore, he who was slain before the pavilion and the King spake forthwith to Sir Gawain, bidding him arise from his seat, and he led him by the hand even unto the bier, weeping bitterly – for the corpse that lay thereon.

Now hearken to that which the King spake: "Great is the loss that ye lie thus, 'tis even the destruction of kingdoms. God grant that ye be avenged so that the folk be only more joyful, and the land repeopled, which by ye and by this sword are wasted and made void." With that he drew the sword, and lo! 'twas broken, so that he held but the half thereof. Weeping for bitter sorrow he gave it unto Sir Gawain, and that good knight laid hold on it, the half that was lacking lay on the corpse of the dead knight. The King took it in his hand, and spake these words, neither less nor more: "Fair Sir, and gentle knight, an God will this sword shall by ye be resoldered; put ye now the two pieces together so that the one steel shall cleave to the other, so shall ye know verily and without doubt that ye shall be held the best knight in the world so long as it may endure." Then did Sir Gawain take the pieces and set them each to the other, but in no wise might he achieve that the steel should hold together, and the brand be resoldered.

Then was the King sore vexed, and he laid the one half again lightly above the breast of the dead knight, even as it had lain afore, and the other half he set in the scabbard, but know ye that he was ill-pleased that the twain might not come together. He bare the sword in one hand and with the other he laid hold on Sir Gawain, and led him into a chamber where he found knights enow, and a great gathering of other folk. They sat themselves down on a costly silken cloth, spread before a couch, and the King spake gently: "Fair sweet friend, take not amiss that which I tell ye, the quest on which ye came hither may not be achieved by thee; but an God so advance your prowess that He grant your return hither, then may ye perchance achieve it, and then may ye resolder the sword. For know of a truth that none save he who maketh the sword whole again may fulfil the quest. Sir knight, he who had undertaken the emprise hath remained in your country, I know not what hath delayed him, but long have we awaited his coming. Well I know that 'twas of your great hardiness that ye came hither; and would ye ask any treasure that we have in this land, certes, and of good will shall it be given ye. None here will do ye a mischief; and of the marvels ye have beheld ask at your pleasure, fair Sir, and we will tell ye the truth and lie not."

Now Sir Gawain had watched through the foregoing night, and ridden far, and had much travail, and great was his desire of slumber, yet greater was his will to hear of the marvels of the castle, thus did he force himself to be wakeful, and asked of that of which he was most in doubt: "Sire," he said, "but now I saw within the hall a lance that bled right freely, now would I pray and require of ye that ye tell me the truth thereof. Whence cometh the blood that floweth in such plenty from the point of the blade? And of the knight who lieth there dead upon the bier; and the broken sword, how it may be resoldered, and how the slain may be avenged of all that do I ask, for an it vex ye not I would fain know the truth thereof."

"Ye shall know it, fair friend, since ye have asked me, straightway and with no tarrying, otherwise durst no man tell ye. But now shall it in no wise be hidden from ye, and ye shall know all that ye have asked. Now would I tell ye first and at the beginning of the Lance, the great loss and the great grief that came therefrom, and the great honour, even as God, through Whom we are healed and saved, hath willed and established it. Know ye verily 'tis that Lance with which the Son of God was smitten through the side, even unto the heart, in the day that He hung upon the Cross. Longinus was the name of him who smote the blow, but afterwards did he receive mercy even unto the salvation or his soul, and he rests in peace. But all the days since hath that Lance bled, and ever shall it bleed until the Day of Doom, nor may it be removed from that place where now it standeth, for 'tis ordained of God that it remain there until He come again to judge the quick and the dead. Fair Sir, I think me that they who hung Christ on the Cross, and nailed Him there, and smote Him, shall be sore afraid when they shall see Our Lord bleed as freshly as on that day, they shall be in great torment, but we shall depart into joy, for that blood shall be our ransom. The great joy that we won by that stroke, fair Sir, may I not tell ye, but by the other are we so bereft that we have lost all. I speak of the stroke given by this sword, in an ill hour was it fashioned and tempered, never did sword strike so sore a blow, for it hath sent to destruction many a duke, many a prince, many a baron, many a noble dame, many a fair maiden and gentle demoiselle. Ye shall have heard tell of the great destruction through which we came hither, how that the kingdom or Logres was destroyed, and the country laid waste by the stroke of this sword; nor would I hide from ye who he was who lost his life, nor who he was who smote him; such marvel ye never heard."

With that he began to weep, and weeping, to tell the tale the truth whereof he knew right well, but even as he would begin he saw that Sir Gawain slept, nor would he waken him, but ceased speaking and left him to his slumber. And I tell ye truly that Sir Gawain slept through the night, and wakened not till the morning, when he found himself on a lofty cliff beside the sea, and nigh at hand, on a rock, were his arms and his steed.

Strangely did he marvel in that he found himself there, and saw neither house nor castle, neither hail nor keep; and he bethought him 'twere an ill sojourning there, so he did on his armour and mounted in haste – he knew well that he was shamed in that he had fallen asleep, for by slumber had he lost hearing of the wonders he had seen, and for that was he grieved at heart.

"Ha! God," quoth he, "so gently did that gracious King, the brave, the wise, the courteous, tell unto me the secret of the great marvels I beheld! Surely do I repent me in that I fell asleep." Then he said unto himself that he would so strive in travail of arms that an it might be he would again find that court, and ask once more concerning the service of the Grail, which he had seen the even before in that goodly hail. "Never," quoth he, "will I return again to Britain till I have done such deeds of arms as may pertain thereto." Then he set spur to his horse, and rode thence swiftly, and never might one behold a land so fairly garnished with wood, with water, and with fair pastures. Yet 'twas the Waste Kingdom, but at midnight had God made it even as he saw it; for so soon as Sir Gawain asked of the Lance, wherefore it bled thus freshly the waters flowed again through their channels, and all the woods were turned to verdure. So was the land in part repeopled, but more it might not be, since he had asked no more.

All the folk whom he beheld blessed him as he passed them by, and cried with one voice upon him: "Sir knight, thou hast slain and betrayed us! Yet great ease hast thou given to us of a truth, and for that are we glad and joyful; and yet must we needs be wroth with thee. Certes, greatly should we hate thee, in that thou didst not ask concerning the Grail and the service thereof. None may tell the joy that should have followed on thine asking – thus it behoveth us to be sad and wrathful." In such fashion spake all whom he met, yet know, that of great love they did it.

Know ye that Sir Gawain rode through many lands, and suffered much travail of arms, for many a long day ere he bethought him to return to Britain. Of the combats that beset him, and the marvels he beheld 'tis not fitting that I tell more; nor will I speak further of him who was slain at the pavilion, who he was, and whence he came, for here doth the tale pass to another matter, even to tell of Guiglain, Sir Gawain's son, and the first deeds which he wrought.

Part II
The Achieving of the Quest

ONG AND WEARY were the journeyings that good knight, Sir Gawain, made in search of the Grail; for he came even to a land wherein from the waxing to the waning of the moon there lacked not adventures stiff and stern. Yet his manhood stood him in good stead at need, otherwise had the toil and the strife weakened him overmuch. Howsoe'er it vexed him sorely. Yet the road led him at the last to a rich and goodly land, so well tilled that naught was lacking of the fruits of the earth, corn, and vines, and fair trees, all whereby man might live grew freely on either hand. That was right pleasing to Sir Gawain, who was worn with travel, for the land was like unto a garden, green, and in nowise bare, and of right sweet odour; it might well be held for an earthly Paradise, since 'twas full of all delights that heart of man might desire.

But ere ever he came within its borders a strange adventure befell him, for he saw a fiery sword, the breadth whereof he might not measure, which kept the entry to a fastness, within which stood a dwelling, cunningly builded, but the walls whereof were clear and transparent as glass; naught that passed therein might be held secret but 'twould have been seen without. I wot not how it chanced, but 'twas void and bare, and Sir Gawain deemed it strange and of ill omen; I think me well 'twas of ill, for 'twas a wild land, but therewith he left it behind him.

So the knight journeyed through that fair country, where he found all that heart desired, or that was needful to the body, so that his strength came again unto him, and he was wholly recovered of the pains which he had endured. And when he had ridden a twelve days' journey through the woodland he came again to an open country, and there he did meet with his comrades, Sir Lancelot and Sir Calogreant, whereat he was greatly rejoiced. The twain had wandered far astray, and save for their arms he might scarce have known them. He found them sleeping under a tree, whither his road led him, and for very joy he wakened them. Then they greeted each other gladly, and told each to the other the toils and the troubles that had befallen them as they rode singly or in company on their quest.

No longer might they abide there, for it drew towards nightfall; and as they went their way they beheld and saw how on the same track a squire spurred swiftly towards them, nor would he slacken his pace ere they met; right friendly was his mien as he bade Sir Gawain and his comrades be welcome to God, and to his lord, and to himself, in sooth he spoke truly and in no mockery, for good token he gave thereafter of his truth. He prayed them, in the name of his lord, that since they were come into his land they would do him so much honour as to turn aside unto his dwelling, for they were on the right road, and 'twas nigh at hand.

Sir Gawain made answer, "I thank ye right heartily, ye and your lord, know that we will gladly come unto your dwelling an' we be not forbidden by sword-thrust." The squire spake again, "This will I tell ye surely, follow ye this road straight unto the Burg, 'tis here full nigh at hand; I, having shown ye the road, will hasten thither, and ride ye as softly as ye will," With that he turned him again, and had swiftly outridden them.

Know ye that the knights were not over-long upon the road, for the twain, Sir Lancelot and Sir Calogreant, were sore a-hungered; sudden they saw before them a castle, fair to look upon, and they deemed they should find a goodly lodging therein. Without, on a meadow, was a great company of knights, who vied with each other in skilful horsemanship, as knights are wont to do. Without spear or shield, in courteous wise they rode hither and thither on the open field; but when the three had come so near that they took knowledge of them, that noble folk left their sport, and rode swift as flight over the meadow toward the road, and received the guests with gentle greeting, as is love's custom, bidding them welcome to their lord's land. With that they took them in safe-conduct, and led them even to the castle – I wot Sir Gawain there found gladsome gain!

The Burg was fairly builded, and therein dwelt a great folk, knights and ladies, who were right joyful as was fitting, that did Sir Gawain mark right well, and drew comfort therefrom. So well did they receive him that it grieved him naught that he was come unto their company; they beheld him right gladly, and all that was needful to him they gave him with full hand. So went he with the twain, Sir Lancelot and Sir Calogreant, unto the lord of the castle, even as they showed him the road.

'Twas the fairest palace ever builded, an the tale lie not no richer might tongue of man describe, or heart of man conceive. Never might the host be vexed through poverty, a courteous prince he was and good, and wise withal I ween. For the summer's heat his hall was all bestrewn with roses, whereof the perfume rejoiced him greatly. White was his vesture, cunningly wrought and sewn with diaper work of gold, 'twas a skilful hand that wrought it! Before him sat two youths of noble birth, whom he ever kept in his company; they jested lightly, the one with the other, the while they played at chess before his couch, and the lord leaned him over towards the board, for it gladdened him to behold the game, and to hearken to their jesting.

When Sir Gawain entered the hall the host received him and his two comrades well, and bade them be seated; Sir Gawain he made to sit beside him on the couch, on a cushion of rose-coloured silk did they sit together. In sooth there was pleasure enow of question and answer, and of knightly talk betwixt the host and Sir Gawain; and they who sat at the chessboard jested and made merry. Thus they made pastime till nightfall, and then were the tables set that all might eat, nor was any man forgotten, there was space for all.

Then the knights arose, and Sir Gawain also, but the host spake to them all by name, for right well he knew them, and bade them sit by him, which they were nothing loth to do. With that there came a great company of knights and ladies, who saluted the host, as is the fashion of women, and sat them all down. Long was the hall and wide, yet 'twas full in every part, and all the tables filled. After them came full twenty chamberlains, young men of noble birth and courteous bearing, who bare napkins and basins, that did the knights mark well; behind them were a great company, bearing candles and candlesticks without number, with that was the hall so light 'twere hard to tell whether 'twere day or night. And there followed thirty minstrels, and others who sang full many a tuneful melody, all with one accord rejoiced and sang praises.

The two knights and Sir Gawain sat beside their host, yet not on a level, for Sir Gawain sat above, and they below, and all around the hall, and ate each twain together, a knight with his lady.

And when all were seated, and were fain to eat, then there came into the hall a wondrous fair youth, of noble bearing, and in his hand he held a sword, fair and broad, and laid it down before the host. With that Sir Gawain 'gan to bethink him what this might betoken. After the youth came cupbearers, who passed through the hall, serving wine to all who were seated ere they might eat. Sir Gawain and his comrades did they serve first of all, the while the host sat beside them and did neither eat nor drink. Nor would Sir Gawain drink, but for his comrades twain they were so sore vexed by thirst, that even though he bade them refrain yet must they drink withal, and thereafter did they fall into a deep slumber, and when Sir Gawain beheld this it vexed him sorely.

Oft-times did the lord of the castle pray Sir Gawain to drink, as a courteous host doth his guest, but otherwise was he minded, and well on his guard, lest he too fall asleep.

At the last came in fair procession, as it were, four seneschals, and as the last passed the door was the palace filled – nor were it fitting that I say more. In the sight of all there paced into the hall two maidens fair and graceful, bearing two candlesticks; behind each maid there came a youth, and the twain held between them a sharp spear. After these came other two maidens, fair in form and richly clad, who bare a salver of gold and precious stones, upon a silken cloth; and behind them, treading soft and slow, paced the fairest being whom since the world began God had wrought in woman's wise, perfect was she in form and feature, and richly clad withal. Before her she held on a rich cloth of samite a jewel wrought of red gold, in form of a base, whereon there stood another, of gold and gems, fashioned even as a reliquary that standeth upon an altar. This maiden bare upon her head a crown of gold, and behind her came another, wondrous fair, who wept and made lament, but the others spake never a word, only drew nigh unto the host, and bowed them low before him.

Sir Gawain might scarce trust his senses, for of a truth he knew the crowned maiden well, and that 'twas she who aforetime had spoken to him of the Grail, and bade him an he ever saw her again, with five maidens in her company, to fail not to ask what they did there – and thereof had he great desire.

As he mused thereon the four who bare spear and salver, the youths with the maidens, drew nigh and laid the spear upon the table, and the salver beneath it. Then before Sir Gawain's eyes there befell a great marvel, for the spear shed three great drops of blood into the salver that was beneath, and the old man, the host, took them straightway. Therewith came the maiden of whom I spake, and took the place of the other twain, and set the fair reliquary upon the table – that did Sir Gawain mark right well – he saw therein a bread, whereof the old man brake the third part, and ate.

With that might Sir Gawain no longer contain himself, but spake, saying, "Mine host, I pray ye for the sake of God, and by His Majesty, that ye tell me what meaneth this great company, and these marvels I behold?" And even as he spake all the folk, knights and ladies alike, who sat there, sprang from their seats with a great cry, and the sound as of great rejoicing. Straightway the host bade them again be seated as before, and make no sound until he bade, and this they did forthwith.

At the sound of the great cry the twain, Sir Lancelot and Sir Calogreant, wakened, for through the wine they had drunk they slept soundly, but even as they beheld the maidens who stood around the board, and the marvels that had chanced, they sank back into slumber, and so it was that for five hours sleep kept fast hold of them, the while the old man spake thus:

"Sir Gawain, this marvel which is of God may not be known unto all, but shall be held secret, yet since ye have asked thereof, sweet kinsman and dear guest, I may not withhold the truth. 'Tis the Grail which ye now behold. Herein have ye won the world's praise, for manhood and courage alike have ye right well shown, in that ye have achieved this toilsome quest. Of the Grail may I say no more save that ye have seen it, and that great gladness hath come of this your question. For now are many set free from the sorrow they long had borne, and small hope had they of deliverance. Great confidence and trust had we all in Perceval, that he would learn the secret things of the Grail, yet hence did he depart even as a coward who ventured naught, and asked naught. Thus did his quest miscarry, and he learned not that which of a surety he should have learned. So had he freed many a mother's son from sore travail, who live, and yet are dead. Through the strife of kinsmen did this woe befall, when one brother smote the other for his land: and for that treason was the wrath of God shown on him and on all his kin, that all were alike lost.

"That was a woeful chance, for the living they were driven out, but the dead must abide in the semblance of life, and suffer bitter woe withal. That must ye know – yet had they hope and comfort in God and His grace, that they should come even to the goal of their grief, in such fashion as I shall tell ye.

"Should there be a man of their race who should end this their sorrow, in that he should demand the truth of these marvels, that were the goal of their desire; so would their penance be fulfilled, and they should again enter into joy: alike they who lay dead and they who live, and now give thanks to God and to ye, for by ye are they now released. This spear and this food they nourish me and none other, for in that I was guiltless of the deed God condemned me not. Dead I am, though I bear not the semblance of death, and this my folk is dead with me. However that may be, yet though all knowledge be not ours, yet have we riches in plenty, and know no lack. But these maidens they be not dead, nor have they other penance save that they be even where I am. And this is by the command of God, that by this His mystery, which ye have here beheld, they shall nourish me once, and once alone, in the year. And know of a truth that the adventures ye have seen came of the Grail, and now is the penance perfected, and for ever done away, and your quest hath found its ending."

Therewith he gave him the sword, and told him he were right well armed therewith, and however much he might bear it in strife never would it break, and he bade him wear it all his days. Thus did he end his tale, telling no more, save that he might now leave the quest he had undertaken, and that for the rest, on the morrow should his toil be ended. And in so far as concerned the maidens 'twas through their unstained purity, and through no misdoing, that God had thus laid on them the service of the Grail; but now was their task ended, and they were sad at heart, for they knew well that never more should the Grail be so openly beheld of men, since that Sir Gawain had learned its secrets, for 'twas of the grace of God alone that mortal eyes might behold it, and its mysteries henceforth no tongue might tell.

With this speaking the night had passed, and the day began to dawn, and as his tale was done, lo! from before Sir Gawain's eyes the old man vanished, and with him the Grail, and all that goodly company, so that in the hall there abode none save the three knights and the maidens.

And Sir Gawain was somewhat sorry, when he saw his host no more, yet was he glad when the maiden spake, saying that his labour was now at an end, and he had in sooth done all that pertained unto the Quest of the Grail, for never elsewhere in any land, save in that Burg alone, might the Grail have been beheld. Yet had that land been waste, but God had hearkened to their prayer, and by his coming had folk and land alike been delivered, and for that were they joyful.

That day Sir Gawain abode there with his comrades, who rejoiced greatly when they heard the tale, and yet were sorrowful in that they had slumbered when the Grail passed before them, and so beheld it not. Good hostelry they found in that Burg, and when the morning dawned and they must needs depart then was many a blessing called down upon Sir Gawain by those maidens, that he might live many years in bliss and honour, this they prayed of a true heart, since he had set them free, and one blessing surely seeketh another. So the good knight departed from among them. Thus doth the Quest of Sir Gawain find an ending.

Part III
Castle Corbenic

NOW THE TALE telleth how it chanced on a day that Sir Gawain had departed from Sir Hector, with whom he had some time held company, and rode on his way alone through a forest, till that it drew nigh to nones. Then he saw on his right hand where a pavilion was set up nigh to the brink of a fountain; thither did

he turn himself to know if any were within. And when he came to the entry he beheld knights, to the number of six, who sat at meat on the green grass. Sir Gawain had eaten naught through the day, so he made fast his steed to one tree, and hung his shield on another, and entered within the pavilion, and saluted those who sat at meat; yet not one of them answered him a word, but all looked upon him with evil looks.

When Sir Gawain saw that none would speak unto him he was in no wise daunted, but sat him down beside them with his sword yet girt about him, and did off his helmet from his head, and set it nigh at hand, and began to eat right heartily, as one sore hungered, saying to him that sat beside him, "Eat, fair Sir, and be of good cheer!"

"In the Name of God, Sir knight," quoth the other, "good cheer may I not have of my meat, an ye thus prevent me, for perchance I have as great need of food as ye! Therefore I forbid ye to lay hand thereto, for by my head ye shall pay full dearly for it!" And all the others spake saying an Sir Gawain made not haste to depart they would slay him without more ado. And Sir Gawain said he would not budge for the six of them – "But it grieveth me for my steed, for he hath naught to eat!"

Then all who were within sprang to their feet, and laid hands on swords and axes, of which there were enow in the tent, and ran upon him to slay him. When Sir Gawain saw that he laced his helm and took again his shield, and refused none who came against him, but smote the first, who was unarmed, so hardly that he clave his head in twain, and he fell dead. Then he ran upon the others who would do their best to slay him, and smote the one so that he severed his arm, 'twixt neck and shoulder, and the others turned to flight when they saw their comrades in such evil case.

Sir Gawain deigned not to pursue them, but mounted his steed, and rode on his way, and held it even till vespertide. And with that he came into a great valley, and he looked before him and saw at the far end thereof a castle that stood right well, for water ran all around it and it was circled with stout walls and battlements. The good knight turned his horse toward it, for there would he lie that night, and when he came to the water he found a bridge of wood by which one might come unto the castle.

So he came unto the chief street, and rode even toward the master-tower, and as he drew nigh he praised it much, for of its size 'twas the fairest and the richest and the strongest he had yet beheld. He looked on the right hand, and he bethought him that he heard a woman cry out, nigh unto him, and he turned him to that side whence he heard the cry, and came unto a great hall. And when he entered therein he saw a damsel in a marble bath, who cried aloud: "Holy Mary! Who will lift me out?"

Sir Gawain came thither, and saw that the bath was half full of water, so that the damsel sat therein up to the waist. And when she saw him she cried, "For God's sake, Sir knight, lift me out!" And Sir Gawain set his hands on her two sides, but for all the power he put forth he might in no wise move her, though he made trial twice or thrice.

And when she saw that he might not move her she said, "Ha, Sir knight, ye have failed; now may ye know of a surety that ye shall not depart from this castle unshamed!"

"Damsel," saith he, "if I have not delivered ye I am right heavy at heart. Yet in that I have thereto set all my strength no man should blame me. But now would I pray ye of your friendship tell me wherefore ye be thus, and by what chance, and if ye may in no wise He delivered?"

"By my faith," said she, "I am set here in such wise that I endure sore torment and anguish, nor may I be delivered ere the best knight in the world shall lift me out, nor may I tell to ye or to another wherefore I be thus tormented until his coming, yet is that nigh at hand, for it shall be even in this very year."

"And how may it be," saith he, "that ye suffer torment?"

"How?" saith she. "Put ye your hand in the water, and ye shall know." With that Sir Gawain put his hand therein, but he might scarce draw it back swiftly enough, for 'twas so hot he deemed he had done his hand a lasting mischief.

"Sir knight," said she, "now ye know well the anguish that I suffer."

"Certes, damsel," quoth he, "I see not how ye may long endure."

"Wherefore?" saith she.

"Because," saith he, "ye suffer too much anguish and torment."

"'Tis not the will of God," saith she, "that I shall die, for as yet hath He not taken full vengeance of a sin which I wrought, for the which I suffer this penance. But now may ye go hence, when it please ye, for naught may ye do to aid me. And since ye have failed in this matter ye may know no more."

When Sir Gawain saw he might do no more he went his way to the master-palace. And squires more than twenty sprang to meet him, and aided him to dismount, and stabled his steed. Then they led him up into the palace to disarm him, and there Sir Gawain found a great company of the fairest knights he had beheld in any land, who arose to greet him when they were ware of his coming. And they said that he was welcome among them, and he saluted them, and prayed might God bless them.

With that they made him unarm, and gave him a rich robe for vesture, and set him down among them, and asked him whence he came. And he said from the kingdom of Logres, and the house of King Arthur.

Then they made the greatest joy in the world, and asked of him news of the court, and he told them such as he knew, but 'twas a while since he had heard aught.

As he spoke there came forth from a chamber a knight, who led with him many other knights; and he was the fairest man that Sir Gawain had beheld since he left his own land, and had the semblance of one of noble birth. And when they who were within saw him coming they spake to Sir Gawain, saying, "Behold the King!"

With that Sir Gawain rose to his feet, and bade him welcome, and the other returned his greeting with a right fair countenance and bade him sit beside him; and he asked him who he was, and he told him the truth. Then was the King right joyful, for greatly did he desire to see Sir Gawain, and to have his friendship, so he spake to him and they took knowledge of each other.

While they spake thus Sir Gawain beheld, and saw where there entered through a window a white dove, which bare in its beak a censer of richest gold. And so soon as it came therein the palace was filled with the sweetest odours that heart of man might conceive, or tongue of man might tell. And all that were in the hall became mute, and spake never a word more, but kneeled down as soon as they beheld the dove. And it entered straightway into a chamber, and forthwith the folk of the palace made ready with all haste, and set the tables on the date, and they sat them down the one and the other, and never a man of them spake a word, nor had need of summons. Sir Gawain marvelled greatly at this adventure, but he sat him down with the others, and beheld and saw how they were all in prayers and orisons.

With that there came forth from the chamber wherein the dove had entered a damsel, the fairest he had beheld any day of his life; and without fail was she the fairest maiden then alive, nor was her peer thereafter born. Her hair was cunningly plaited and bound, and her face was fair to look upon. She was beautiful with all the beauty that pertaineth unto a woman, none fairer was ever seen on earth. She came forth from the chamber bearing in her hands the richest vessel that might be beheld by the eye of mortal man. 'Twas made in the semblance of a chalice, and she held it on high above her head, so that she ever bowed before it.

Sir Gawain looked on the vessel, and praised it much, yet might he not know whereof 'twas wrought; for 'twas not of wood, nor of any manner of metal; nor was it in any wise of stone, nor of horn, nor of bone, and therefore was he sore abashed. Then he looked on the maiden, and marvelled more at her beauty than at the wonder of the vessel, for never had he seen a damsel with whom she might be compared; and he mused so fixedly upon her that he had no thought for aught beside. But for the King and his knights, as the damsel passed them by, all kneeled low before the holy vessel; and forthwith were the tables replenished with the choicest meats in the world, and the hall filled with sweetest odours.

When the damsel had passed the dais once she returned into the chamber whence she came, and Sir Gawain followed her with his eyes as long as he might, and when he saw her no more he looked on the table before him, and saw naught that he might eat, for 'twas void and bare; yet was there none other but had great plenty, yea a surfeit of victuals, before him. And when he saw this he was sore abashed, and knew not what he might say or do, since he deemed well that he had in some point transgressed, and for that transgression was his meat lacking to him. So he withheld him from asking till that they were risen from the table, but then all gat them forth from the palace, the one here, the other there, so that Sir Gawain wist not what had become of them, and knew naught but that he was left alone; and when he himself would have gone forth into the courtyard below he might no longer do so, for all the doors were fast shut.

When he saw this he leaned him against one of the windows of the hall and fell into deep thought. Then there came forth from a chamber a dwarf, bearing a staff in his hand, and when he saw Sir Gawain he cried upon him: "Who be this caitiff knight, who by ill chance leaneth here against our window? Flee ye from hence, here may ye not remain, for in ye is too great villainy! Go, get ye to rest in one of these chambers that none behold ye here!" Then he raised his staff to smite Sir Gawain, but he put forth his hand and took it from him. And when the dwarf saw this he cried, "Ha! Sir knight, 'twill avail ye nothing, for ye may not escape hence without shaming!"

With that he gat him into a chamber; and Sir Gawain looked toward the head of the hall, and saw there one of the richest couches in the world, and he made haste towards it, for there would he lie. But even as he set him down he heard a maiden cry upon him, "Ha! Sir knight, thou diest an thou liest there unarmed, for 'tis the Couch Adventurous, but look ye, yonder lie arms, take them, and lie ye down an ye will."

Sir Gawain ran swiftly where he saw the armour, and armed himself as best he might, and when he was armed he sat him down straightway. But scarce had he set him down when he heard a cry, the most fell he had ever heard, and he thought him well 'twas the voice of the foul fiend. With that there came forth swiftly from a chamber a lance whereof the blade was all afire, and it smote Sir Gawain so hardly that despite shield and hauberk it pierced his shoulder through and through. And he fell swooning, but anon he felt how one drew out the lance, yet he saw not who laid hand to it. Then was he much afeard, for the wound bled sorely, yet would he not rise up from the couch, but said within himself that though he died for it yet would he behold more of the marvels – yet he wist well that he was sore wounded.

Long time did Sir Gawain abide there, and when night fell – so that he saw but ill save for the light of the moon, which shone through more than forty windows, which were all open – then he looked towards the chamber which was nighest to him and beheld a dragon, the greatest he had ever seen, never a man but had felt dread at the sight. In all the world were there no more diverse colours than might be seen upon it, for 'twas red, and blue, and yellow, and green, and black, and white: and its eyes were red and swollen, and its mouth huge and gaping.

The dragon began to go up and down in the chamber, making play with its tail, and lashing the ground: and when it had thus made sport awhile it turned over on its back, and began to writhe and utter cries, even as it died a hard death. When it had striven thus awhile it stretched itself out as it were indeed dead, and Sir Gawain marvelled much, for he saw how that it cast forth from its mouth young dragons, even to the number of five hundred, all of which were living.

When it had done this it came forth even unto the great hall, and lo! it found there a leopard, the greatest in the world, and the twain ran the one upon the other, and a mighty battle began betwixt them. And the dragon deemed well it would get the better of the leopard, yet might it not do so. And as they fought thus it befell Sir Gawain that he lost his sight, and for awhile saw naught – yet did the moon shine brightly – but after awhile his sight returned to him, and he saw how the dragon and the leopard ever strove together.

Long while did the strife of the twain endure, so that Sir Gawain wist not the which had the better, and the which the worse; but when the dragon saw that it might not vanquish the leopard, it turned again to the chamber whence it came, and so soon as it entered therein, the young dragons fell upon it, and they fought together right hardily, and the melee endured great part of the night, till that in the end the old dragon slew the young, and the young the old.

Then the windows of the hall clapt to, the one after the other, with so great a noise it seemed as if the palace must fall; and there came therein a wind, so great and so strong that it swept clear the rushes from the floor. At this adventure did Sir Gawain marvel much, more than at aught that had aforetime befallen, yet would he wait awhile to see what should chance further.

Long time after that the windows of the palace were closed Sir Gawain hearkened and heard the sound of bitter weeping and lamentation, he deemed well 'twas the voice of women. And when he would have arisen to seek the cause he saw come forth from a chamber twelve maidens, who made the greatest lamentation in the world; they came the one after the other and said, weeping, "Dear Lord God, when shall we be delivered from this pain?" And when they came unto the door of the chamber where the dove had entered the even before, they kneeled them down and made prayers and orisons, and withal wept bitterly. And when they had been there a great while they turned them again whence they came.

When the maidens were departed Sir Gawain saw come forth from a chamber a great knight, all armed, shield at neck, and sword in hand; and he said unto Sir Gawain, "Sir knight, arise, go slumber in one of these chambers, for here may ye not remain!" But he said he would abide there an he died for it.

"Not so, fair Sir," quoth the other, "for it behoves ye to fight with me ere ye may abide here!"

"To fight," quoth Sir Gawain, "will I assent, an I must needs suffer it, nevertheless I were liever to fight than to get me hence!"

"I' faith," quoth the knight, "an ye will not do it of courtesy ye must needs do it of force – guard ye well, for here I do defy ye!"

Then he ran on him with uplifted sword, and Sir Gawain arose and defended him as best he might, but the knight pressed him hard. So their shields and helmets were cloven, and their hauberks rent on shoulder and on side and on thigh, and the blood ran from their bodies. But greatly was Sir Gawain vexed for the wound in his shoulder, for it might not be stanched, and that wound had well nigh put him to the worse; yet he suffered and endured as best he might, and covered him with his shield as one who knew well what it behoved him to do. And the knight pressed upon him with sword thrust, as one of great valour and prowess, and drave him hither and thither.

Thus Sir Gawain endured even until he had taken breath, then he ran vigorously upon the knight, and dealt him many a hardy blow on helmet and shield, and the knight did likewise. And the battle endured long, till the one and the other had lost their force, and the strength of their bodies, and were so mazed they might no longer hold their feet, but fell to the ground, the one on the one side, the other on the other. And they had fought so long and so hardily that the hall was bestrewn with the mails of their hauberks, and the splinters of their shields. And so spent and so weary were they that they might not lift their heads, but lay on the ground even as they had swooned.

Great while they lay thus, Sir Gawain beside the couch and the knight anear him, then the palace began to shake, and the windows to clap together, and it began to thunder and lighten, as 'twas the worst weather in the world, save that it rained not. Of this adventure was Sir Gawain much dismayed, yet so spent was he that he might not lift his head, and with that was his brain so bemused with the thunder claps that he knew not if it were day or night.

Then there swept through the hall a breeze so soft and sweet, 'twas a marvel, and there came the sound of many voices as it were descending into the hall, which sang so sweetly that naught in the world could liken them, there might well be even two hundred. And Sir Gawain might not hear what they sang, save they oft-times chanted, "Glory, and praise, and honour be unto the King of Heaven!" And a little afore they heard the voices 'twas as if the sweetest perfumes in the world were shed forth therein.

Sir Gawain hearkened well the voices, and they seemed to him so sweet and so pleasant that he deemed not they were of earth, but rather things spiritual, and without doubt 'twas even so. Then he opened his eyes and saw naught, and he knew verily that these were no earthly voices, since his eyes might not behold them. He was fain to have arisen from the ground, yet might not do so since he had lost the strength of his limbs and the power of his body.

Then he saw come forth from a chamber the damsel who the even afore had borne the holy vessel before the table. And before her came two tapers and two censers. And when she came even to the middle of the palace she set the Holy Grail afore her on a table of silver. And Sir Gawain beheld all around censers to the number of ten which ceased not to give forth perfume. And all the voices began to sing together more sweetly than heart of man might think, or mouth speak. And all said with one voice, "Blessed be the Father of Heaven."

When the song had endured long time the damsel took the vessel and bare it into the chamber whence she came, and then were the voices silent as they had departed thence, and all the windows of the palace opened and closed them again and the hall grew dark so that Sir Gawain saw naught, but of this was he well aware that he felt hale and whole as naught had ailed him, nor might he feel aught of the wound in his shoulder, for 'twas right well healed. Then he arose joyous and glad at heart, and went seeking the knight who had fought with him, but he found him not.

Then he heard as it were a great folk that drew nigh to him, and he felt how they laid hold on him by the arms and the shoulders, and the feet and the head, and bare him forth from the hall, and bound him fast to a cart that was in the midst of the court, and forthwith he fell asleep.

In the morning when the sun was risen Sir Gawain awoke, and lo! he was in the vilest cart in the world, and he saw that his shield was bound on the shaft afore him, and his steed was made fast behind. But in the shafts was a horse so thin and so meagre to look at that it seemed scarce worth twopence. And when he found himself in such sorry case he made sore lament; for it seemed to him that no man was ever so sorely shamed, and he were liever he were dead than living.

With that came towards him a damsel, bearing a scourge in her hand, and she began to smite the steed and to lead it swiftly through the streets of the town. And when the minstrels saw the knight in the cart they followed shouting and crying, and they threw on him mud, and dirt and old clouted rags in great plenty. Thus they followed him forth from the town, pelting him with all the dirt they might find.

And when he had passed the bridge the damsel stayed, and unbound him, and bade him descend from the cart, for there had he been over long. And he sprang down forthwith and mounted his steed and asked of the damsel the name of the castle, and she said 'twas the castle of Corbenic. And he went his way, making bitter lamentation, and cursing the hour he was born and that he was made knight. For now had he lived over long, since that he had been held the vilest and the most shamed among men.

So Sir Gawain went his way, making lament and weeping right bitterly. Thus he wandered all day without meat or drink till at even he came to a hermitage, where dwelt one whom men called the Secret Hermit, and 'twas even as he was about to chant vespers. Sir Gawain hearkened right willingly; and when they were done the holy man entered his cell and asked of Sir Gawain who he might be, and Sir Gawain told him the truth.

"Ha! Sir knight, ye be right welcome. Certes of all the knights in the world ye be the knight I most desired to see; but tell me, for God's sake, where did ye lie overnight?"

Sir Gawain was that wrathful he might not speak, but the tears came even to his eyes; and the holy man saw well that some matter had vexed him, so that he left speaking, save that he said: "Sir, be not vexed at aught that hath befallen ye, for there liveth no man so valiant but mischance o'ertaketh him at times."

"Certes, Sir," quoth Sir Gawain, "I know right well that there be none so valiant but he findeth ill-luck now and again, yet never to my thinking did one man alone have such ill-hap as hath fallen to me this fortnight past." Then he began to tell him all that had befallen him at the castle of Corbenic, and the holy man looked on him, and became sore amazed, so that for awhile he spake no word; and when he might speak he said, "Ha, Sir, God help ye, for truly 'twas great mischance when ye saw, and yet wist not what ye saw!"

"Ha, fair Sir," quoth Sir Gawain, "an ye know what 'twas that I beheld tell me, I pray ye!"

"Certes," quoth the Hermit, "'twas the Holy Grail, in the which the blood of Our Lord was received and held, and when ye beheld it not in humility and lowliness ye merited right well punishment, and so were ye forbidden to partake of its Bread, and that saw ye right well, for when all the others were served ye were passed over."

"For God's sake, Sir," quoth Sir Gawain, "tell me the truth of the marvels I beheld."

"Through me," quoth the Hermit, "may ye not know them, yet shall it be but a short while ere ye shall learn."

"Ha, fair Sir," saith the knight, "tell me at least the signification of the dragon, an ye know."

"That will I tell ye," quoth the Hermit, "but after shall ye ask me no more, for no more may ye hear as at this time.

"Verily did ye see in the chamber a dragon, which cast forth from its mouth fire and flame and young dragons, which it left even in the chamber, and went forth and entered into the great hall. And when it came thither it found a leopard, against which it battled mightily, but might not overcome it. And when it saw it might not have the victory it returned back into the chamber whence it came forth, and there did the young dragons fall upon it, and they slew each the other – and that did ye behold."

"Yea, 'twas even so," quoth Sir Gawain.

"Now will I tell ye," quoth the holy man, "the signification thereof. The mighty and great dragon figureth the King Arthur, your uncle, who shall depart from his land, even as the dragon departed from the chamber, leaving therein his knights and kinsmen, even as the dragon left its young. And like as the dragon fought against the leopard, yet might not overcome, so shall King Arthur make war upon a knight, but shall not vanquish him, though he strive with all his power. And like as the dragon returned to his lair when it might not put the leopard to the worse, even so shall the King get him back to his own land when he seeth that he may in no wise get the better of that knight. And then shall a marvellous adventure befall ye, for even as ye lost your sight, the while that the dragon and the leopard strove together, so shall the light of your prowess be put out. But when the King shall return to his land it shall chance unto him as it chanced unto the dragon, for his own men shall fall upon him, even as the young fell upon the old dragon, and the conflict shall endure till all shall alike be slain.

"Now have ye heard the signification of the dragon, so have I done your behest, even as I will ye shall do mine, when that I shall ask ye."

And Sir Gawain said even so would he do.

"Now," quoth the holy man, "it behoveth ye to swear upon these relics that never in your life will ye speak of that which ye have seen, or tell it unto man or woman." And he sware, yet in his heart was he sore dismayed for the words that he had heard, yet did he make good cheer, though his heart misgave him.

That night he lay within, and was well served of all that the holy man might have, and the morrow, so soon as he had heard Mass from the lips of the Hermit, he armed himself, and mounted his steed, and commended the holy man to God, and went his way as before. But now doth the tale cease speaking of Sir Gawain, and telleth awhile of Hector, who had set himself to search for Sir Lancelot.

The Legend of Sir Gawain

Studies upon Its Original Scope and Significance: Chapters I, II, III, VI and IX
by Jessie L. Weston

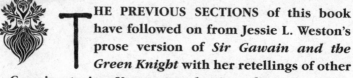

THE PREVIOUS SECTIONS of this book have followed on from Jessie L. Weston's prose version of *Sir Gawain and the Green Knight* with her retellings of other Gawain stories. Verse reproductions from the Percy Folio have also shown remarkable similarities to the content of the more famous Green Knight story, though with notable differences. In conclusion to this volume it would seem fitting to delve further into the legend surrounding Gawain, and so we have included a selection of chapter extracts from Weston's own foundational studies on the subject.

This intriguing work explores the origins of the Gawain legend, along with the contradictory elements of his character and the varied interpretations over the centuries. Chapter I introduces the ideas covered in Weston's studies, with Chapter II discussing early conceptions of Gawain and drawing fascinating parallels to the Irish Cuchulinn from the Ulster cycle. Chapter III provides useful summaries of the legend as it appears by the poets Chrétien de Troyes and Wolfram von Eschenbach. Chapter VI touches on the role of women in Gawain's adventures, and the conflicting ways in which he acts towards them. Finally, Chapter IX takes *Sir Gawain and the Green Knight* as its focus, comparing the various forms of the story and highlighting its most significant aspects.

Chapter I
Introductory

EVER SINCE THE DAYS when Geoffrey of Monmouth gave to the world that fascinating combination of fact and fiction which he dignified by the title of 'History', the fame of King Arthur and his knights has been one of the most precious heritages of the English people – one of the most fruitful sources of inspiration to writers other than English. For if we alone may claim King Arthur as ours by right of birth, he has become, as it were, the property of the whole world by right of literary inspiration.

Indeed, if to have been the first to enshrine the story of a hero in undying literary form were to constitute a prior right to that hero, then France and Germany, rather than England, might claim King Arthur as their own; for though he was to English minds a tradition, an ideal (dare we say, a *memory*?), the English tongue was, at the time of King Arthur's highest glory, but in its childhood – too halting, too unformed, to give full expression to England's pride in her national hero.

It was a curious fate that befell us, one surely unique in the literary experience of any nation, that of being compelled, by lack of means of expression, to have recourse to a foreign tongue in order to preserve the record of the king we delighted to honour. The poems that formed the basis of the extant Arthurian Romances were, doubtless, many of them, composed in England, but their writers were Anglo-Norman, and their language French. It was not till the end of the fifteenth century that England clothed in fitting words, and in her own tongue, the records of Arthur's deed. The majority of the Arthurian Romances are French, some of the very finest of the entire cycle German.

Previous to Malory's immortal composition, English Arthurian literature consisted of scattered ballads and metrical romances, the majority of which own Gawain, rather than Arthur, as their hero. In the form in which we possess them, these are rarely older than the fourteenth or fifteenth century, though the subject-matter doubtless is of much earlier date. But, though English literature generally abounded with Arthurian allusions, the feats of the hero King and his knight were at no time, earlier or later, woven into an epic poem. We have nothing in our literature to set over-against the works of such writers as Chrétien de Troyes, Hartmann von Aue, Gottfried von Strassbourg, or Wolfram von Eschenbach.

Malory's prose epic, which, fine as it is, is an example rather of excellence of style than a faithful representation of the original legend, was till this nineteenth century the sole great monument which English literature had dedicated to the memory of Arthur. Tennyson's collection of Arthurian poems and Idylls has freed us from a well-deserved reproach, though, from a critical point of view, it must be admitted that his work is open to much the same objection as is Malory's – it is admirable considered as *literature*, as *legend* it does even less justice to the original characters of the story.

This feature of the question, viz., that the great mass of Arthurian romance is in a foreign tongue, ought to be borne in mind; it goes far to explain the fact – for it is a fact – that the labours of English scholars in this field have hitherto been productive of less solid results than have been achieved either in France or in Germany. It must be admitted that it strikes an English student disagreeably to find that, in taking up the study of a subject so essentially national in spirit, the English books which can be relied upon for information are so few in number, and, with some honourable exceptions, of so little value in comparison with the foreign literature.

It has long been a matter of discussion whether there ever were an historical Arthur or not. Our minds are not so easily satisfied as was Caxton's – who tells us, in his preface to Malory's *Morte d'Arthur*, how he hesitated whether to print the romance or not, doubting whether Arthur had ever lived; but was reassured by those who had seen the King's tomb at Glastonbury, and Gawain's skull at Dover Castle. Such evidence as this would scarcely satisfy us nowadays, though for the sake of English literature we may well rejoice that it satisfied Caxton.

But without committing ourselves to a faith in these interesting relics, or in Arthur's victories far afield, we may, so scholars tell us, believe that he really lived, and was a valiant warrior and successful general. Both Professor Rhys and Mr. Alfred Nutt adhere to the view that the historic Arthur occupied a position equivalent to that of the *Comes Britannia*, who under the Romans held a roving commission to defend the province wherever attacked. It is quite in keeping with this identification that we find Arthur warring in all parts of the island: now in Northumberland – crossing the border into Scotland to take counsel with the allied princes for an attack on the Saxons; now journeying southward to give the invaders battle on Salisbury Plain.

That mythical elements also entered largely into the popular conception of Arthur is doubtless true, as the curious story of his birth and election to the crown seem to testify, but whether he really represents a Celtic God or Culture Hero, or is a representative of a widespread Aryan myth, we have but scanty data to determine.

Dr. Oskar Sommer predicts that when all the leading MSS. of the cycle have been carefully edited, and all the romances dissected and compared, we shall find that the original Arthur saga is very simple in form – it is the stories connected with the other heroes who gathered round the British king, which have crossed and complicated the primitive legend. One, and that an important step in the great work of elucidating this confused tangle of romance, would therefore be the careful sifting of the stories connected with the individual knights; the attempt to discover what was the original form of each legend; to find out, if we can, how much they have borrowed – in the case of the leading knights, how much they have lent; and thus by separating, as far as may be, the threads of the fabric, to discover the nature of the ground-work. But this is a task which is only practicable, and indeed only serviceable, in the case of the leading figures of the legend – such characters as Gawain, Perceval, Kay, Tristan, Lancelot, and Galahad. The great crowd of minor characters who cross and recross the stage are in many instances only understudies of the principal heroes; their adventures but reflections of deeds originally attributed to other and more important actors in the drama. Many of these characters would well repay study of the details of their story, but in the case of those above named the work is not merely desirable, but absolutely essential, if we are ever to arrive at a clear idea of the growth of this great legend.

Something has already been done in this direction. Mr. Nutt's *Studies on the Legend of the Holy Grail* have gone far towards the elucidation of the original *données* of the Perceval story. Professor Zimmer's study on the Tristan saga has thrown light upon the genesis of that legend; but there is still a vast field to be explored. The most perplexing, and in many ways the most important, of all the knights surrounding King Arthur, Gawain, has hitherto failed to meet with the favour accorded to his companions; true, the materials for an examination of his legend have in a great measure been prepared by Sir Frederick Madden in his collection of English metrical romances, and by M. Gaston Paris, in his study of the episodic romances connected with the hero; but the varying legends have not hitherto been examined and compared with a view to determining what was the original form of the Gawain Legend.

The more one studies the Arthurian cycle, the more one becomes convinced of the importance of this character, and of the necessity of discovering his original role. The materials at our disposal grow with every year, and we are now far better furnished for the task than was the case when Sir Frederick Madden undertook to collect the romances connected with Sir Gawain. These Studies therefore have been undertaken with the view of leading to a truer appreciation of one of the most puzzling, and at the same time most fascinating, characters of the Arthurian cycle, a character which later developments of the legend have greatly obscured, and most unjustly vilified. If in the course of these Studies certain points are established which may impel those better qualified than the present writer to pursue the investigation yet further, they will have amply fulfilled their object.

Chapter II
Early Conceptions of Gawain

THERE IS practically no doubt that, as mentioned in the previous chapter, the Arthurian legend proper has become greatly obscured by the introduction of legends connected with other heroes; there is but little more doubt that the first of all the heroes with whom Arthur gradually became connected was he whom we know from the Anglo-Norman and French romances as *Walwein, Gauvain, Gawain*, and from Welsh texts as *Gwalchmai*. The first M. Gaston Paris looks upon as the oldest form of the name by which the knight is best known, and it is no unusual thing to find both Walwein and Gawain employed in the same romance. That the French *Gawain* and Welsh *Gwalchmai* are the same character is certain, but the connection of these two forms is not so clear.

Any student of the Arthurian cycle could, without difficulty, name romances in which such leading heroes as Tristan, Lancelot, or Galahad are not even mentioned, but it would be difficult to recall one in which *Gawain* does not figure – sometimes even more prominently than the ostensible hero of the romance. Always closely connected with Arthur, his uncle on the mother's side, he is found in the historical accounts of that king, even as in the romantic. M. Gaston Paris gives, as the earliest mention of him, a quotation from William of Malmesbury (1125), relating to the discovery of Walwain's tomb at Ross in Pembrokeshire; he is there mentioned as Arthur's nephew, and 'not unworthy of Arthur'. Professor Zimmer, in his criticism of M. Paris' views, carries the literary evidence further back, by referring to Signor Rajna's discovery of names of Breton heroes in Italian deeds of the early twelfth century; *Artusius* (*Arthur*) and *Galvanus* (*Gawain*) are names of frequent recurrence. The German scholar is of opinion that these names justify the conclusion that the heroes were well known in Italy by 1090 – arguing a widespread continental acquaintance with the romances during the last thirty years of the eleventh century, at the latest – a date considerably anterior to that of any romance we now possess. Of those which have descended to us we may take Chrétien de Troyes' poems both as the earliest in themselves, and as representing a more primitive and less complicated form of the respective stories with which they deal. In all these poems, and also in the earlier prose romances, such as the *Merlin* (even in its extended form), Gawain appears as the beau-idéal of courage and courtesy, and this character he preserves in the English metrical romances. But in the later stage of the Arthur-saga, in those versions which are devoted to the most highly developed and ecclesiasticised form of the Grail legend, the character of Gawain undergoes a remarkable and striking change: he becomes a mere libertine, cruel and treacherous. Even his valour is no longer unquestioned. In the earlier romances Gawain is practically invincible; at the most, as in the case of Iwein, his opponent succeeds in achieving a drawn battle. Wirnt von Gravenberg, in his *Wigalois*, apologises eagerly for having repeated in his poems a statement to the effect that Gawain had been defeated by an unknown knight; if he had not been assured of it by his authority he would never have ventured to do so.

In the *Suite de Merlin* we find the enchanter prophesying Gawain's glory, and foretelling that he shall only be overcome by *one* knight; but when we reach Malory (Book iv. chap. 18) we find a list of *six* knights, each of whom has proved superior in valour to the once invincible hero.

But Malory, who drew from various sources, and represents a late stage in the evolution of the legend, is remarkably inconsistent in his treatment of Gawain: the earlier and later conceptions strive together in his version, and he makes statements utterly at variance the one with the other. Thus in Books vii. chap. 35, and x. chap. 58, we find Gareth refusing to have anything to do with his brother Gawain, on the ground that he is *treacherous, vengeable, a murderer of good knights*, and *a hater of all knights of the Round Table*; while, in Book xiii. chap. 16, Gawain and Gareth ride together in search of the Grail; and in Book xx. chap. 1, Gawain, Gareth, and Gaheris together refuse to countenance

Mordred and Agravain in their betrayal of Lancelot and Guinevere to King Arthur. It is in revenge for the death of Gareth at Lancelot's hands that Gawain urges the King to the fatal war with Lancelot; he can forgive the death of his sons, but not that of his dearly loved brother. And, when Gawain himself dies, both Arthur and Lancelot lament him in terms utterly out of keeping with Malory's previous indications; to Arthur he is *the man in the world I loved most*; to Lancelot, *a ful noble knyght as ever was borne.* It is not easy to account for this change in the estimation in which Gawain was held; Sir F. Madden thinks that the original offender was the compiler of the prose *Tristan*, who desired to exalt the fame of his special hero at the expense of the better-known Gawain. It seems, however, more probable that the reason may rather be sought in the strongly moralising tendencies of the later romances, there being certain features of the original Gawain story difficult to combine with edification. If it were the author of the *Tristan* only who was in fault, we should expect to find the old conception of Gawain obtaining in romances not affected by the *Tristan*, but all the later versions show this same declension.

But, whatever the original reason, it is unfortunately the case that later writers have followed in the track of Malory rather than in that of Chrétien; and the English nineteenth-century representations of Gawain are even more unjust to the original than are the fifteenth. Tennyson depicts him as *light of love, false, reckless,* and *irreverent*; and when we find Morris speaking of *gloomy Gawain*, we have indeed travelled far from the early English *Sir Gawayne*, the *gay, gratious,* and *gude* who

> *plus volt faire que il ne dist,*
> *Et plus doner qu'il ne promist.*

Scholars are now practically unanimous in admitting that, though the development of Gawain as a model of chivalrous knighthood is due largely to the Northern French poets, the character is, in its origin, *Celtic*. M. Gaston Paris says that Gawain belongs '*certainement à la tradition celtique la plus ancienne*'; but what was the special '*tradition celtique*' relating to the hero it is now difficult to say. The very popularity which

Gawain so long enjoyed has operated disastrously, by making him the hero of such a perplexing crowd of adventures that it might well seem labour thrown away to endeavour to separate from the mass any incidents which may be regarded as forming the kernel, so to speak, of his story, and yet, at the outset, he must have been the hero of certain definite adventures, certain special feats, which caused him to be looked upon as worthy to be allied with the hero-king of the Britons. It is possible that at first he may have been even a more notable hero than Arthur himself.

It ought not to be impossible to single out from among the various versions of Gawain's adventures certain features which, by their frequent recurrence in the romances devoted to him, and their analogy to ancient Celtic tradition, seem as if they might with probability be regarded as forming part of his original story. It is scarcely to be hoped that we can ever construct a coherent account on which we may lay our finger and say '*This*, and no other, was the original Gawain story'; but we may, I think, be able to specify certain incidents, saying, 'This belongs to Gawain and to no other of King Arthur's knights. *That* adventure is a necessary and integral part of his story.'

One of the most striking characteristics of Gawain, and one which may undoubtedly be referred to the original conception of his character, is that of the waxing and waning of his strength as the day advances and declines. Probably the earliest version of this is the one given by Chrétien's continuator, Gautier de Doulens:

> *Hardemens et force doubloit*
> *Toustans puis ke midis passoit,*
> *Por voir, a monsignor Gauvain,*
> *Tout en devons estre certain;*
> *Quant la clartés del jor faloit*
> *Icelle force tresaloit*
> *Et de miedi en avant*
> *Li recroissoit tot autretant.*

The *Merlin* gives it somewhat differently, e.g. '*quant il se levoit au matin il avoit la force al millor chevalier del monde; et quant vint à eure de prime si li doubloit, et à eure de tierce ausi. et quant ce vint à eure de midi si revenoit à sa première force, ou il avoit esté au matin; et quant vint à eure de nonne et à toutes lts eures de la nuit estoit il toudis en sa premiere force.'*

Malory has again another version: *'but Sir Gawayne fro it passed 9 of the clok waxed ever stronger and stronger / for thenne hit cam to the hour of noone and thryes his myghte was encreaced. / And thenne. whan it was past noone / and whan it drewe toward evensong Syre Gawayne's strengthe febled and waxt passynge faint that unnethe he myght dure ony lenger.'*

And later on: *'Then had Syr Gawayne suche a grace and gyfte that an holy man had gyven to hym / That every day in the year from underne tyl hyghe noone hys myght encreaced tho thre houres as moche as thryse hys strengthe.'*

This, though the latest version, and ascribing a reason for the peculiarity utterly out of keeping with Gawain's general character in the romance (for he is certainly no favourite with 'holy men') agrees better with the *Perceval* than with the *Merlin.*

Scholars have seen in this growth and waning of Gawain's power, directly connected as it is with the waxing and waning of the sun, a proof that this Celtic hero was at one time a solar divinity.

Another characteristic of Gawain, in which he differs from the other knights, is that he possesses a steed, which is known by a special name. *Gringalet*, or *le Gringalet*, is the form generally found in the French romances, but Professor Zimmer maintains that the name is more correctly *Gingalet* or *Guingalet*, a view to which the Welsh form of the word, *Keincaled*, lends support. This horse figures repeatedly in the old romances; the *Merlin* gives a long account of how Gawain at the outset of his knightly career won it by force of arms from the Saxon king, Clarions. There has been a great deal of discussion as to the original meaning of the name; the author of the *Merlin* says the steed was so called *'por sa grant bonté'*; Bartsch, commenting on the names given in the *Parzival*, gives as its meaning *'cheval maigre et alerte'*; Zimmer prefers *'schön-ausdauernd'* (as we should say, *of good staying power*); M. Gaston Paris more cautiously says that the name was originally Celtic, but that its signification has been lost. In any case it doubtless referred to some special virtue in the steed, which, judging from the frequency with which it was stolen, or taken by stratagem, from its rightful owner, was a highly desirable possession.

One point which Zimmer brings out, in the article above referred to, is of special interest and significance in its bearing on the direction in which we must seek for light on the earliest forms of the Gawain story. The name of this horse, so closely connected with the hero, and that in romances admittedly belonging to an early stage of the Arthurian cycle, only occurs *once* in Welsh literature, and then in a triad preserved in a late twelfth-century ms., where it is found in company with the horse of a certain Gilbert, identified by Zimmer as an Anglo-Norman follower of Henry I. Even in stories of which we possess parallel versions, such for instance as the Erec (Geraint), which has come down to us in French, German, and Welsh, the *Welsh* writer refrains from mentioning Gawain's famous steed, where, in the parallel French passages, the name occurs. Zimmer opines that the omission was of set purpose, the name being a foreign one. Without entering into the question as to which of the versions, the French or the Welsh, is dependent on the other, it seems clear that the Northern French poets and romancers did not get the *Gringalet* tradition from *Wales*, yet the horse figures in stories which manifestly represent the oldest version we at present possess of Gawain's adventures. The inference seems to be that we must go *behind* the Welsh stories to arrive at the earliest form of the legend; that we need even pass through them on our journey to the remote Celtic antiquity in which the key to the main problem of our study will be found, seems increasingly doubtful.

It is practically certain that if Gawain were ever looked upon as a solar hero he would in that character have been possessed of a steed of especial beauty and value. Teutonic mythology is on this point very instructive. Siegfried's famous horse *Grani* was undoubtedly originally such a sun-horse. Odin and Freyr have each of them their own steed.

But besides the horse the 'solar' hero ought also to possess a sword, and in the early romances we find Gawain in possession of a sword, and that no other than *Excalibur*.

Chrétien mentions Escalibur as Gawain's sword without any comment, but as if his possession of it were a well-known fact. In the *Merlin* we have an account of how Arthur, on the occasion of bestowing knighthood on his nephew, presented him with Escalibur; and Gawain throughout the romance wields that weapon, Arthur having the sword he won from the giant king, Rion. Sir F. Madden, in his 'Introduction', says that Arthur *lent* the sword to his nephew, an error into which he probably fell by yielding to the preconceived idea that Escalibur could belong to no one but Arthur. But there is no trace of a *loan* in the *Merlin*; it is a permanent *gift*.

Here, Escalibur is not the sword given by the mysterious Lady of the Lake, but that fixed in the block of stone, which Arthur alone can withdraw, thereby proving his right to the kingdom – an adventure attributed in the *Queste* to Galahad, and which probably finds its earliest form in the famous sword of the Branstock, which, as we know, was a divine weapon.

A peculiarity of Escalibur, mentioned in the *Merlin*, is that it throws so great a light when drawn that it is as if two torches had been kindled – a peculiarity distinctly suggestive of a 'sun' weapon. Professor Zimmer identifies this sword *Caliburnus* (Latin), *Escalibor* (French), *Caledvwlch* (Welsh), with *Caladbolg*, the great sword of the early Irish, or Ultonian, cycle. This sword was forged in Fairyland, and when drawn from the sheath 'waxed greater than the rainbow', – a somewhat curious simile, which though doubtless understood by the chronicler as referring simply to the far-reaching sweep of the weapon, yet may not improbably indicate some original 'light-giving' quality, analogous to that mentioned above of Escalibur.

Students of the legend will remember that there is a decided confusion as to the sword which Arthur wields: it is sometimes that drawn from the stone, sometimes that won from King Rion, sometimes the gift of the Lady of the Lake; the name Escalibor (Excalibur) is given both to the first and last named of these weapons. Judging from analogy, the sword of the stone, which finds its parallel in early Northern saga, should be the original sword of the story, and the only one to which a really divine origin can justly be ascribed. It is *this* sword, and not either of the other two, which Arthur gives to Gawain.

The fact that the weapon can also be traced back to early Irish legend in no way militates against the suggestion that Gawain may have been, in Arthurian legend, its original possessor; quite the contrary. We shall find in the progress of this investigation that between Gawain, and the great hero of the Ultonian cycle, Cuchulinn, there exist many striking parallels. There is probably no hero of the Arthurian cycle, not excepting Arthur himself, who stands in so close a relation to the heroes of early Irish legend, or presents so many points of contact with their stories as the gallant nephew of the British king.

We shall scarcely go far astray if we believe that Gawain, at the outset of his career, was equipped as befitted a 'solar' hero, with a steed and sword of exceptional virtue; nor shall we, I believe, be wrong if we accept the statement of the early romance-writers and believe that the sword was *Excalibur*.

Chapter III
The Legend in Chrétien's 'Conte de Graal' and Wolfram's 'Parzival'

HAVING THUS, as far as possible, ascertained what was the primitive conception of Gawain in the Celtic mind, we will endeavour to discover what were the details of the story connected with him. The task is a difficult one, but it may be simplified if we take, as basis for our inquiry, that Romance which is now generally considered to be the earliest of the Gawain cycle, and in which his adventures are related in the clearest and most coherent manner – the *Perceval*, or *Conte del Graal* of Chrétien de Troyes. I have also coupled with Chrétien's poem at the heading of this chapter the *Parzival* of Wolfram von Eschenbach. The source of this poem is undoubtedly closely related to that of Chrétien, and it also gives the conclusion of Gawain's adventures, which Chrétien, who left his work unfinished, was unable to do.

I would guard against being supposed to hold that the version of these two poets represents the *original* Gawain legend, but by taking this as a basis of comparison, and ascertaining which of the incidents there related figure most persistently in other romances of the cycle, we may be assisted in arriving at a conclusion as to the character of the fundamental *données* of the story.

In both poems, that of Chrétien and of Wolfram, the ostensible hero of the Romance is Perceval, but a large proportion, practically half of the entire work, is dedicated to the adventures of Gawain. These adventures are kept distinct from those of the original hero (though Wolfram, at least, is careful never to lose sight entirely of Parzival) and are far simpler and less complicated than is the case with other 'Gawain' romances.

In both poems Gawain makes his first appearance on the scene in connection with the love-trance into which Perceval is plunged by the sight of the blood-drops on the snow, a trance which keeps him motionless and unconscious in close proximity to Arthur's camp. It is Gawain who breaks the spell by covering the blood-stains, and after revealing his name to Perceval conducts him to the presence of the king. During the subsequent feast held in Perceval's honour, the loathly messenger of the Grail appears and curses Perceval for his failure to ask the question at the Grail Castle; she also tells of the imprisoned queens in the Château-Merveil, and, in Chrétien, of other adventures of which no more is heard, and which therefore need not be specified here. Immediately on her departure, the knight, Guingambrésil (Chrétien) or Kingrimursel (Wolfram) arrives on the scene, and accusing Gawain of having treacherously murdered his lord, challenges him to single combat, and fixes the place and time of their meeting. The feast breaks up in disorder, and the two heroes ride forth on their respective quests.

Gawain's first adventure, which is related with much more charm and felicity by the German than by the French poet, is to aid an old knight whose castle is besieged by the rejected lover of his elder daughter. Gawain takes part in the tournament as the chosen knight of the younger, a mere child, and by his valour determines the fortunes of the day in favour of his side. Leaving the castle, Gawain rides to Escavalon, or Askalon, the scene of the proposed combat, where he is met by the king of the land, who, ignorant of his identity, sends him to his castle, commending him to the care of his sister.

The lady proves to be of surpassing beauty, and Gawain makes overtures of love, to which she readily responds. They are interrupted by an old knight, who recognises Gawain as the supposed murderer of his master, and incites the inhabitants of the city to attack him. Gawain and the lady take refuge in a tower, and defend themselves with a chessboard and the stone pieces belonging to it. The king returns in company with Guingambrésil, by whose representations the strife is ended, the single combat deferred for a year, and Gawain allowed to depart in safety, having undertaken in the meanwhile to ride in search of either the Bleeding Lance of the Grail Castle (Chrétien), or the Grail itself (Wolfram).

Gawain next falls in with a maiden and a wounded knight, whom he assists and is warned by them of the dangers of the way. He, however, continues, and soon meets a lady of dazzling beauty, sitting beside a spring of water. Gawain makes advances to her, to which she replies with scant courtesy, but tells him if he will fetch her horse from a garden near at hand she will ride with him. The knight does this, and is again warned by the dwellers in the garden of the maiden's evil designs.

They ride off together, followed at a distance by a hideous dwarf, according to Wolfram, the lady's attendant.

Reaching the wounded knight, Gawain dismounts to bind his wounds, when the former, by a *ruse*, gains possession of Gawain's horse, and rides off, thus forcing Gawain either to go on foot or to mount the wretched steed belonging to the dwarf. The lady mocks him continuously, and, on their arrival at a meadow bounded by water, on the farther side of which is seen a magnificent castle, deserts him, and is ferried over the water by a boatman, while Gawain is attacked by a knight mounted on his (Gawain's) steed, *le Gringalet*. The hero overthrows him, on which the boatman appears, and claims the steed of the vanquished knight as his toll. Gawain represents that the horse is, in truth, his own, and offers the rider in exchange. They cross the water, and Gawain is courteously entertained for the night by the boatman.

In the morning the hero is attracted by the appearance of the castle, at the windows of which he sees many richly dressed ladies. His host endeavours to dissuade him from attempting the adventure of the castle, which is enchanted, 'Le Château Merveil'; but Gawain persists, enters the building, and seats himself on a wonderful couch, the 'Lit merveil'. He is immediately assailed by invisible foes with a storm of stones, and bolts shot from the crossbow; and, having successfully withstood these assaults, by a furious lion, which he slays.

The enchantments of the castle are now at an end. The inhabitants acclaim Gawain as their lord, and he is presented to the queens of the castle, three in number (according to Wolfram, *four*), one old and white-haired, the others respectively her daughter and granddaughter. The old queen is in reality Arthur's mother, who has either eloped with, or been carried off by, the magician who built the castle; the other two, mother and sister to Gawain himself, but neither side is aware of the relationship.

A curious trait occurs at this point in Chrétien's version. The boatman tells Gawain that whoever achieves the adventure of the castle must remain there; '*que jamais de cette maison n'istroit u fust tors u raison,*' at which Gawain is exceedingly angry; but nothing comes of the prohibition. In both poems he leaves the castle the following morning to fight with a knight whom the lady who had accompanied him to the castle brings to oppose him.

Gawain vanquishes this knight, all the ladies of the castle looking on at the combat, and then with the lady of his choice (*l'Orgueilleuse de Logres* in Chrétien; *Orgeluse* in Wolfram), who is still contemptuous, rides on a further quest – to weave a garland from the flowers, or pluck the bough of a tree, guarded by Guiromelans or Gramoflanz. To do this Gawain has to brave the adventure of the 'Perilous Ford' (crossing a river which flows through a rocky ravine), which he does successfully, wins his garland, is challenged by Guiromelans to single combat, and learns from him the rank and identity of the queens of the Château Merveil. On his return to the 'Proud Lady' she receives him kindly, and apologises for her former contemptuous conduct, which was simply meant to spur him on to avenge her wrongs upon Guiromelans, who had slain her lover.

They return to the castle, where Gawain is received with great honour. He sends a messenger to Arthur to invite him to assist with all his court at the approaching conflict between the hero and Guiromelans. The messenger finds the court plunged in grief at Gawain's supposed death.

Here Chrétien's version breaks off abruptly, but the story is continued, as follows by Wolfram:

Arthur and Guinevere eagerly promise to go to the trysting-place named by Gawain, and the messenger returns with the news. Gawain weds Orgeluse (the connection between the two is somewhat vague in Chrétien), and so soon as Arthur's court has been seen to pass on the farther side of the water, follows them. He makes all the ladies whom he has freed from captivity draw rein in a ring round the tent of King Arthur, a display which excites Kay's wrath and envy,

> 'Got mit den liutne wunder tuot,
> Wer gaþ Gâwân die frouwen luot?'

> ['God worketh with some His wonders,
> Who gave Gawain this woman-folk?']

The next morning Gawain, riding forth to prove if he be sufficiently recovered from the wounds received at the Château Merveil, meets Parzival; neither recognizes the other, and a fierce conflict ensues in which Gawain is worsted, and would be slain, save that his pages, passing at the critical moment, call upon him by name, and Parzival, learning that his opponent is his friend and kinsman, throws away his sword. The single combat between Gawain and Gramoflanz is deferred for another day, and finally, by the efforts of King Arthur and Brandelidelein, Gramoflanz's uncle, prevented altogether; Gramoflanz wedding Gawain's sister, whose love he had won while she was imprisoned in the Château Merveil.

Gawain's adventures are now completed, and he retires into the background, the remaining books of the poem being devoted to the principal hero, Parzival.

It has been supposed by critics that the latter part of Wolfram's poem, as well as the first two books, which are also independent of Chrétien, was the invention of the German poet, but I shall hope to show, in the progress of these Studies, that incidents parallel to those related in Wolfram are to be found elsewhere; and even in the portion which he shares in common with Chrétien there is at least one important incident of which the French poet knows nothing, but which is preserved in an independent romance.

Critics have also objected that the Grail quest, undertaken by Gawain, is allowed to drop into oblivion, and that this must be owing to the fact that Chrétien left his poem unfinished. Had he completed it, he would, they say, have brought Gawain, as well as Perceval, to the Grail castle; and Wolfram, taking Chrétien for his guide, would have done the same, instead of leaving Gawain, as he does, simply lord of the Château Merveil, and its bevy of fair ladies.

But this is, I believe, an entirely mistaken view. When the Gawain adventures are examined in the light of earlier parallels, it will, I think, become apparent that it is exactly at this point that the story *should* end; that the Grail quest is entirely independent of Gawain, and its introduction due to the growing popularity of this feature of the Arthurian cycle, a popularity which eventually issued in sending *all* the knights of the Round Table, without distinction, in search of the Grail.

It will follow from this that we shall find that the German poet was not giving reins to his fancy, but following a genuine tradition, identical in source, though varying in detail, with that followed by Chrétien.

Chapter VI
The Loves of Gawain

IF WE accept the conclusion arrived at in the preceding chapter (Chapter V – The Magic Castle), that Gawain's quest was originally of the nature of a visit to the other-world, and that

in a form most consonant with Celtic myth, we should naturally expect to find some surviving traces of his connection with the queen of this other-world.

Of all the knights of King Arthur's Court, Gawain is certainly the one whose love-affairs, if we accept later tradition, we should expect to find, from the first, the most numerous and the least edifying. On the contrary, tradition on this point is curiously vague and incomplete. In all Gawain's story there is no trace of a *liaison* under circumstances of deception and treachery, such as is attributed to Lancelot or Tristan. How he came to win the reputation of a faithless libertine, such as later tradition represents him, it would be impossible, regarding his story merely on the surface to say. M. Gaston Paris points out that the name of no special lady is associated with his, as that of Enid is with Erec, or Guinevere and Iseult with the two heroes just mentioned. Gawain is rather the courteous and disinterested champion of *all* maidens than the lover of one. This vagueness of tradition, coupled with the hero's reputation as a model of chivalry, led in later romances to the association of his name, now with one, now with another; the same romance (as e.g. *Diu Krône*) sometimes crediting him with two distinct lady-loves.

It seems probable that the real cause of this conflict of evidence lies in the fact that Gawain's expedition to and residence in the Maidens' Isle (Isle of Women) was an essential part of his story. The lady of his love was really the queen of that other-world, and he was, naturally enough, regarded as the champion of all the dwellers in it. The romances give us no really good reason for the title of 'the Maidens' Knight', as ascribed to Gawain; and it does not seem improbable that it may have been part of the original tradition. Gradually, as Christian ideas gained ascendency, this Celtic other-world would come to be looked upon somewhat in the light of a Mohammedan paradise, and the character of Gawain, as dweller in it, suffered proportionately.

Without going so far as Professor Rhys, who looks upon Gawain as a pattern of chastity, and practically equates him with Galahad, a view which can hardly be sustained by examination of the romances, we may, I think, maintain with truth that the attribution of indiscriminate amours to this knight is not in accordance with original tradition.

The real truth was, I believe, that Gawain's love was not only a denizen of another world, but also, as is frequently the case in such stories, originally *nameless*. It was not till, at a later date, certain attributes of the Goddess of Love had been passed over to the queen of the other-world, that she received a name. Thomas the Rhymer's love is as nameless as the queen who led Bran and Connla to her island court, though Tännhauser's lady is Venus.

There certainly was a persistent tradition to the effect that Gawain's love was no mere earthly maiden. The traces of such a tradition have, in Chrétien's poem, been partially, but not entirely, obscured. The circumstances of Gawain's meeting with the lady are in themselves suspicious; she is more or less closely connected with the enchanted castle, and she is certainly nameless. Wolfram's *Orgeluse* is only a misreading of *L'Orgueilleuse de Logres*, the only title by which Chrétien knows her.

Elsewhere we find it distinctly stated that Gawain's love was a *fairy*. In *Guinglain or Le Bel Inconnu* the hero is said to be the son of Gawain and the fairy *Blancemal*. In *Rigomer* Gawain is delivered from prison by the fairy *Lorie*, '*qui moult l'amoit.*' *Florie* is also the name attributed to the mother of Gawain's son in the German *Wigalois*, and in the version P of the *Livre d'Artus*.

In connection with this latter it is interesting to note that the lady is said to be the daughter of the king of *Escavalon*. Now, the lady with whom Gawain had the chessboard adventure was the daughter of the king of Escavalon (Askalon in the *Parzival*), and Wolfram, commenting on the extreme beauty of this lady and her brother, mentions the fact that they came of fairy race.

Florî is again the name of Gawain's *amie* in *Diu Krône*, though the lady he marries is Amurfina, the niece of Gansguoter, the magician of the enchanted castle. Amurfina is, however, said to be of *Forei*, which may be, a reminiscence of *Florî*. We may add to this list of Gawain's fairy mistresses the fay Karmente, who in *Saigremor* detains him in her isle.

But there are two distinct lines of tradition to be noted in the different accounts of Gawain's unearthly love; she is sometimes, as we have seen, a fairy, nothing being said as to her relatives, at others the close connection of a powerful magician. This would appear to have been the case with Chrétien and Wolfram's lady, as it is with Amurfina, whose uncle, Gansguoter, plays the same part as that of the enchanter of the Château Merveil in both French and German poems, viz. that of abductor of King Arthur's mother.

We may remark here that the appearance in this character of the Lord of the Castle finds support in early legend. *E.g.* in Irish tradition, Lug, one of the lords of the Irish other-world, abducts Dechtire, sister of Conchobar, and mother of Cuchulinn, with whom, as we have shown, Gawain has important points of contact. It will be remembered that both in Chrétien and in Wolfram the mother of *Gawain*, as well as of Arthur, is a prisoner in the Magic Castle, and is freed by her son.

That Amurfina is none other than the lady otherwise known as l'Orgueilleuse de Logres, or Orgeluse, seems very probable; and the special interest of Heinrich's presentment lies in the fact that he connects her so closely with the magician. We found in a preceding chapter that Emer, whose wooing by Cuchulinn affords a parallel to the Gawain-Proud-Lady episode, is the daughter of Forgall the Wily, a prince renowned for his magical powers, a feature which suggests an originally closer connection between the magician and the lady in the French and German poems than the authors of those poems were aware of; and which has been, in a measure, preserved in *Diu Krône*.

This relationship however survives, in slightly varying forms, in the English metrical romances. In the fragmentary poem of the *The Marriage of Sir Gawayne* we find the hero, in order to rescue King Arthur from the snares of a powerful enchanter, chivalrously wedding the magician's sister, a lady of unexampled hideousness. On the marriage night she reveals herself as beautiful as she was previously repulsive, and gives her husband the choice whether he will have her beautiful by night, and hideous by day, or vice versa. Gawain, with that courtesy for which he was famous, leaves the decision to the lady; whereupon she tells him she has been laid under a spell to preserve this repulsive form till she finds a knight courteous enough 'to give her her will'. The spell is now broken, and she will be beautiful alike by night and by day.

I am indebted to Mr. Alfred Nutt for having pointed out the existence of a most striking Irish parallel to this story, which, as seeming to indicate the source of the incident itself, and also as strengthening the argument for the Celtic origin of the Gawain legend, we may well insert here. The tale deals with the adventures of the five Lugaids, sons of Dáire Doimtech, one of whom it was prophesied should obtain the kingship of Ireland. 'It had been foretold that the future ruler should bear the name of *Lugaid*, wherefore Dáire, apparently anxious to show no favouritism, gave the name to each of his sons. Pressed for a further indication, the Druid foretold that a golden fawn should come into the assembly, and the son who should take it should win the kingship or sovranty. The fawn appears, and all the sons pursue it; one, Lugaid Laigde (Macniad), caught it, while another brother cut it up. Snow began to fall heavily, and the youths sought for a shelter. They came to a great house, with fire and food in abundance, the mistress of which was a horrible hag. She is ready to give them lodging for the night, provided one of them will share her couch. The youths, not unnaturally, demur at this, but finally Lugaid Laigde (who had caught the fawn) accepts the offer, and the tale runs thus: *Howbeit the hag went into the couch of white bronze, and Macniad followed her; and it seemed to him that the radiance of her face was the sun rising in the month of May, and her fragrance was likened by him to an odorous herb-garden, and she said to him, "Good is thy journey, for I am the Sovranty, and thou shall obtain the sovranty of Erin."* The following morning they find themselves horseless, on a level plain, with their hounds tied to their spears.

Now this story is certainly as old as the eleventh century, probably older, and there seems little doubt that in it we have the earliest form of the incident found in the *Marriage of Sir Gawayne*. As Mr. Nutt points out, there is a similar motif in the two tales; in the Irish, the lady is 'the Sovereignty'; in the English, the question Arthur has to solve is 'What do women most desire?' The answer is 'Sovereignty', *i.e.* their will. When Gawain practically exemplifies this by giving his bride her own way, the spell is broken.

In the Irish tale the lady herself is the enchanter, and not subject to a spell laid on her by another.

It is an interesting point that both Mr. Whitley Stokes and Mr. Nutt connect this lady with the 'Loathly Messenger' of the Grail, who both in the *Peredur*, and the *Gautier* continuation of the *Perceval* is transformed to a fairer shape. Neither Chrétien nor Wolfram retain this feature, but the latter, besides his hideous Kondrie, has also a Kondrie *la Belle*; this latter is a resident in the Magic Castle, and is Gawain's sister. If she really be, as has been suggested, a survival of the messenger in her transformed shape, the connection with Gawain is curious and interesting. An Irish parallel of certain aspects of this character is Leborcham, the female messenger of King Conchobar, and one of Cuchulinn's loves; she bore him two sons.

A later version of the English ballad makes the lady the mother of Gyngalyn, known otherwise as *Libeaus Desconus*, and amusingly remarks that though Gawain 'was weddyd oft in his days' yet he never loved any other lady so well. Altogether, this question of Gawain and the Loathly Lady scarcely seems as if it had yet been fully worked out.

Another English romance, *The Carle of Carlile*, in its later form weds Gawain to the 'Carle's' daughter, the hero having previously freed the father from enchantment by striking off his head. It may also be that the amorous advances made to Gawain by the wife of the *Green Knight*, a story with which we shall deal fully later on, owe their origin to a reminiscence of this early feature.

What then, we may ask, is the conclusion to be drawn from this special inquiry? *Firstly*, I think we must admit that Gawain's connection with a lady of supernatural origin is a remarkably well-attested feature of his story. *Secondly*, that between this lady, as represented in the most consecutive accounts of Gawain's adventures, and the queen of the other-world, as represented in Irish tradition, there exists so close a correspondence as to leave little doubt that they were originally one and the same character. *Thirdly*, that in these earlier stories we find, side by side with the lady, a magician, whose connection with her is obscure, but who is certainly looked upon as lord and master of the castle to which she conducts the hero, and which the latter wins. In such stories as the *Carle of Carlile* and the *Green Knight* the character of the magician has been preserved, while the lady has lost her supernatural qualities.

This remark may also hold good for *The Marriage of Sir Gawain*, where the magician is found, but the lady is apparently unable to free herself, unaided, from the spell laid upon her. *Fourthly*, we examined the nature of the castle ruled over by this magician, and we found it to be undoubtedly an 'other-world' dwelling.

Taking all these points into consideration the inference to be deduced from them seems clear – Gawain's love in the earliest instance was regarded as being either the *Daughter of the King of the Other-world*, or as herself the *Queen of that Other-world*. The presence of the magician points to the first of these characters, the parallels with the 'Island of Women' to the second – but, essentially, both characters are one and the same.

It is interesting in this connection to note that Professor Rhys in his *Arthurian Studies* considers Lot, Gawain's father, as having been originally identical with Lug, the Irish Light-god, father of Cuchulinn, and, like Lug, later on a king of the Other-world, or Isles of the Dead. If we are right in the above reading of the problems contained in the Gawain story, the hero was originally a sun-deity (therefore probably son of a light-god), and at the same time *son-in-law* to the lord of the other-world.

Another, and not less important, point must also be considered. We saw in the case of the Gawain-Proud-Lady episodes that no parallel to them is found in the *Peredur*, which contains such striking parallels to the *Perceval* portion of Chrétien and Wolfram's work. Again, in the special features characterizing these episodes, which seem to have so far-reaching a bearing on the Gawain story, we have found ourselves compelled to go further back, to seek in *Irish* rather than in *Welsh* tradition for parallels and explanations – and this search has been fruitful of result. So far as I can speak from personal study, the close connection between Gawain and a magician, or magician's daughter, seems to have completely dropped out of Welsh literature, and yet there seems little doubt that it represents a feature of the primitive story. The French and German romances retain it, so do the English metrical tales. Whence then did they obtain the tradition? The English romances probably drew, at least partially, from French sources; the Germans certainly owed their knowledge of Arthurian legend to France. The question really is, Where did the French poets get their version? Judging from the silence, on so many important points, of Welsh tradition, it seems most probable that, as Professor Zimmer maintains, they obtained their knowledge *direct* from their Breton neighbours, and not from Wales through the medium of England – a view which M. Gaston Paris favours.

It seems probable that this Breton version represented more closely the original form of the story than the tradition preserved in Wales. Otherwise one can hardly account for Chrétien and Wolfram, not to mention Heinrich von dem Türlin, being in possession of a version so capable of explanation by Irish parallels, which version is at the same time unrepresented in extant Welsh literature. It may be that the Gawain story, thoroughly and carefully examined, will eventually throw important light on the vexed question of the transmission of these fascinating legends.

But, however transmitted, it is, I think, clear that in the solution suggested in these last two chapters we have a key to the conflicting versions of Gawain's amours, as well as an explanation of that change of character which in the later romances operated so disastrously for his fame.

[Note: Mr. Nutt points out that a parallel to this deterioration may be found in the character of Ninian or Nimue, Merlin's love. At first a sympathetic and attractive personality, she gradually, in the expanded Merlin romances, undergoes a change for the worse, developing finally into the repulsive Vivien of the Tennyson Idylls. Kay also declines in the estimation of the romancers, though hardly to the same extent, or on the same lines.]

Chapter IX
Sir Gawain and the Green Knight

AMONG the Metrical Romances, which, as we have already said, formed, previous to Malory, the English contribution to Arthurian literature, the most important is that known as *Syr Gawayne and the Grene Knyght*; important not only from the

point of view of literary merit, which is considerable (M. Gaston Paris considers it 'le joyau de la litterature Anglaise au Moyen Age'), but also from its subject-matter – the adventure which it relates being found in varying forms in other romances, and, there is reason to believe, going back to an early stage of Celtic saga.

As the story, while it preserves with singular fidelity its archaic character, is yet given at greater length, and with more elaboration, in the English poem than in the other versions, we will first consider the adventure as there related, and then compare the other accounts with it, thus endeavouring to discover what were the original features of the story, and who was its earliest hero.

The poem, as given by Sir F. Madden in his *Sir Gawayne*, is printed from a ms., believed to be unique, in the Cottonian collection. From internal evidence it appears to have been *written* in the reign of Richard II, *i.e.* towards the end of the fourteenth century, though it may have been composed somewhat earlier; and the authorship has been ascribed to the Scottish poet, Huchown, whose *Morte d' Arthur*, preserved in the Lincoln Library, was used, among other romances, by Malory in his compilation.

The story is as follows: – On a New Year's Day, while Arthur is keeping his Christmas feast at Camelot, a gigantic knight, clad in green, mounted on a green horse, and carrying in one hand a holly bough, and in the other a 'Danish' axe, enters the hall and challenges one of Arthur's knights to stand him 'one stroke for another'. If any accept the challenge he may strike the first blow, but he must take oath to seek the Green Knight at a twelve-months' end and receive the return stroke. Seeing the gigantic size and fierce appearance of the stranger the knights hesitate, much to Arthur's indignation. Finally Gawain accepts the challenge, and, taking the axe, smites the Green Knight's head from the body. To the dismay of all present the trunk rises up, takes up the head, and, repeating the challenge to Gawain to meet him on the next New Year's morning at the Green Chapel, rides from the hall.

Faithful to his compact, Gawain, as the year draws to an end, sets forth amid the lamentations of the court to abide his doom, which all look upon as inevitable. He journeys north, and on Christmas Eve comes to a castle, where the lord receives him kindly, tells him he is within easy reach of his goal, and bids him remain over the feast as his guest. Gawain accepts. The three last days of the year the host rides forth on a hunting expedition, leaving Gawain to the care of his wife, and making a bargain that on his return they shall mutually exchange whatever they have won during the day. Gawain is sorely tempted by the wiles of his hostess, who, during her lord's absence, would fain take advantage of Gawain's well-known courtesy and fame as a lover. But he turns a deaf ear to her blandishments, and only a kiss passes between them, which he, in fulfilment of his compact, passes on to the husband on his return. The next day the result is similar: Gawain receives and gives two kisses. The third day, besides three kisses, the lady gives him a green lace, which, if bound round the body, has the property of preserving from harm. In view of the morrow's ordeal, from which Gawain does not expect to escape with his life, he cannot make up his mind to part with this talisman, but gives his host the kisses, and says nothing about the lace. The following morning at day-break he rides forth, and comes to the Green Chapel, apparently a natural hollow, or cave, in a wild and desolate part of the country. The Green Knight appears, armed with his axe, and bids Gawain kneel to receive the blow. As the axe descends, Gawain instinctively flinches, and is rebuked for his cowardice by the knight, who tells him he cannot be Gawain. The second time he remains steady, but the axe does not touch him. The third time the knight strikes him, inflicting a slight cut on the neck.

Gawain promptly springs to his feet, drawing his sword, and announces that he has now stood 'one stroke for another', and that the compact is at an end; whereon the Green Knight reveals himself as his erewhile host. He was cognisant of his wife's dealings with Gawain; the three strokes equalled the three trials of his guest's fidelity, and, had not Gawain proved partially faithless to his compact by concealing the gift of the lace, he would have escaped unharmed. The name of the Green Knight is Bernlak de Hautdesert, and he had undertaken this test of Gawain's valour at the instance, and by help of the skill, of Morgan le Fay, who desired to vex Guinevere by shaming the Knights of the Round Table.

Gawain returns to court, tells the whole story, concealing nothing, and all the knights vow henceforward to wear a green lace in his honour.

This is a summary of the wild and fantastic story, the origin of which Sir F. Madden believed he had discovered in the first continuation (by Gautier de Doulens) of Chrétien's *Conte del Graal*. But this theory, though at first favourably received, cannot, we think, be maintained.

In the French poem the story is connected with a certain Carados, Arthur's nephew, and the son, unknown to himself, of a powerful enchanter. This latter makes his appearance as does the Green Knight (only he is not dressed in green, and the colour of his steed is 'fauve'), while Arthur is holding high court, at Pentecost – not at Christmas. He is armed with a sword instead of an *axe* (which latter seems to be the original weapon), and proceeds at once to explain to Arthur what he means by 'one blow for another' – viz. that he will allow one of Arthur's knights to cut off his head on condition that he may be allowed at a year's interval to do the same for the knight. This, M. Gaston Paris observes, at once marks a corrupted form of the story, revealing as it does the superhuman nature of the challenger.

But we are not sure that this does not really correspond to the original form, *only*, and this is an important difference, in the primitive version the hero knows from the first that it is a magician with whom he is dealing, and there is no masquerading in the form of a knight. This will become clear as we proceed in our investigation. To proceed with the story: – All refuse, with the exception of the new-made knight, Carados, who, in spite of the remonstrances of king and queen, seizes the sword and strikes off the knight's head. The latter takes it up, replaces it on his shoulders (not riding off with it in his hands, as in the English poem), and, bidding Carados look for his return in a year's time, departs. At the expiration of the year the knight returns and finds Carados ready to submit to the test, but at the prayer of the queen and her ladies he forbears the blow (thus omitting the real test of the valour of the hero), and reveals the true relationship, that of father and son, between himself and Carados.

It seems difficult to understand how any one could have regarded this version, ill-motived as it is, and utterly lacking in the archaic details of the English poem, as the source of that work. It should probably rather be considered as the latest in *form*, if not in *date*, of all the versions.

Two other accounts, which seem, so far as can be judged from the comparison of an abstract with an original to be practically the same, again connect the story with Gawain.

They are those of the German *Diu Krône*, already often quoted, and the French romance *La Mule sans Frein*.

In the first, the hero arrives at a turning castle, the battlements of which, with one exception, are surmounted by human heads. Waiting till the entrance of the castle comes opposite to him, Gawain spurs his mule through the doorway, and is welcomed by a dwarf, and led to a chamber. From the window of this room he sees a man of strange appearance, who changes semblance in an extraordinary manner. Presently he enters the room, richly attired, and carrying an axe (halberd) over his shoulder. He entertains Gawain hospitably, and, after the meal, gives the astonished hero the choice of smiting off the host's head that evening, on condition that the host in his turn shall do the same for him on the morrow; or of allowing his host to smite off his head there and then.

Gawain naturally accepts the first alternative, and strikes off the stranger's head, which the trunk seeks for, takes up by the hair, and departs. The next morning he returns, and calls upon Gawain to fulfil his compact, which the hero is willing to do, presenting his neck without flinching to the axe. After two feints at striking off his head, the stranger avows that his only aim has been to test Gawain's courage. He, himself, is Gansguoter, a magician with whom Arthur's mother had eloped, and the uncle of Amurfina, Gawain's lady-love. This identification of the magician with the lover of King Arthur's mother connects the story with the poems of Chrétien and Wolfram, but the account, as it stands, is peculiar to Heinrich, and we cannot tell whence he drew it. The features of the 'turning' castle, and the heads on the battlements are found elsewhere, and have a decidedly archaic flavour.

In the *Mule sans Frein* Gawain arrives at the castle of a giant. The building is surrounded by poles, on each of which is a human head. The giant makes Gawain the same offer as does Gansguoter, viz. to strike off his head that evening on condition of his own being struck off on the morrow, or to allow the giant to strike off his at once. Gawain accepts the first, and smites off the head of the giant, who departs with it, returning the next morning to claim fulfilment of the pledge, which, as in *Diu Krône*, has only been a test of Gawain's valour.

The strong resemblance between these two versions – which agree in the severed heads being *en évidence*, and in the terms of the offer, as well as in the *motive* of the test, which here appears directed to *Gawain* in particular, and not, as in the English romance, to all the knights of Arthur's court – seems to point unmistakably to their derivation from a common source.

It will be noted that in neither of these last versions is there the interval of a year between the pledge and its fulfilment.

Another version, that of the prose *Perceval*, attributes the adventure to Lancelot. The hero arrives at the 'Gaste Cité'. At the steps of the palace he is confronted by a richly dressed knight, who demands that Lancelot shall cut off his head, taking an oath that he will return in a year's time and submit to the same ordeal. Lancelot complies, and the knight falls dead. At the expiry of the year the hero returns, and is met by the brother of the first knight. Lancelot kneels down, commends his soul to God, and prepares to receive the blow; but as the axe descends he flinches, and is rebuked by the knight – 'So did not my brother.' Before he can strike again two damsels interpose, and at their prayer Lancelot's life is spared. Twenty knights have already been slain without their slayer having dared to keep his part of the compact by returning. Lancelot's courage, and fidelity to his word, have broken the spell; the 'Gaste Cité' is re-peopled.

It will be seen here that there is no trace of a magician, and it is evidently a late form of the story.

We have already referred (chapter vi.) to the story of Gawain disenchanting the Carle of Carlile by striking off his head; and in Malory's Seventh Book, previously quoted, we find Gareth, Gawain's brother, arriving at the castle of his lady, Dame Liones. During the night he is attacked by a knight in armour, and strikes off his head. The knight is healed by an ointment applied by the damsel Linet, and returning the following night, fights again with Gareth, is again beheaded and restored to life by the same means. The story seems to lack point, and both it and the *Carle of Carlile* incident are probably reminiscences of the 'Green Knight' legend.

But to all appearance the oldest version now accessible is that of the *Fled Bricrend* (Bricriu's Feast), an Irish tale preserved in mss. written towards the end of the eleventh or beginning of the twelfth century, but representing a tradition considerably older, and showing no trace of Christianity. The story there given is as follows: –

The three heroes, Cuchulinn, Loégairé, and Conall, dispute as to which of them is entitled to the chief place and 'portion of the hero' at the feast. The king, Conchobar, declines to decide the question himself, and after appealing to several judges, they are finally referred to the giant Uath Mac Denomain, who dwells near a lake. They seek the giant, and submit the questions to him. He promises a decision if they, on their part, will observe a certain preliminary condition – which they undertake to do.

This proves to be of the nature of a bargain – "Whoever of you says Uath will cut off my head today, and allow me to cut off his tomorrow, to him shall belong 'the portion of the hero.'"

Loégairé and Conall either refuse to submit to the test, or having cut off the giant's head fly without waiting for the return blow, there appear to be two versions – Cuchulinn, on the contrary, declares himself willing to submit to the test. Uath, giving his axe to Cuchulinn, lays his head on a stone, the hero smites it from the body, and the giant, clasping it to his breast, springs into the lake. The next morning he reappears, whole as before. Cuchulinn presents his neck to the axe. The giant makes three feints at striking him, and pronounces that he has fulfilled the conditions, and is alone entitled to 'the portion of the hero'.

The versions of Irish sagas preserved in the eleventh- and twelfth-century mss. seem not infrequently to contain 'doublets' of the same incident, and thus at the conclusion of the *Fled Bricrend* the incident occurs again, in a fragmentary form in the oldest ms. (the Book of the Dun Cow), but complete in a later ms. from which it has been translated by Professor Kuno Meyer. This version differs from the one given above in a manner important for our inquiry. The stranger, a gigantic figure, carrying axe and block, arrives at the court of Conchobar during the absence of the three heroes, Cuchulinn, Conall, and Loégairé. He excludes the king, and his councillor Fergus, from his challenge, but directs it to all the other heroes. The terms agree with the earlier version. The first who accepts is Munremar, who smites off the stranger's head; he takes it up, and departs with it in his hand. The following night he returns, but Munremar does not appear to fulfil his part of the bargain. The chief heroes are, however, present, and declare their readiness to accept the challenge. Loégairé and Conall follow Munremar's example in evading the fulfilment of their pledge; Cuchulinn, as before, comes triumphantly through the ordeal. The giant only strikes him once, with the blunt edge of his axe, and proclaims him the chief hero of Ulster. He likewise reveals his own identity; he is Curoi Mac Dairé, the famous Munster warrior and magician, to whom the settlement of the supremacy of the Ulster champions had been remitted by Ailill and Medbh, whom Conchobar had first chosen as judges of the matter.

It will be seen here that the *conditions* of the test resemble more closely those of *Diu Krône* and *La Mule sans Frein*; but the three blows of the oldest Irish ms. are only found in the English version.

The story is then an exceedingly old one, and the first recorded hero with whom it is connected is the Ultonian hero Cuchulinn. We have already noted the many striking resemblances between this hero and Gawain; it seems therefore, *prima facie*, likely that if the story were connected with one of the knights of the Arthurian cycle, it would be with that one who is admittedly of Celtic origin, and moreover already connected with Cuchulinn; and when we examine the stories as they have descended to us, we find that the three versions ascribing the adventure to Gawain undeniably present more archaic features than either of the remaining two – *two* out of these three giving the challenge in the same terms as in the Irish stories; in *one*, the *Mule sans Frein*, the opponent of the hero is a giant, while in the *Green Knight* he is of gigantic size, thus again recalling the primitive version.

Further, it is significant that in the two remaining versions the hero is in one instance a young knight of whom little or nothing is known, but who is here said to be *Arthur's nephew*; in the other, the very knight who, as we saw in the last chapter, gradually superseded Gawain, *i.e.* Lancelot.

But so much has been claimed for the *Carados* version, which, as we said above, has been held to be the source of the English poem, that it cannot fairly be put on one side without a careful examination of the reasons for so rejecting it. As a point in favour of its priority it has been held that the close relationship between magician and hero, there existing, represents a feature of real antiquity which has dropped out, even of the Irish story. The father of Cuchulinn, the primitive hero of the adventure, was not merely a god, but also one of the *Tuatha de Danann*, a god turned magician.

This is true so far as it goes, but the point for us is, Was the giant who tested the valour of the Ultonian hero represented in any version as being that hero's father? If he were, no trace of it has come down to us, and it seems creating unnecessary confusion to postulate such a lost version, when, as we hope to show, the evidence all points to a much simpler solution.

If it be true that Cuchulinn was the son of a magician, it is also quite as true that he married a magician's daughter. The real question seems to be, Which of the two characters does this weird enchanter of the Green Knight story represent – the hero's father or his father-in-law, the lord of the Chateau Merveil?

On this point the *Diu Krône* version, which, as we have seen, agrees in the terms of the challenge with the *Fled Bricrend*, and possesses some specially archaic features, is very explicit – the magician is Lord of the Magic Castle, abductor of King Arthur's mother, and uncle to the lady whom Gawain eventually marries.

Nor are indications of this lacking even in the *Carados* version. The story there told of the liaison between the mother of the hero and the enchanter closely resembles the account of the loves of Klingsor, lord of the Chateau Merveil, and Iblis, wife of the king of Sicily, as related by Wolfram. The English poem, as we noted in a preceding chapter, seems also to have retained a hint of this, in the relations between Gawain and the wife of the knight-magician, who exerts all her fascinations to induce the hero to make love to her. *The Carle of Carlile* story, which relates how Gawain struck off the *Carle's* head, thus freeing him from enchantment, and wedded his daughter, belongs to the same group, and adds its testimony to strengthen the suggested identification.

But if the magician of the story *was* originally the lord of the Chateau Merveil, then we have, I think, a clear indication of how the story first came to be connected with Gawain: *it was one of the tests he had to undergo in order to prove himself a worthy mate for the enchanter's daughter.*

Connected with Cuchulinn, the point of the story was clear and definite; it was no mere vague, chance adventure; there was something to be won by submitting to the ordeal. Why transfer *this*, among all Cuchulinn's innumerable feats, to Gawain, unless he, too, was to be tested for a definite purpose? This original *motif* of the story has dropped out, but the idea that the trial was designed as a special test of Gawain's valour still survives.

And, if this was really the original meaning of the story, I do not think it is difficult to see how the magician came in the French poem, and in that alone, to be represented as the hero's *father*. The version of the story known to the poet had lost the lady, for whose sake the feat was undertaken, altogether. There is no trace of the magician's daughter here surviving. At the same time it is possible that the idea of a near relationship between magician and hero still lingered, and the author, either of the *Carados* version, or of its source, accounted for this relationship in a manner accordant with the story he already knew of the enchanter's *liaison* with a queen. If we reject this, which seems an easy and natural solution, and prefer to consider the French story as a genuine survival of the connection between the Ultonian hero and his supernatural father, *then* we must postulate, (a) the existence of a hypothetical original, differing in at least one important point from the *Fled Bricrend* story, (b) that this original descended by a different line than that of the Gawain versions, where the Magicians = Lord of the Magic Castle, and the hero's father-in-law.

Now we are tolerably certain that this was not the case, for not only is there a similar story told of the enchanter in the French poem to that told of the Lord of the Castle, but the hero is *Arthur's nephew, i.e.* the tale has been affected by the Gawain versions.

In estimating the relative value of the versions, as representatives of the original form, it is interesting to note that they fall apparently into two classes, in one of which the magician seeks the hero, and the scene passes at Arthur's court, in the other the hero goes to find the magician (or meets him accidentally), and the adventure falls out at the castle of the latter.

Now this variation of form *may* correspond to the two versions of the *Fled Bricrend*, in one of which Cuchulinn seeks the giant in his home, in the other the giant comes to Conchobar's court, or it *may* be due to the growing popularity of the Arthurian legend, which encouraged the placing of such adventures in the brilliant frame provided by the famous court. If the former were the case we should expect to find very little difference in detail and character between the two groups. As a matter of fact, those which have kept the visit *to* the magician offer, as a rule, much more archaic features, though we must except from this rule the prose *Perceval*. The oldest form of the story may therefore be said to be represented by the Book of the Dun Cow version of the *Fled Bricrend*, *Diu Krône* and *La Mule sans Frein*; in these three cases the hero visits the magician, and the blows are given on succeeding days.

The *Green Knight* poem, which represents the magician seeking Gawain at Arthur's court, and Gawain visiting the magician for the return blow, is an ingenious combination of the two forms – the only version we possess which does attempt to combine them. The introduction of a year's interval between the two strokes is probably due to this variation, which necessitated a double journey, on the part of the magician and on that of the hero. The author of the *Green Knight*, or his source (probably his source), was either the first to make the magician visit Arthur's court (if due to the influence of the Arthurian legend), or already knew two forms of the story. The original author of the *Carados* version, on the other hand, only knew one, and that not the oldest form. So he never suggests the visit of the hero to the magician, and keeps the year's interval between the blows, for which, in his case, there was no need, as they were to be given on the same spot. The challenger might just as well have returned the next day, as he does in the *Fled Bricrend* continuation, which seems to show that the visit to the court was not due to a knowledge of that early variant.

Further, the knight in the French poem is armed with a *sword*, not with an axe, which was undoubtedly the original weapon; he replaces his head on his shoulders, instead of going off with it in his hand, a touch which adds much to the weird horror of the original story; finally, and this is the most decisive proof of all, the return blows are entirely omitted, so the hero is spared the real and crowning test of his valour, a test which, unless we greatly mistake, was the *raison d'être* of the whole story. On all these grounds there seems little doubt that the story, as told by Chrétien's continuator, represents a very late, and eminently unsatisfactory, version of this popular adventure.

The *Perceval* or *Lancelot* version, on the other hand, though manifestly late, is much better motived. There is a real test of the hero's courage in his returning after a year's interval to face what is, practically, certain death; nor is he spared the ordeal of the return blows. But the fact that the challenger is no magician, but is really slain, shows conclusively that the author had only a late and confused form of the story before him.

So far as we can tell, taking the Irish story as our basis, the *Diu Krône* and *Mule sans Frein* versions are the oldest, the *Lancelot* the youngest of the series. *The Green Knight* and the *Carados* versions come in between them, and the English poem is certainly the older of these two.

This, of course, would practically settle the point of the identity of the original hero, did not the fact that the feat belongs to the Cuchulinn-Gawain parallels place it beyond doubt. It is Gawain and 'not Lancelot nor another' to whom it should rightfully be ascribed.

There is one interesting feature in the story, which hitherto does not appear to have attracted much attention, viz. the *lace* which the wife of the Green Knight bestows upon Gawain, and which has the power of conferring invulnerability on its wearer. In *Diu Krône*, too, we find Gawain in possession of a magic girdle, wrought by a fairy, which also has the power of preserving the wearer from harm. Gawain apparently wins it to give to Guinevere; but the story is confused, and it is evident from numerous allusions in the poem that he himself retains, if not the *girdle* itself, the *stone* in which its magic power resides, and which is eventually won from him by a trick.

We find the girdle again in the *Wigalois*, when a knight appears with it at the Court, offering it as a gift to Guinevere; bidding her, if she will not accept it, to send a knight to fight with him. Guinevere at first takes the girdle, but the following day, by Gawain's advice, returns it. One after another, the stranger overthrows all Arthur's champions. Finally, Gawain himself is overcome, and forced to ride with the newcomer to his own land. On the way the knight gives the girdle to *Gawain*. This hero weds the niece of the king of the land (as we saw in chapter vii), and it is because he has parted with this girdle, which is enchanted, to his wife, that he cannot find his way back to her. The story is not very clear, but the point of importance for us is that here again we find this hero possessed of a magic girdle.

Now *Cuchulinn* also had such a girdle, and scholars have seen in the powers conferred by it a connection with the invulnerability generally ascribed to the northern hero Siegfried. It seems therefore not unlikely that this feature, preserved only in the English poem, may also be referred to an early Celtic source. In any case it is undoubtedly interesting, and seems to demand closer examination.

On the whole, the adventure which we have discussed in this chapter stands on a different footing to that which we studied in the preceding. There, the conclusion seemed to be that, though there was a strong body of evidence in favour of Gawain as the original hero, yet that that evidence was not of a character to lead us to conclude that the story need necessarily have formed part of the *original* Gawain legend.

Here it is otherwise. There is practically no doubt that, as connected with Arthurian legend, it was Gawain, and Gawain alone, who was the hero of the adventure. The Celtic parallels are strong evidence for an early date, and in more than one version we find traces of a connection with the adventure which demonstrably formed part of the primitive Gawain story, *i.e.* the *Chateau Merveil* episode. Taking all these points into consideration, there seems strong grounds for concluding that in the stories classed under the heading of this chapter we have a genuine survival of a feat which formed part of the very earliest adventures attributed to the hero – if we mistake not, one of the special deeds of valour by which he won the favour and the hand of his 'other-world' bride.